Praise for *Maybe in Another Life*

A *People* Magazine Pick

Us Weekly Must Pick

Named a Best Book of the Summer by
*Glamour, Good Housekeeping, USA TODAY,
Cosmopolitan*, POPSUGAR, Working
Mother, Bustle, and Goodreads

"Entertaining and unpredictable; Reid makes a compelling argument for happiness in every life."

—*Kirkus Reviews* (starred review)

"Reid makes you think about love and destiny and then shows you the *what could have been*; I loved every word. A heartfelt, witty, and scintillating journey from one parallel universe to another, *Maybe in Another Life* takes the concept of fate and makes it tangible and engrossing; I couldn't put this book down!"

—Renee Carlino, *USA Today* bestselling author

"Readers looking for a romance with a twist won't be disappointed."

—*Library Journal*

Praise for *After I Do*

"Written in a breezy, humorous style familiar to fans of Jane Green and Elin Hilderbrand, *After I Do* focuses on Lauren's journey of self-discovery. The intriguing premise and well-drawn characters contribute to an emotionally uplifting and inspiring story."

—*Booklist*

"uplifting as it is brutally honest—a must-read."

—*Kirkus Reviews*

"Taylor Jenkins Reid offers an entirely fresh and new perspective on what can happen after the 'happily ever after.' With characters who feel like friends and a narrative that hooked me from the first page, *After I Do* takes an elegant and incisively emotional look at the endings and beginnings of love. Put this book at the top of your must-read list."

—Jen Lancaster, *New York Times* bestselling author

"Taylor Jenkins Reid delivers a seductive twist on the timeless tale of a couple trying to rediscover love in a marriage brought low by the challenges of domestic togetherness. I fell in love with Ryan and Lauren from their passionate beginning, and I couldn't stop reading as they followed their unlikely road to redemption. Touching, perceptive, funny, and achingly honest, *After I Do* will keep you hooked to the end, rooting for husbands and wives and the strength of true love."

—Beatriz Williams, *New York Times* bestselling author

"Taylor Jenkins Reid writes with ruthless honesty, displaying an innate understanding of human emotion and creating characters and relationships so real I'm finding it impossible to let them go. *After I Do* is a raw, unflinching exploration of the realities of marriage, the delicate nature of love, and the enduring strength of family. Simultaneously funny and sad, heartbreaking and hopeful, Reid has crafted a story of love lost and found that is as timely as it is timeless."

—Katja Millay, author of *The Sea of Tranquility*

Praise for *Forever, Interrupted*

"Touching and powerful . . . Reid masterfully grabs hold of the heartstrings and doesn't let go. A stunning first novel."

—*Publishers Weekly* (starred review)

"Moving, gorgeous and, at times, heart-wrenching. Taylor Jenkins Reid writes with wit and true emotion that you can *feel*. Read it, savor it, share it."

—Sarah Jio, *New York Times* bestselling author of *The Violets of March*

"A moving novel about life and death."

—*Kirkus Reviews*

"You'll laugh, weep, and fly through each crazy-readable page."

—*Redbook*

"Sweet, heartfelt, and surprising, *Forever, Interrupted* is a story about a young woman struggling to find her way after losing her husband. These characters made me laugh as well as cry, and I ended up falling in love with them, too."

—Sarah Pekkanen, internationally bestselling author of *The Opposite of Me*

"Taylor Jenkins Reid has written a poignant and heartfelt exploration of love and commitment in the absence of shared time that asks 'what does it take to be the love of someone's life?'"

—Emma McLaughlin and Nicola Kraus, *New York Times* bestselling authors

"This beautifully rendered story explores the brilliance and rarity of finding true love, and how to find our way back through the painful aftermath of losing it. These characters will leap right off the page and into your heart."

—Amy Hatvany, author of *Somewhere Out There*

"*Forever, Interrupted* weaves a beautiful love story with a terrible tragedy. Told in alternating timelines, each chapter progresses sequentially from two different arcs: one of a blooming, forever love and another of overcoming a sudden, inexplicable loss. Each storyline moves effortlessly and seamlessly through the connected stages, while also emphasizing the strengthening of old friendships and the forging of new ones. Whether told in past or present voice, Reid's debut is a superb read from start to finish!"

—*Romantic Times*

Also by Taylor Jenkins Reid

Forever, Interrupted
After I Do
Maybe in Another Life

ONE TRUE LOVES

~ A Novel ~

TAYLOR JENKINS REID

WASHINGTON SQUARE PRESS
New York   Toronto   London   Sydney   New Delhi

Washington Square Press
An Imprint of Simon & Schuster, Inc.
1230 Avenue of the Americas
New York, NY 10020

First Washington Square Press trade paperback edition June 2016

WASHINGTON SQUARE PRESS and colophon are registered trademarks of Simon & Schuster, Inc.

For information about special discounts for bulk purchases, please contact Simon & Schuster Special Sales at 1-866-506-1949 or business@simonandschuster.com.

The Simon & Schuster Speakers Bureau can bring authors to your live event. For more information or to book an event, contact the Simon & Schuster Speakers Bureau at 1-866-248-3049 or visit our website at www.simonspeakers.com.

Manufactured in the United States of America

10 9 8 7 6 5 4 3 2 1

Library of Congress Cataloging-in-Publication Data

Names: Reid, Taylor Jenkins.
Title: One true loves : a novel / by Taylor Jenkins Reid.
Description: First Washington Square Press trade paperback edition. | New York: Washington Square Press, [2016]
Subjects: LCSH: Triangles (Interpersonal relations)—Fiction. | Man-woman relationships—Fiction. | Mate selection—Fiction. | GSAFD: Love stories.
Classification: LCC PS3618.E5478 O54 2016 | DDC 813/.6—dc23
LC record available at http://lccn.loc.gov/2015035902

ISBN 978-1-4767-7690-3
ISBN 978-1-4767-7691-0 (ebook)

This is a book about Acton, Massachusetts.
So naturally, I would like to dedicate it to Andy Bauch
of Boxborough.
And to Rose, Warren, Sally, Bernie, Niko, and Zach
of Encino, California.

ONE TRUE LOVES

I am finishing up dinner with my family and my fiancé when my husband calls.

It is my father's sixty-fourth birthday. He is wearing his favorite sweater, a hunter green cashmere one that my older sister, Marie, and I picked out for him two years ago. I think that's why he loves it so much. Well, also because it's cashmere. I'm not kidding myself here.

My mother is sitting next to him in a gauzy white blouse and khakis, trying to hold in a smile. She knows that a tiny cake with a candle and a song are coming any minute. She has always been childlike in her zeal for surprises.

My parents have been married for thirty-five years. They have raised two children and run a successful bookstore together. They have two adorable grandchildren. One of their daughters is taking over the family business. They have a lot to be proud of. This is a happy birthday for my father.

Marie is sitting on the other side of my mother and it is times like these, when the two of them are right next to each other, facing the same direction, that I realize just how much they look alike. Chocolate brown hair, green eyes, petite frames.

I'm the one that got stuck with the big butt.

Luckily, I've come to appreciate it. There are, of course, many songs dedicated to the glory of a backside, and if my thirties have taught me anything so far, it's that I'm ready to try to be myself with no apologies.

My name is Emma Blair and I've got a booty.

I am thirty-one, five foot six, with a blond, grown-out pixie cut. My hazel eyes are upstaged by a constellation of freckles on the top of my right cheekbone. My father often jokes he can make out the Little Dipper.

Last week, my fiancé, Sam, gave me the ring he has spent over two months shopping for. It's a diamond solitaire on a rose gold band. While it is not my first engagement ring, it is the first time I've ever worn a diamond. When I look at myself, it's all I can see.

"Oh no," Dad says, spotting a trio of servers headed our way with a lit slice of cake. "You guys didn't . . ."

This is not false modesty. My father blushes when people sing to him.

My mother looks behind her to see what he sees. "Oh, Colin," she says. "Lighten up. It's your birthday . . ."

The servers make an abrupt left and head to another table. Apparently, my father is not the only person born today. My mother sees what has happened and tries to recover.

". . . Which is why I did not tell them to bring you a cake," she says.

"Give it up," my dad says. "You've blown your cover."

The servers finish at that table and a manager comes out with another slice of cake. Now they are all headed right for us.

"If you want to hide under the table," Sam says, "I'll tell them you're not here."

Sam is handsome in a friendly way—which I think might just be the best way to be handsome—with warm brown eyes that seem to look at everything with tenderness. And he's funny. Truly funny. After Sam and I started dating, I noticed my laugh lines were getting deeper. This is most likely because I am growing older, but I can't shake the feeling that it's because I am laughing more than I ever have. What else could you want in a person other than kindness and humor? I'm not sure anything else really matters to me.

The cake arrives, we all sing loudly, and my father turns beet red. Then the servers turn away and we are left with an oversized piece of chocolate cake with vanilla ice cream.

The waitstaff left five spoons but my father immediately grabs them all. "Not sure why they left so many spoons. I only need one," he says.

My mother goes to grab one from him.

"Not so fast, Ashley," he says. "I endured the humiliation. I should get to eat this cake alone."

"If that's how we are playing it . . ." Marie says. "For my birthday next month, please put me through this same rigmarole. Well worth it."

Marie drinks a sip of her Diet Coke and then checks her phone for the time. Her husband, Mike, is at home with my nieces, Sophie and Ava. Marie rarely leaves them for very long.

"I should get going," Marie says. "Sorry to leave, but . . ."

She doesn't have to explain. My mom and dad both stand up to give her a hug good-bye.

Once she's gone and my father has finally agreed to let us all eat the cake, my mom says, "It sounds silly but I miss that. I miss leaving someplace early because I was just so excited to get back to my little girls."

I know what's coming next.

I'm thirty-one and about to be married. I know exactly what is coming next.

"Have you guys given any thought to when you might start a family?"

I have to stop myself from rolling my eyes. "Mom—"

Sam is already laughing. He has that luxury. She's only his mother in an honorary capacity.

"I'm just bringing it up because they are doing more and more studies about the dangers of waiting too long to have a child," my mom adds.

There are always studies to prove I should hurry and studies to prove that I shouldn't and I've decided that I will have a baby when I'm goddamn good and ready, no matter what my mother reads on the *Huffington Post*.

Luckily, the look on my face has caused her to backpedal. "Never mind, never mind," she says, waving her hand in the air. "I sound like my own mother. Forget it. I'll stop doing that."

My dad laughs and puts his arm around her. "All right," he says. "I'm in a sugar coma and I'm sure Emma and Sam have better things to do than stay out with us. Let's get the bill."

Fifteen minutes later, the four of us are standing outside the restaurant, headed to our cars.

I'm wearing a navy blue sweater dress with long sleeves and thick tights. It is just enough to insulate me from the cool evening air. This is one of the last nights that I'll go anywhere without a wool coat.

It's the very end of October. Autumn has already settled in and overtaken New England. The leaves are yellow and red, on their way to brown and crunchy. Sam has been over to my parents' house once already to rake the yard clean. Come December, when the temperature free-falls, he and Mike will shovel their snow.

But for now the air still has a bit of warmth to it, so I savor it as best I can. When I lived in Los Angeles, I never savored warm nights. You don't savor things that last forever. It is one of the reasons I moved back to Massachusetts.

As I step toward the car, I hear the faint sound of a ringing cell phone. I trace it back to my purse just as I hear my father rope Sam into giving him a few guitar lessons. My father has an annoying habit of wanting to learn every instrument that Sam plays, mistaking the fact that Sam is a music teacher for Sam being *his* music teacher.

I dig through my purse looking for my phone, grabbing the only thing lit up and flashing. I don't recognize the number. The area code 808 doesn't ring a bell but it does pique my interest.

Lately, no one outside of 978, 857, 508, or 617—the various area codes of Boston and its suburbs—has reason to call me.

And it is 978 specifically that has always signified home no matter what area code I was currently inhabiting. I may have spent a year in Sydney (61 2) and months backpacking from Lisbon (351 21) to Naples (39 081). I may have honeymooned in Mumbai (91 22) and lived, blissfully, for years, in Santa Monica, California (310). But when I needed to come "home," "home" meant 978. And it is here I have stayed ever since.

The answer pops into my head.

808 is Hawaii.

"Hello?" I say as I answer the phone.

Sam has turned to look at me, and soon, my parents do, too.

"Emma?"

The voice I hear through the phone is one that I would recognize anywhere, anytime—a voice that spoke to me day in and day out for years and years. One I thought I'd never hear again, one I'm not ready to even believe I'm hearing now.

The man I loved since I was seventeen years old. The man who left me a widow when his helicopter went down somewhere over the Pacific and he was gone without a trace.

Jesse.

"Emma," Jesse says. "It's me. I'm alive. Can you hear me? I'm coming home."

~

I think that perhaps everyone has a moment that splits their life in two. When you look back on your own timeline, there's a sharp spike somewhere along the way, some event that changed you, changed your life, more than the others.

A moment that creates a "before" and an "after."

Maybe it's when you meet your love or you figure out your life's passion or you have your first child. Maybe it's something wonderful. Maybe it's something tragic.

But when it happens, it tints your memories, shifts your perspective on your own life, and it suddenly seems as if everything you've been through falls under the label of "pre" or "post."

I used to think that my moment was when Jesse died.

Everything about our love story seemed to have been leading up to that. And everything since has been in response.

But now I know that Jesse never died.

And I'm certain that *this* is my moment.

Everything that happened *before* today feels different now, and I have no idea what happens *after* this.

BEFORE

~

Emma and Jesse

Or, how to fall in love and fall to pieces

I have never been an early riser. But my hatred for the bright light of morning was most acute on Saturdays during high school at ten after eight a.m.

Like clockwork, my father would knock on my door and tell me, "The bus is leaving in thirty minutes," even though the "bus" was his Volvo and it wasn't headed to school. It was headed to our family store.

Blair Books was started by my father's uncle in the sixties, right in the very same location where it still stood—on the north side of Great Road in Acton, Massachusetts.

And somehow that meant that the minute I was old enough to legally hold a job, I had to ring up people's purchases some weekdays after school and every Saturday.

I was assigned Saturdays because Marie wanted Sundays. She had saved up her paychecks and gotten a beat-up navy blue Jeep Cherokee last summer.

The only time I'd been inside Marie's Jeep was the night she got it, when, high on life, she invited me to Kimball's Farm to get ice cream. We picked up a pint of chocolate for Mom and Dad and we let it melt as we sat on the hood of her car and ate our own sundaes, comfortable in the warm summer air.

We complained about the bookstore and the fact that Mom always put Parmesan cheese on potatoes. Marie confessed that she had smoked pot. I promised not to tell Mom and Dad.

Then she asked me if I'd ever been kissed and I turned and looked away from her, afraid the answer would show on my face.

"It's okay," she said. "Lots of people don't have their first kiss until high school." She was wearing army green shorts and a navy blue button-down, her two thin gold necklaces cascading down her collarbone, down into the crevice of her bra. She never buttoned her shirts up all the way. They were always a button lower than you'd expect.

"Yeah," I said. "I know." But I noticed that she didn't say, "*I* didn't have my first kiss until high school." Which, of course, was all I was really looking for. I wasn't worried that I wasn't like anyone else. I was worried that I wasn't like *her*.

"Things will get better now that you're going to be a freshman," Marie said as she threw away the rest of her mint chocolate chip. "Trust me."

In that moment, that night, I would have trusted anything she told me.

But that evening was the exception in my relationship with my sister, a rare moment of kinship between two people who merely coexisted.

By the time my freshman year started and I was in the same building as her every day, we had developed a pattern where we passed each other in the hallways of home at night and school during the day like enemies during a cease-fire.

So imagine my surprise when I woke up at eight ten one Saturday morning, in the spring of ninth grade, to find out that I did not have to go to my shift at Blair Books.

"Marie is taking you to get new jeans," my mom said.

"Today?" I asked her, sitting up, rubbing my eyes, wondering if this meant I could sleep a little more.

"Yeah, at the mall," my mom added. "Whatever pair you want, my treat. I put fifty bucks on the counter. But if you spend more than that, you're on your own."

I needed new jeans because I'd worn holes into all of my old ones. I was supposed to get a new pair every Christmas but I was so particular about what I wanted, so neurotic about what I thought they should look like, that my mother had given up. Twice now we had gone to the mall and left after an hour, my mother trying her best to hide her irritation.

It was a new experience for me. My mother always wanted to be around me, craving my company my entire childhood. But I had finally become so annoying about something that she was willing to pass me off to someone else. And on a Saturday, no less.

"Who's going to work the register?" I said. The minute it came out of my mouth, I regretted it. I was suddenly nervous that I'd poked a hole in a good thing. I should have simply said, "Okay," and backed away slowly, so as to not startle her.

"The new boy we hired, Sam," my mom said. "It's fine. He needs the hours."

Sam was a sophomore at school who walked into the store one day and said, "Can I fill out an application?" even though we weren't technically hiring and most teenagers wanted to work at the CD store down the street. My parents hired him on the spot.

He was pretty cute—tall and lanky with olive skin and dark brown eyes—and was always in a good mood, but I found myself incapable of liking him once Marie deemed him "adorable." I couldn't bring myself to like anything she liked.

Admittedly, this type of thinking was starting to limit my friend pool considerably and becoming unsustainable.

Marie liked everyone and everyone liked Marie.

She was the Golden Child, the one destined to be our parents' favorite. My friend Olive used to call her "the Booksellers' Daughter" behind her back because she even *seemed* like the sort of girl whose parents would own a bookstore, as if there was a very specific stereotype and Marie was tagging off each attribute like a badge of honor.

She read adult books and wrote poetry and had crushes on fictional characters instead of movie stars and she made Olive and I want to barf.

When Marie was my age, she took a creative writing elective and decided that she wanted to "become a writer." The quotation marks are necessary because the only thing she ever wrote was a nine-page murder mystery where the killer turned out to be the protagonist's little sister, Emily. I read it and even I could tell it was complete garbage, but she submitted it to the school paper and they loved it so much they ran it in installments over the course of nine weeks in the spring semester.

The fact that she managed to do all of that while still being one of the most popular girls in school made it that much worse. It just goes to show that if you're pretty enough, cool comes to you.

I, meanwhile, had covertly read the CliffsNotes in the library for almost every book assigned to us in English 1. I had a pile of novels in my room that my parents had given me as gifts and I had refused to even crack the spines.

I liked music videos, NBC's Thursday Must-See TV lineup, and every single woman who performed at Lilith Fair. When I was bored, I would go through my mom's old issues of *Travel + Leisure*, tearing out pictures and taping them to my wall. The space above my bed became a kaleidoscope of magazine covers of Keanu Reeves, liner notes from Tori Amos albums, and centerfolds of the Italian Riviera and the French countryside.

And no one, I repeat no one, would have confused me for a popular kid.

My parents joked that the nurse must have given them the wrong child at the hospital and I always laughed it off, but I had, more than once, looked at pictures of my parents as children and then stared at myself in the mirror, counting the similarities, reminding myself I belonged to them.

"Okay, great," I told my mom, more excited about not having to go to work than spending time with my sister. "When are we leaving?"

"I don't know," my mom said. "Talk to Marie. I'm off to the store. I'll see you for dinner. I love you, honey. Have a good day."

When she shut my door, I lay back down on the bed with vigor, ready to relish every single extra minute of sleep.

Sometime after eleven, Marie barged into my room and said, "C'mon, we're leaving."

We went to three stores and I tried on twelve pairs of jeans. Some were too baggy, some too tight, some came up too high on my waist.

I tried on the twelfth pair and came out of the dressing room to see Marie staring at me, bored senseless.

"They look fine; just get them," she said. She was wearing head-to-toe Abercrombie & Fitch. It was the turn of the millennium. All of New England was wearing head-to-toe Abercrombie & Fitch.

"They look weird in the butt," I said, staying perfectly still.

Marie stared at me, as if she expected something.

"Are you gonna turn around so I can see if they are weird in the butt, or what?" she finally said.

I turned around.

"They make you look like you're wearing a diaper," she told me.

"That's what I just said."

Marie rolled her eyes. "Hold on." She circled her finger in the air, indicating that I should go back into the dressing room. And so I did.

I had just pulled the last pair of jeans off when she threw a pair of faded straight-leg ones over the top of the door.

"Try these," she said. "Joelle wears them and she has a big butt like yours."

"Thanks a lot," I said, grabbing the jeans from the door.

"I'm just trying to help you," she said, and then I could see her feet walk away, as if the conversation was over simply because she wasn't interested in it anymore.

I unzipped the fly and stepped in. I had to shimmy them over my hips and suck in the tiniest bit to get them buttoned. I stood tall and looked at myself in the mirror, posing this way and that, turning my head to check out what I looked like from behind.

My butt was growing shapelier by the day and my boobs seemed to have stagnated. I had read enough of my mother's *Glamour* magazines to know that this was referred to as "pear shaped." My stomach was flat but my hips were growing. Olive was starting to gain weight in her boobs and her stomach and I wondered if I wouldn't prefer that sort of figure. Apple shaped.

But, if I was being honest with myself, what I really wanted was all that my mother had passed on to Marie. Medium butt, medium boobs, brown hair, green eyes, and thick lashes.

Instead, I got my father's coloring—hair neither fully blond nor fully brunette, eyes somewhere in between brown and green—with a body type all my own. Once, I asked my mother where I got my short, sturdy legs from and she said, "I don't know, actually," as if this wasn't the worst thing she'd ever said to me.

There was only one thing about my appearance that I truly loved. My freckles, that cluster of tiny dark spots under my right eye. My mom used to connect the dots with her finger as she put me to bed as a child.

I loved my freckles and hated my butt.

So as I stood there in the dressing room, all I wanted was a pair of jeans that made my butt look smaller. Which these seemed to do.

I stepped out of the dressing room to ask Marie's opinion. Unfortunately, she was nowhere to be found.

I stepped back into the dressing room, realizing I had no one to make this decision with but me.

I looked at myself one more time in the mirror.

Maybe I liked them?

I looked at the tag. Thirty-five bucks.

With tax, I'd still have money left over to get teriyaki chicken from the food court.

I changed out of them, headed to the register, and handed over my parents' money. I was rewarded with a bag containing one pair of jeans that I did not hate.

Marie was still missing.

I checked around the store. I walked down to the Body Shop to see if she was there buying lip balm or shower gel. Thirty minutes later, I found her buying earrings at Claire's.

"I've been looking all over for you," I said.

"Sorry, I was looking at jewelry." Marie took her change, delicately put it back into her wallet, and then grabbed the tiny white plastic bag that, no doubt, contained fake gold sure to stain her ears a greenish gray.

I followed Marie as she walked confidently out of the store and toward the entrance where we'd parked.

"Wait," I said, stopping in place. "I wanted to go to the food court."

Marie turned toward me. She looked at her watch. "Sorry, no can do. We're gonna be late."

"For what?"

"The swim meet," she said.

"What swim meet?" I asked her. "No one said anything about a swim meet."

Marie didn't answer me because she didn't have to. I was already following her back to the car, already willing to go where she told me to go, willing to do what she told me to do.

It wasn't until we got in the car that she deigned to fill me in. "Graham is the captain of the swim team this year," she said.

Ah, yes.

Graham Hughes. Captain of every team he's on. The front-runner for "best smile" in the yearbook. Exactly the sort of person Saint Marie of Acton would be dating.

"Great," I said. It seemed clear that my future entailed not just sitting and watching the fifty-meter freestyle, but also waiting in Marie's car afterward while she and Graham made out in his.

"Can we at least hit a drive-through on the way there?" I asked, already defeated.

"Yeah, fine," she said.

And then I mustered up as much confidence as I possibly could and said, "You're paying."

She turned and laughed at me. "You're fourteen. You can't buy your own lunch?"

She had the most amazing ability to make me feel stupid even at my most self-assured.

We stopped at a Burger King and I ate a Whopper Jr. in the front seat of her car, getting ketchup and mustard on my hands and having to wait until we parked to find a napkin.

Marie ditched me the minute we smelled the chlorine in the air. So I sat on the bleachers and did my best to entertain myself.

The indoor pool was full of barely clothed, physically fit boys my age. I wasn't sure where to look.

When Graham got up on the diving block and the whistle blew, I watched as he dove into the water with the ease of a bird flying through the air. From the minute he entered the water, it was clear he was going to win the race.

I saw Marie, over in the far corner, bouncing up and down, willing him to win, believing in him with all of her might. When Graham claimed his throne, I got up and walked around, past the other side of the bleachers and through the gym, in search of a vending machine.

When I came back—fifty cents poorer, a bag of Doritos richer—I saw Olive sitting toward the front of the crowd with her family.

One day last summer, just before school started, Olive and I were hanging out in her basement when she told me that she thought she might be gay.

She said she wasn't sure. She just didn't feel like she was totally straight. She liked boys. But she was starting to think she might like girls.

I was pretty sure I was the only one who knew. And I was

also pretty sure that her parents had begun to suspect. But that wasn't my business. My only job was to be a friend to her.

So I did the things friends do, like sit there and watch music videos for hours, waiting for Natalie Imbruglia's "Torn" video to come on so that Olive could stare at her. This was not an entirely selfless act since it was my favorite song and I dreamt of chopping off my hair to look just like Natalie Imbruglia's.

Also not entirely selfless was my willingness to rewatch *Titanic* every few weeks as Olive tried to figure out if she liked watching the sex scene between Jack and Rose because she was attracted to Leonardo DiCaprio or Kate Winslet.

"Hey!" she said as I entered her sight line that day at the pool.

"Hey," I said back. Olive was wearing a white camisole under an unbuttoned light blue oxford button-down. Her long jet-black hair hung straight and past her shoulders. With a name like Olive Berman, you might not realize she was half-Jewish, half-Korean, but she was proud of where her mother's family had come from in South Korea and equally proud of how awesome her bat mitzvah was.

"What are you doing here?" she asked me.

"Marie dragged me and then ditched me."

"Ah," Olive said, nodding. "Just like the Booksellers' Daughter. Is she here to see Graham?" Olive made a face when she said Graham's name and I appreciated that she also found Graham to be laughable.

"Yeah," I said. "But . . . wait, why are you here?"

Olive's brother swam until he graduated last year. Olive had tried but failed to make the girls' swim team.

"My cousin Eli swims for Sudbury."

Olive's mom turned away from the swim meet and looked

at me. "Hi, Emma. Come, have a seat." When I sat down next to Olive, Mrs. Berman turned her focus back to the pool.

Eli came in third and Mrs. Berman reflexively pumped her hands into frustrated fists and then shook her head. She turned and looked at Olive and me.

"I'm going to go give Eli a conciliatory hug and then, Olive, we can head home," she said.

I wanted to ask if I could join them on their way home. Olive lived only five minutes from me. My house was more or less between theirs and the highway exit. But I had trouble asking things of people. I felt more comfortable skirting around it.

"I should probably find Marie," I said. "See if we can head out."

"We can take you," Olive said. "Right, Mom?"

"Of course," Mrs. Berman said as she stood up and squeezed through the crowded bleachers. "Do you want to come say good-bye to Eli? Or should I meet you two at the car?"

"The car," Olive said. "Tell Eli I said hi, though."

Olive put her hand right into my Doritos bag and helped herself.

"Okay," she said once her mom was out of earshot. "Did you see the girl on the other side of the pool, talking to that guy in the red Speedo?"

"Huh?"

"The girl with the ponytail. Talking to somebody on Eli's team. I honestly think she might be the hottest girl in the world. Like ever. Like, that has ever existed in all of eternity."

I looked toward the pool, scanning for a girl with a ponytail. I came up empty. "Where is she?" I said.

"Okay, she's standing by the diving board now," Olive said as she pointed. "Right there. Next to Jesse Lerner."

"Who?" I said as I followed Olive's finger right to the diving board. And I did, in fact, see a pretty girl with a ponytail. But I did not care.

Because I also saw the tall, lean, muscular boy next to her.

His eyes were deep set, his face angular, his lips full. His short, light brown hair, half-matted, half-akimbo, the result of pulling the swimming cap up off his head. I could tell from his swimsuit that he went to our school.

"Do you see her?" Olive said.

"Yeah," I said. "Yeah, she's pretty. But the guy she's talking to . . . What did you say his name was?"

"Who?" Olive asked. "Jesse Lerner?"

"Yeah. Who is Jesse Lerner?"

"How do you not know who Jesse Lerner is?"

I turned and looked at Olive. "I don't know. I just don't. Who is he?"

"He lives down the street from the Hughes."

I turned back to Jesse, watching him pick up a pair of goggles off the ground. "Is he in our grade?"

"Yeah."

Olive kept speaking but I had already started to tune her out. Instead, I was watching Jesse as he headed back to the locker room with the rest of his team. Graham was right next to him, putting a hand on his shoulder for a brief moment before jumping ahead of him in the slow line that had formed. I couldn't take my eyes off of the way Jesse moved, the confidence with which he put one foot in front of the other. He was younger than any of the other swimmers—a freshman on the varsity team—and yet seemed right at home, standing in front of everyone in a tiny swimsuit.

"Emma," Olive said. "You're staring."

Just then, Jesse turned his head ever so slightly and his gaze landed squarely on me, for a brief, breathless second. Instinctively, I looked away.

"What did you say?" I asked Olive, trying to pretend I was engaged with her side of the conversation.

"I said you were staring at him."

"No, I wasn't," I said.

It was then that Mrs. Berman came back around to our side of the bleachers. "I thought you were meeting me at the car," she said.

"Sorry!" Olive said, jumping up onto her feet. "We're coming now."

"Sorry, Mrs. Berman," I said, and I followed them both behind the bleachers and out the door.

I paused, just before the exit, to see Jesse one last time. I saw a flash of his smile. It was wide and bright, toothy and sincere. His whole face lit up.

I wondered how good it would feel to have that smile directed at me, to be the cause of a smile like that—and suddenly, my new crush on Jesse Lerner grew into a massive, inflated balloon that was so strong it could have lifted the two of us up into the air if we'd grabbed on.

That week at school, I noticed Jesse in the hallway almost every day. Now that I knew who he was, he was everywhere.

"That's the Baader-Meinhof phenomenon," Olive said when I mentioned it at lunch. "My brother just told me about this. You don't notice something and then you learn the name for it and suddenly it's everywhere." Olive thought for a moment. "Whoa. I'm pretty sure I have the Baader-Meinhof phenomenon *about* the Baader-Meinhof phenomenon."

"Are you seeing Jesse everywhere, too?" I asked, entirely missing the point. Earlier that day, I'd walked right by him coming out of Spanish class. He was talking to Carolyn Bean by her locker. Carolyn Bean was the captain of the girls' soccer team. She wore her blond hair back in a bun, with a sporty headband every day. I'd never seen her without lip gloss. If that was the kind of girl Jesse liked, I stood no chance.

"I'm not seeing him any more than normal," Olive said. "But I always see him around all the time. He's in my algebra 1 class."

"Are you friends with him?" I asked.

"Not really," Olive said. "But he's a nice guy. You should just say hi to him."

"That's insane. I can't just say hi to him."

"Sure you can."

I shook my head and looked away. "You sound ridiculous."

"*You* sound ridiculous. He's a boy in our class. He's not Keanu Reeves."

I thought to myself, *If I could just talk to Jesse Lerner, I wouldn't care about Keanu Reeves.*

"I can't introduce myself, that's crazy," I said, and then I gathered my tray and headed toward the trash can. Olive followed.

"Fine," she said. "But he's a perfectly nice person."

"Don't say that!" I said. "That just makes it worse."

"You want me to say he's mean?"

"I don't know!" I said. "I don't know what I want you to say."

"You're being sort of annoying," Olive said, surprised.

"I know, okay?" I said. "Ugh, just . . . come on. I'll buy you a pack of cookies."

Back then, a seventy-five-cent bag of cookies was enough to make up for being irritating. So as we walked over to the counter, I dug my hand into my pocket and counted out what silver coins I had.

"I have one fifty exactly," I said just as I followed Olive to the back of the line. "So enough for both of us." I looked up to see Olive's eyes go wide.

"What?"

She directed me forward with the glance of her eyes.

Jesse Lerner was standing right in front of us. He was wearing dark jeans and a Smashing Pumpkins T-shirt with a pair of black Converse One Stars.

And he was holding Carolyn Bean's hand.

Olive looked at me, trying to gauge my reaction. But instead, I stared forward, doing a perfect impression of someone unfazed.

And then I watched as Carolyn Bean let go of Jesse's hand, reached into her pocket, took out a tube of lip balm, and applied it to her lips.

As if it wasn't bad enough she was holding his hand, she had the audacity to let go of it.

I hated her then. I hated her dumb, soccer-playing, headband-wearing, Dr-Pepper-flavored-lip-balm-applying guts.

If he ever wanted to hold my hand, I'd never, ever, ever let go.

"Let's get out of here," I said to Olive.

"Yeah," she said. "We can get something from the vending machine instead."

I walked off, depressed and lovesick, heading for the vending machine by the band room.

I bought two Snickers bars and handed one of them to Olive. I chomped into mine, as if it were the only thing that could fill the void in my heart.

"I'm over him," I said. "Totally dumb crush. But it's done. I'm over it. Seriously."

"Okay," Olive said, half laughing at me.

"No, really," I said. "Definitely over."

"Sure," Olive said, scrunching her eyebrows and pursing her lips.

And then I heard a voice coming from behind me.

"Emma?"

I turned to see Sam coming out of the band room.

"Oh, hey," I said.

"I didn't know that you had this lunch period."

I nodded. "Yep."

His hair was a bit disheveled and he was wearing a green shirt that said "Bom Dia!"

"So, I guess we've got our first shift together," he said. "Tomorrow at the store, I mean."

"Oh," I said. "Yeah." On Tuesday, Marie had borrowed my Fiona Apple CD without asking, prompting me to call her a "complete asshole" within hearing distance of my parents. My punishment was a Friday shift at the store. In my family, instead of getting grounded or having privileges revoked, you redeemed yourself by working more. Extra shifts at the store were my parents' way of both teaching lessons and extracting free labor. Assigning me Friday evening in particular meant I couldn't hang out with Olive and they could have a date night at the movies.

"Tomorrow?" Olive said. "I thought we were going to hang out at my house after school."

"Sorry," I said. "I forgot. I have to work."

The bell rang, indicating that it was time for me to start walking toward my world geography class.

"Ah," Olive said. "I have to go. I left my book in my locker."

Olive didn't wait for me, didn't even offer. Nothing stood between her and being on time for anything.

"I should get going, too," I said to Sam, who didn't seem to be in a rush to get anywhere. "We have a test in geo."

"Oh, well, I don't want to keep you," Sam said. "I just wanted to know if you wanted a ride. Tomorrow. To the store after school."

I looked at him, confused. I mean, I wasn't confused about what he was saying. I understood the simple physics of getting into a car that would take me from school to work. But it surprised me that he was offering, that he would even think to offer.

"I just got my license and I inherited my brother's Camry,"

he said. In high school, it seemed like everyone was inheriting Camrys or Corollas. "So I just thought . . ." He looked me in the eye and then looked away. "So you don't have to take the bus, is all."

He was being so thoughtful. And he barely knew me.

"Sure," I said, "that would be great."

"Meet you in the parking lot after school?" he asked.

"That sounds great. Thank you. That's really cool of you."

"No worries," he said. "See you tomorrow."

As I walked toward the double doors at the end of the hall, heading to class, it occurred to me that maybe it was time to just be friends with whomever I wanted to be friends with, to not try quite so hard to reject everything Marie liked.

Maybe it was time to just . . . be myself.

The next day I wore a red knit sweater and flat-front chinos to school, cognizant of my parents' request to never wear jeans at the store. And then, ten minutes after the last bell rang, I saw Sam leaning against the hood of his car in the school parking lot, waiting for me.

"Hey," I said as I got closer.

"Hey." He went around to my side of the car and opened the car door. No one had ever opened a car door for me before except my father, and even then, it was usually a joke.

"Oh," I said, taking my backpack off and putting it in the front seat. "Thank you."

Sam looked surprised for a moment, as if he wasn't sure what I was thanking him for. "For the door? You're welcome."

I sat down and sunk into the passenger's seat as Sam made his way to his side of the car. He smiled at me nervously when he got in and turned on the ignition. And then, suddenly, jazz music blasted through the speakers.

"Sorry," he said. "Sometimes I really have to psych myself up in the morning."

I laughed. "Totally cool."

He turned the music down but not off and I listened as it softly filled the air in the car. Sam put the car in reverse and twisted his body toward me, resting his arm on the back of my seat and then backing out of the spot.

His car was a mess. Papers at my feet, gum wrappers and guitar picks strewn across the dashboard. I glanced into the backseat and saw a guitar, a harmonica, and two black instrument cases.

I turned back to face the front. "Who is this?" I said, pointing to the stereo.

Sam was watching the steady stream of cars to his left, waiting for his chance to turn onto the road.

"Mingus," he said, not looking at me.

There was a small opening, a chance to enter the flow of traffic. Sam inched up and then swiftly turned, gracefully joining the steady stream of cars. He relinquished his attention, and turned back to me.

"Charles Mingus," he said, explaining. "Do you like jazz?"

"I don't really listen to it," I said. "So I don't know."

"All right, then," Sam said, turning up the volume. "We'll listen and then you'll know."

I nodded and smiled to show that I was game. The only problem was that I knew within three seconds that Charles Mingus was not for me and I didn't know how to politely ask him to turn it off. So I didn't.

My father was at the register when we came in through the doors. His face lit up when he saw me.

"Hi, sweetheart," he said, focused on me. And then he turned for a brief second. "Hey, Sam!"

"Hi, Dad," I said back. I didn't love the idea of my father calling me "sweetheart" in front of people from school. But groaning about it would only make it worse, so I let it go.

Sam headed straight for the back of the store. "I'm going to run to the bathroom and then, Mr. Blair, I'll be back to relieve you."

My dad gave him a thumbs-up and then turned to me. "Tell me all about your day," he said as I put my book bag down underneath the register. "Start at the beginning."

I looked around to see that the only customer in the store was an older man reading a military biography. He was pretending to peruse it but appeared to be downright engrossed. I half expected him to lick his fingertip to turn the page or dog-ear his favorite chapter.

"Aren't you supposed to be taking Mom on a date?" I asked.

"How old do you think I am?" he asked, looking at his watch. "It's not even four p.m. You think I'm taking your mother to an early bird special?"

"I don't know," I said, shrugging. "You two are the ones who made me work today so you could go see a movie together."

"We made you work today because you were being rude to your sister," he said. His tone was matter-of-fact, all blame removed from his voice. My parents didn't really hold grudges. Their punishments and disappointments were perfunctory. It was as if they were abiding by rules set out before them by someone else. *You did this and so we must do that. Let's all just do our part and get through this.*

This changed a few years later, when I called them in the middle of the night and asked them to pick me up from the police station. Suddenly, it wasn't a fun little test anymore. Suddenly, I had actually disappointed them. But back then, the stakes were low, and discipline was almost a game.

"I know that you and Marie are not the best of friends," my dad said, tidying up a stack of bookmarks that rested by the register. When the store opened, sometime in the sixties, my great-uncle who started it had commissioned these super cheesy bookmarks with a globe on them and an airplane cir-

cling it. They said "Travel the World by Reading a Book." My father loved them so much that he had refused to update them.
He had the same exact ones printed time and time again.

Whenever I picked one of them up, I would be struck by
how perfectly they symbolized exactly what I resented about
that bookstore.

I was going to travel the world by *actually traveling it*.

"But one day, sooner than you think, the two of you are
going to realize how much you need each other," my dad continued.

Adults love to tell teenagers that "one day" and "sooner or
later" plenty of things are going to happen. They love to say
that things happen "before you know it," and they really love
to impart how fast time "flies by."

I would learn later that almost everything my parents told
me in this regard turned out to be true. College really did "fly
by." I did change my mind about Keanu Reeves "sooner or later."
I was on the other side of thirty "before I knew it." And, just as
my father said that afternoon, "one day" I was going to need my
sister very, very much.

But back then, I shrugged it off the same way teens all over
the country were shrugging off every other thing their parents
said at that very moment.

"Marie and I are not going to be friends. Ever. And I wish
you guys would let up about it."

My father listened, nodding his head slowly, and then looked
away, focusing instead on tidying up another stack of bookmarks. Then he turned back to me. "I read you loud and clear,"
he said, which is what he always said when he decided that he
didn't want to talk about something anymore.

Sam came out of the back and joined us up by the registers.

The customer reading the book came over to the counter with the book in his hand and asked us to keep it on hold for him. No doubt so he could come back and read the same copy tomorrow, as if he owned the thing. My father acted as if he was delighted to do it. My father was very charming to strangers.

Right after the man left, my mom came out of her office in the back of the store. Unfortunately, Dad didn't see her.

"I should tell your mother it's time to go," he said. I tried to stop him but he turned his head slightly and started yelling. "Ashley, Emma and Sam are here!"

"Jesus Christ, Colin," my mom said, putting a hand to her ear. "I'm right here."

"Oh, sorry." He made a scrunched face to show that he'd made a mistake and then he gently touched her ear. It was gestures like that, small acts of intimacy between them, that made me think my parents probably still had sex. I was both repulsed and somewhat assuaged by the thought.

Olive's parents always seemed on the edge of divorce. Marie's friend Debbie practically lived at our house for two months a few years earlier when her parents were ironing out their own separation. So I was smart enough to know I was lucky to have parents who still loved each other.

"All right, well, since you're both here, we will take off," my mom said, heading toward the back to grab her things.

"I thought you weren't leaving for your date until later," I said to my father.

"Yeah, but why would we hang around when our daughter is here to do the work?" he said. "If we hurry, we can get home in time to take a disco nap."

"What is a disco nap?" Sam asked.

"Don't, Sam; it's a trap," I said.

Sam laughed. I never really made people laugh. I wasn't funny the way Olive was funny. But, suddenly, around Sam I felt like maybe I could be.

"A disco nap, dear Samuel, is a nap that you take before you go out and party. You see, back in the seventies . . ."

I walked away, preemptively bored, and started reorganizing the table of best sellers by the window. Marie liked to sneak her favorite books on there, giving her best-loved authors a boost. My only interest was in keeping the piles straight. I did not like wayward corners.

I perked up only when I heard Sam respond to my father's story about winning a disco contest in Boston by laughing and saying, "I'm so sorry to say this, but that's not a very good story."

My head shot up and I looked right at Sam, impressed.

My dad laughed and shook his head. "When I was your age and an adult told a bad story, do you know what I did?"

"Memorized it so you could bore us with it?" I piped in.

Sam laughed again. My father, despite wanting to pretend to be hurt, gave a hearty chuckle. "Forget it. You two can stay here and work while I'm out having fun."

Sam and I shared a glance.

"Aha. Who's laughing now?" my dad said.

My mom came out with their belongings and within minutes, my parents were gone, out the door to their car, on their way to take disco naps. I was stunned, for a moment, that they had left the store to Sam and me. Two people under the age of seventeen in charge for the evening? I felt mature, suddenly. As if I could be trusted with truly adult responsibilities.

And then Margaret, the assistant manager, pulled in and I realized my parents had called her to supervise.

"I'll be in the back making the schedule for next week,"

Margaret said just as soon as she came in. "If you need any-thing, holler."

I looked over at Sam, who was standing by the register, lean-ing over the counter on his elbows.

I went into the biography section and started straightening that out, too. The store was dead quiet. It seemed almost silly to have two people out in front and one in the back. But I knew that I was here as a punishment and Sam was here because my parents wanted to give him hours.

I resolved to sit on the floor and flip through Fodor's travel books if nobody else came in.

"So what did you think of Charles Mingus?" Sam asked. I was surprised to see that he had left the area by the cash regis-ter and was just a few aisles down, restocking journals.

"Oh," I said. "Uh . . . Very cool."

Sam laughed. "You liar," he said. "You hated it."

I turned and looked at him, embarrassed to admit the truth. "Sorry," I said. "I did. I hated it."

Sam shook his head. "Totally fine. Now you know."

"Yeah, if someone asks me if I like jazz, I can say no."

"Well, you might still like jazz," Sam offered. "Just because you don't like Mingus doesn't mean . . ." He trailed off as he saw the look on my face. "You're already ready to write off all of jazz?"

"Maybe?" I said, embarrassed. "I don't think jazz is my thing."

He grabbed his chest as if I'd stabbed him in the heart.

"Oh, c'mon," I said. "I'm sure there are plenty of things I love that you'd hate."

"Try me," he said.

"*Romeo + Juliet*," I said confidently. It had proven to be a definitive dividing line between boys and girls at school.

Sam was looking back at the journals in front of him. "The play?" he asked.

"The movie!" I corrected him.

He shook his head as if he didn't know what I was talking about.

"You've never seen *Romeo + Juliet* with Leonardo DiCaprio?" I was aware of the fact that there were other versions of *Romeo and Juliet*, but back then, there was no Romeo but Leo. No Juliet but Claire Danes.

"I don't really watch that many new movies," Sam said.

A mother and son came in and headed straight for the children's section in the back. "Do you have *The Velveteen Rabbit*?" the mom asked.

Sam nodded and walked with her, toward the stacks at the far end of the store.

I moved toward the cash register. When they came back, I was ready to ring them up, complete with a green plastic bag and a "Travel the World by Reading a Book" bookmark. When she was out the door, I turned to Sam. He was standing to the side, leaning on a table, with nothing to do.

"What do you like to do, then?" I asked. "If you're not into movies, I mean."

Sam thought about it. "Well, I have to study a lot," he said. "And other than that, between my job here and being in the marching band, orchestra, and jazz band . . . I don't have a lot of time."

I looked at him. I was thinking less and less about whether Marie thought he was cute, and more and more about the fact that I did.

"Can I ask you something?" I said as I turned away from the stacks in front of me and walked toward him.

"I think that's typically how conversations go, so sure," he said, smiling.

I laughed. "Why do you work here?"

"What do you mean?"

"I mean, if you're so busy, why do you spend so much time working at a bookstore?"

"Oh," Sam said, thinking about it. "Well, I have to buy my own car insurance and I want to get a cell phone, which my parents said was fine as long as I pay for it myself."

I understood that part. Almost everyone had an after-school job, except the kids who scored lifeguard jobs during the summer and somehow ended up making enough to last them the whole year.

"But why *here*? You could be working at the CD store down the road. Or, I mean, the music store on Main Street."

Sam thought about it. "I don't know. I thought about applying to those places, too. But I . . . I think I just wanted to work at a place that had nothing to do with music," he said.

"What do you mean?"

"I mean, I play six instruments. I have to be relentless about practicing. I play piano for at least an hour every day. So it's nice to just have, like, one thing that isn't about minor chords and tempos and . . ." He seemed lost in his own world for a moment but then he resurfaced. "I just sometimes need to do something totally different."

I couldn't imagine what it was like to be him, to have something you were so passionate about that you actually needed to make yourself take a break from it. I didn't have any particular passion. I just knew that it wasn't my family's passion. It wasn't books.

"What instruments?" I asked him.

"Hm?"

"What are the six that you play?"

"Oh," he said.

A trio of girls from school came in the door. I didn't know who they were by name, but I'd seen them in the halls. They were seniors, I was pretty sure. They laughed and joked with one another, paying no attention to Sam or me. The tallest one gravitated toward the new fiction while the other two hovered around the bargain section, picking up books and laughing about them.

"Piano," Sam said. "That was my first one. I started in second grade. And then, let's see . . ." He put out his thumb, to start counting, and then with each instrument another finger went up. "Guitar—electric and acoustic but I count that as one still—plus bass, too—electric and acoustic, which I also think counts as one even though they really are totally different."

"So five so far but you're saying that's really only three."

Sam laughed. "Right. And then drums, a bit. That's my weakest. I just sort of dabble but I'm getting better. And then trumpet and trombone. I just recently bought a harmonica, too, just to see how fast I can pick it up. It's going well so far."

"So seven," I said.

"Yeah, but I mean, the harmonica doesn't count either, not yet at least."

In that moment, I wished my parents had made me pick up an instrument when I was in second grade. It seemed like it was almost too late now. That's how easy it is to tell yourself it's too late for something. I started doing it at the age of fourteen.

"Is it like languages?" I asked him. "Olive grew up speaking English and Korean and she says it's easy for her to pick up other languages now."

Sam thought about it. "Yeah, totally. I grew up speaking Portuguese a bit as a kid. And in Spanish class I can intuit some of the words. Same thing with knowing how to play the guitar and then learning the bass. There's some overlap, definitely."

"Why did you speak Portuguese?" I asked him. "I mean, are your parents from Portugal?"

"My mom is second-generation Brazilian," he said. "But I was never fluent or anything. Just some words here and there."

The tall girl headed toward the register, so I put down the book in my hand and I met her up at the counter.

She was buying a Danielle Steel novel. When I rang it up, she said, "It's for my mom. For her birthday," as if I was judging her. But I wasn't. I never did. I was far too worried that everyone else was judging me.

"I bet she'll like it," I said. I gave her the total and she took out a credit card and handed it over.

Lindsay Bean.

Immediately, the resemblance was crystal clear. She looked like an older, lankier version of Carolyn. I bagged her book and handed it back to her. Sam, overlooking, pointed to the bookmarks, reminding me. "Oh, wait," I said. "You need a bookmark." I picked one up and slipped it into her bag.

"Thanks," Lindsay said. I wondered if she got along with Carolyn, what the Bean sisters were like. Maybe they loved each other, loved to be together, loved to hang out. Maybe, when Lindsay took Carolyn to the mall to get jeans, she didn't abandon her in the store.

I knew it was silly to assume that Carolyn's life was better than mine just because she had been holding Jesse Lerner's hand yesterday in line for a pack of cookies. But, also, I knew that simply because she *had* been holding Jesse's hand in line for a pack of cookies, her life *was* better than mine.

The sun was starting to set by then. Cars had turned on their headlights. Often, during the evening hours, the low beams of SUVs were just high enough to shine right into the storefront.

This very thing happened just as Lindsay and her friends were making their way outside. A champagne-colored oversized SUV pulled up and parked right in front of the store, its lights focused straight on me. When the driver turned the car off, I could see who it was.

Jesse Lerner was sitting in the front passenger's side of the car. A man, most likely his father, was driving.

The back door opened and out popped Carolyn Bean.

Jesse got out of his side and hugged Carolyn good-bye and then Carolyn got in her sister's car with her sister's two friends.

Then Jesse hopped back into his father's car, glancing into the store for a moment as he did it. I couldn't tell if he saw me. I doubted he was really *looking*, the way I had been.

But I couldn't take my eyes off of him. My gaze followed his silhouette even as Carolyn and Lindsay's car took off, even as Jesse's father turned the headlights back on and three-point-turned out of the parking lot.

When I spun back to what I was doing, I ached somehow. As if Jesse Lerner was meant to be mine and I was being forced to stare right into the heart of the injustice of it all.

My hand hit the stack of bookmarks, sending them into disarray. I gathered them and fixed them myself.

"So I was wondering," Sam said.

"Yeah?"

"If maybe you'd want to, like, go see a movie together sometime."

I turned and looked at him, surprised.

There was too much overwhelming me in that moment. Jesse with Carolyn, the headlights in my eyes, and the fact that someone was actually, possibly, *asking me out on a date*.

I should have said, "Sure." Or "Totally." But instead I said, "Oh. Uh . . ."

And then nothing else.

"No worries," Sam said, clearly desperate for this awkwardness to end. "I get it."

And just like that, I sent Sam Kemper straight into the friend zone.

Two and a half years later, Sam was graduating.

I had spent a good portion of my sophomore year trying to get Sam to ask me out again. I had made jokes about not having anything to do on a Saturday night and I had vaguely implied that we should hang out outside of the store, but he wasn't getting it and I was too much of a chicken to ask him outright. So I let it go.

And since then, Sam and I had become close friends.

So I went with my mom and dad to support him as he sat outside in the sweltering heat in a cap and gown.

Marie was not yet home for the summer from the University of New Hampshire. She was majoring in English, spending her extracurricular time submitting short stories to literary magazines. She had yet to place one but everyone was sure she'd get published somewhere soon. Graham had gone to UNH with her but she broke up with him two months in. Now she was dating someone named Mike whose parents owned a string of sporting goods stores. Marie would often joke that if they got married, they would merge the businesses. "Get it? And sell books and sports equipment at the same store," she'd explain.

As I told Olive, there was no end to the things Marie could say to make me purge my lunch. But no one else seemed to want to vomit around her, and thus, my parents were promoting her to assistant manager for the summer.

Margaret had just recently quit and Marie had lobbied for the job. I was surprised when my mom was reticent to let her do it. "She should be off enjoying herself in college," she said. "Before she comes back here and takes on all of this responsibility."

But my father was so excited about it that even I had softened to the idea. He made her an assistant manager name badge even though none of us wore name badges. And he told my mom that he couldn't be happier than to spend his summer with both of his daughters at the store.

The smile on his face and the gleam in his eye led me to promise myself to be nicer to Marie. But she hadn't even come home yet and I was already unsure it would take.

I was not looking forward to summer at the store. Sam had given his notice the month before and had worked his last day. Instead of staying in town, he was leaving in a few weeks to take an internship at a music therapy office in Boston. And then he was starting at Berklee College of Music in the fall.

It was his first choice and when he got in, I'd congratulated him with a hug. Then I quickly moved on to teasing him for staying so close to home. But I wasn't entirely joking. I truly couldn't understand why his first choice was to live in a part of the country he'd lived in all his life. I had set my sights on the University of Los Angeles. I got a pamphlet in the mail and I liked the idea of going to school in permanent sunshine.

As Sam's name was called out on the converted football field that afternoon, my parents were disagreeing about whether to restain our back patio. I had to nudge my father in the ribs with my elbow to get his attention.

"Guys," I said. "Sam's up."

"Samuel Marcos Kemper," the principal announced.

The three of us stood and cheered for him, joining his own parents, who were seated on the other side of the crowd.

When Sam sat down, I connected eyes with him for a moment and watched a smile creep across his face.

~

Four hours later, Olive and I were standing in the kitchen of Billy Yen's house, filling up our red Solo cups with generic-looking beer from an ice-cold steel keg.

Almost seventeen, I had made out with two guys and dated Robby Timmer for four weeks, during which time I let him get to a tame third base. It was safe to say I was looking to ditch my v-card as soon as the moment was right and I was hoping that moment was sooner rather than later.

Olive, for her part, had come out to her parents as bisexual and then confused them when she started dating Matt Jennings. Olive patiently explained to her parents that bisexual did not mean gay, it meant *bisexual*. And while they seemed to understand, they once again became confused when Olive and Matt broke up and Olive started dating a girl from her after-school job at CVS. They understood gay and they understood straight but they did not understand Olive.

"Did you see who's here?" Olive asked. She took a sip of the beer and made a grimace. "This tastes like water, basically," she said.

"Who?" I asked. I sipped from my cup and found that Olive was right—it did taste watery. But I liked watery beer. It tasted less like beer.

"J-E-S-S-E," Olive said.

"He's here?" I asked.

Olive nodded. "I saw him earlier, by the pool."

Olive and I were not aware, when we heard about the party, that there was a pool and people there would be running around in bikinis and swim shorts, throwing one another in and playing chicken. But even if we had been, we still would have come and we still wouldn't have worn our bathing suits.

I sipped my own drink and then decided to just throw it back in a series of chugs. Then I filled up my cup again.

"All right, well," I said. "Let's just walk around and see if we spot him."

Jesse and Carolyn broke up sometime over spring break earlier that year. It wasn't such a crazy thing to think that Jesse might notice me.

Except that it was. It was totally absurd.

He was now the captain of the swim team, leading our high school to three undefeated seasons. There was an article about him in the local newspaper, titled "Swim Prodigy Jesse Lerner Breaks 500 Meter Freestyle State Record." He was out of my league.

Olive and I took our cups with us out back, joining the chaos surrounding the yard and pool. There were girls on the redwood patio smoking clove cigarettes and laughing together, every single one of them wearing a spaghetti-strap tank and low-cut jeans. I was embarrassed to be wearing the very same thing.

I had on a black tank with flared jeans that came up two inches lower than my belly button. There was a gap between the tank and the jeans, my midriff showing. Olive was wearing flat-front camo-print chinos and a V-neck purple T-shirt, also exposing her lower abs. Now I look at pictures of us back then and I wonder what on earth possessed us to leave the house with our belly buttons hanging out.

"You look great, by the way," Olive said. "This might be your hottest phase yet."

"Thanks," I said. I figured she was referring to the way I'd been wearing my long, blond-brown hair low down my back, parted in the middle. But I also suspected it had something to do with the way that I was growing into my body. I felt more confident about my butt, less shy about my boobs. I stood taller and straighter. I had started wearing dark brown mascara and blush. I had become a slave to lip gloss like every other girl in school. I felt far from a beautiful swan but I no longer felt like an ugly duckling, either. I was somewhere in between, and I think my growing confidence had started showing.

Olive waved a hand in front of her face as the smoke from the cloves drifted over to us. "Why do girls think that just because the cigarette smells vaguely of nutmeg that I would want to smell it any more than a normal one?" She walked away, down toward the pool to put some distance between us and the smoke.

It was only once my feet hit the concrete surrounding the pool that I realized who was about to dive in.

There, in a wet red-and-white bathing suit clinging to his legs, toes lined up perfectly with the edge of the diving board, was . . . Sam.

His hair was wet and mashed down onto his head. His torso was entirely bare. There, underneath the faint chest hair and the sinewy pecks, was a six-pack.

Sam had a six-pack.

What?

Olive and I watched as he bounced slowly, preparing to take flight. And then he was in the air.

He landed with the familiar *thwack* of a belly flop.

Someone yelled, "Ohhhhh, duuude. That had to hurt." And then Sam's head popped up from the water, laughing. He shook the water from his ears and saw me.

He smiled and then started to swim to the edge as a second guy jumped in right after him.

I was suddenly nervous. If Sam came up to me, wet and half-naked, what did I want to happen?

"Another beer?" Olive asked me, holding her cup out to show me it was empty.

I nodded, assuming she would go get them.

But instead she said, "Be a doll," and handed me her cup.

I laughed at her. "You are so annoying."

She smiled. "I know."

I walked up to the keg outside and pumped out enough for one cup before it sputtered out.

"Oh, man!" I heard from behind me.

I turned around.

Jesse Lerner was standing six inches from me in a T-shirt, jeans, and leather sandals. He was smiling in a way that seemed confident but vaguely shy, like he knew how handsome he was and it embarrassed him. "You drained the last of the keg," he said.

It was the first time Jesse had ever said a complete sentence to me, the first time I'd heard a subject followed by a predicate come out of his mouth aimed for my ears.

The only thing that was weird about it was how *not* weird it was. In an instant, Jesse went from someone I saw from afar to someone I felt like I'd been talking to my entire life. I wasn't intimidated, as I always imagined I'd be. I wasn't even nervous. It was like spending years training for a race and finally getting to race it.

"You snooze, you lose," I said, teasing.

"Rules say if you take the last beer you have to chug it," he said.

And then, from the crowd, came the word that no teenager holding a Solo cup ever wants to hear.

"Cops!"

Jesse's head whipped around, looking to confirm that the threat was real, that it wasn't just a bad joke.

In the far corner of the yard, where the driveway ended, you could just make out the blue and red lights across the grass.

And then there was a *whoop*.

I looked around, trying to find Olive, but she'd already taken off into the back woods, catching my eye and pointing for me to do the same.

I dropped the cups on the ground, spilling my beer on my feet. And then I felt a hand on my wrist. Jesse was pulling me with him, off in the opposite direction of everyone else. We weren't going toward the woods in the back; we were headed for the bushes that separated the house from the one next to it.

Everyone was scrambling. What had previously been the controlled type of chaos that rages through a high school kegger became unruly disorder, teenagers running in every direction. It was the closest I'd come to seeing anarchy.

When Jesse and I got to the bushes, he guided me into them first. They were dense and thorny. I could feel the skin on my bare arms and ankles chafing against the tiny sharp blades in every direction.

But the bushes were big enough that Jesse could crawl in next to me and they were dark enough that I felt safe from the police officers. We were far enough away from everyone else that it started to feel quiet—if the background noise of a police siren and heavy running footsteps can ever really be described as quiet.

I could sense Jesse's body right next to me, could feel his arm as it grazed mine.

"Ow!" he said in a stage whisper.

"What?" I whispered back.

"I think I cut my lip on a thorn."

A harsh stream of light cascaded over the bushes we were hiding in and I found myself frozen still.

I could hear my own breath, feel my heart beating against the bone of my chest. I was terrified; there was no doubt about it. I was drunk by this point. Not plastered, by any means, but well past a buzz. There was real danger in getting caught: not only my parents' disappointment, but also the actual threat of being arrested.

That being said, it was impossible to deny the tingle of excitement running through me. It was a rush, to be stifling my own breath as I felt the shadow of a police officer grow closer and closer. It was thrilling to feel adrenaline run through me.

After some time, the coast started to clear. There were no more heavy footsteps, no more flashlights. We heard cars driving away, chattering stop. My ankles had started to itch considerably and I knew I'd been bitten by something or somethings. It was, after all, May in Massachusetts—which meant that every bug in the air was out for blood.

I wasn't sure when to speak up, when to break the silence.

On the one hand, it seemed like it was safe to come out of the bushes. On the other hand, you never want to be wrong about that.

I heard Jesse whisper my name.

"Emma?" he said softly. "Are you okay?"

I didn't even know that he knew my name and there he was, saying it as if it were his to say.

"Yeah," I said. "Maybe a little scraped up but other than that, I'm good. You?"

"Yeah," he said. "I'm good, too."

He was quiet for a moment longer and then he said, "I think it's safe. Are you able to crawl out?"

The way he said it made me think that maybe he'd crawled into the bushes before, that maybe this wasn't the first time Jesse had been at a party he wasn't supposed to be at, doing things he wasn't supposed to be doing.

"Yeah," I said. "I got it."

A few awkward army-crawl-like steps forward and I was standing on the grass in front of Jesse Lerner.

His lip was cut and there was a scrape on the top of his forehead. My arms had a few tiny scratches down them. My ankle still itched. I lifted my foot up and saw a few small welts where my pants met the top of my shoes.

It was pitch-dark, the lights in the house all dimmed. Everything was deadly quiet. The only sound either of us could hear was the sound of our own breath and that of the crickets rubbing their wings together, chirping.

I wasn't sure what we were supposed to do now. How we were supposed to get home.

"C'mon," Jesse said, and then he took my hand again. Twice in one night, holding hands with Jesse Lerner. I had to remind myself not to take it too personally. "We will walk down the street until we find somebody else who escaped and bum a ride with them."

"Okay," I said, willing to follow his lead because I had no better idea. I just wanted to get home quickly so I could call

Olive and make sure she was okay and make sure she knew that I was.

And then, there was Sam. He'd been there, in the pool. Where had he gone?

Jesse and I set out down the dark suburban road, headed nowhere in particular, hoping it would lead us somewhere good.

"How come you weren't swimming?" I asked him once we were a few feet down the road.

Jesse looked at me. "What do you mean?"

"I mean, aren't you supposed to be the greatest swimmer of all time?"

Jesse laughed. "I don't know about that."

"You were written up in the *Beacon*."

"Yeah, but I'm not a fish. I do exist outside of the water," he teased.

I shrugged. "Question still stands, though," I said. "It was a pool party."

He was quiet for a moment. I thought maybe the conversation was over, maybe we weren't supposed to be talking, maybe he didn't want to talk to me. But once he finally started talking again, I realized that he had been caught up in his own head for a moment, deciding how much to say.

"Do you ever feel like everyone is always telling you who you are?" he asked me. "Like, people are acting as if they know better than you what you're good at or who you are supposed to be?"

"Yeah," I said. "I think so."

"Can I let you in on a very poorly kept secret?" he asked me.

"Yeah."

"My parents want me to train for the Olympic trials."

"Ah." He was right. That was a very poorly kept secret.

"Can I let you in on a better-kept secret?" he asked.

I nodded.

"I hate swimming."

He was staring forward, putting one foot in front of the other along the road.

"Do your parents know that?" I asked him.

He shook his head. "Nobody does," he said. "Well, I guess, except for you now."

At the time, I could not, for the life of me, understand why he told me this, why he trusted me with the truth about his life more than anyone else. I thought it meant that I was special, that maybe he had always felt about me the way I felt about him.

Now, looking back on it, I know it was just the opposite. I was a girl in the background of his life—that's what made me safe.

"I never really cared much for swimming anyway," I told him reassuringly. I said it because it was the truth. But there was a large secondary benefit in what I'd said.

Now I knew who he really was and I still liked him. And that made me different from anyone else.

"My parents run the bookstore," I said. "Blair Books."

"Yeah," he said. "I know. I mean, I put that together." He smiled at me and then looked away. We made our way around a corner and found ourselves on the main road.

"They want me to take over the store one day," I told him. "They are always giving me these five hundred–page novels as presents and telling me that one day I'll fall in love with reading just like they have and . . . I don't know."

"What?" Jesse asked.

"I hate reading books."

Jesse smiled, surprised and satisfied. He put his hand up, offering me a high five. He had confided in me because he thought I was a stranger, only to find that I was a comrade.

I laughed and leaned over, raising my palm to his. We slapped and then Jesse held on for a moment.

"Are you drunk?" he asked me.

"A little," I said. "Are you?"

"A little," he answered back.

He didn't let go of my hand and I thought maybe, just maybe, he was going to kiss me. And then I thought that was an insane thing to think. *That would never happen.*

Later on, when Jesse and I would tell each other everything, I asked him what he was thinking back then. I'd say, "That moment when you held on to my hand, right before the cops found us, were you going to kiss me?" He'd say he didn't know. He'd say that all he remembered was that he had just realized, for the first time, how pretty I was. "I just remember noticing the freckles under your eye. So, maybe. Maybe I was going to kiss you. I don't know."

And we will never know.

Because just as I built up enough confidence to look Jesse right in the eye in the wee hours of the morning, we were blinded by the stunning bright light of a police officer's flashlight, aimed directly into our eyes. We were drunk on the sidewalk, caught red-handed.

A litany of half-assed lies and two failed Breathalyzers later, Jesse and I sat handcuffed along the wall of the Acton Police Department waiting to be picked up.

"My parents are going to kill me," I said to him. "I don't think I've ever heard my dad as pissed as he was on the phone." In the bright light of the police station, the cut on Jesse's lip looked burgundy, the bug bites on my ankles almost terra-cotta.

I thought Jesse would react by telling me how much worse he had it, how much more unbearable his parents would un-doubtedly be. But he didn't. Instead he said, "I'm sorry."

"No," I said, shaking my head. I never realized how often I used my hands to talk until they were constrained. "It's not your fault."

Jesse shrugged. "Maybe," he said. "But I'm still sorry."

"Well, then, I'm sorry, too."

He smiled. "Apology accepted."

There was a list of recent detainments on the table just to our left. I kept sneaking peeks at it to see if anyone else had been caught. I saw a few names of seniors I recognized but no Olive, no Sam. I felt confident I'd been the only one of us picked off.

"Are you worried about your parents?" I said.

Jesse thought about it and then shook his head. "My parents have a very specific set of rules and as long as I don't break any of those, I can pretty much do whatever I want."

"What are the rules?" I asked.

"Break state records and don't get anything below a B-minus."

"Seriously?" I said. "Those are the only rules you have to live by?"

"Do you know how hard it is to break state records *and* get a B-minus in all of your classes?" Jesse wasn't angry at me, but there was an edge to his voice.

I nodded.

"But the upside is they didn't seem too angry on the phone when I called them from the police station at one a.m. So I have that."

I laughed and then fiddled with my arms in the cuffs, trying to keep them from rubbing against the bone of my wrists.

"Why are they making us wear these?" I asked. "They didn't even arrest us. What do they think we are going to do? Run away?"

Jesse laughed. "Maybe. We could escape out of here. Go all Bonnie and Clyde." I wondered if he knew Bonnie and Clyde were lovers. I thought about telling him.

"So your parents aren't going to take it as well, huh?" Jesse asked.

I shook my head. "Oh, hell no. No, I'm going to be working shifts at the store from now until I'm ninety-two years old, basically."

"The bookstore?"

"Yeah; that's my parents' favorite mode of punishment. Also, they are under the illusion that my sister and I are going to one day take over the store, so . . ."

"Is that what you want to do?"

"Run a bookstore? Are you kidding me? Absolutely not."

"What do you want to do?"

"Get out of Acton," I said. "That's number one. I want to see the world. First stop, the Pacific Ocean, and then the sky's the limit."

"Oh yeah?" he said. "I've been thinking about applying to a few schools in California. I figured if I'm three thousand miles away, my parents can't force me to train doubles."

"I was thinking about doing that, too," I said. "California, I mean. I don't know if my parents will let me, but I want to go to the University of Los Angeles."

"To study what?"

"No idea. I just know that I want to join, like, every abroad program they have. See the world."

"That sounds awesome," Jesse said. "I want to do that. I want to see the world."

"I just don't know if my parents will go for it," I said.

"If you want to do something, you *have* to do it."

"What? That doesn't even make sense."

"Of course it does. If you want something as passionately as you clearly want this, that means you owe it to yourself to make it happen. That's what I'm doing. I want out so I'm getting out. I'm going far, far away. You should, too," he said.

"I don't think my parents would like that," I said.

"Your parents don't have to be you. You have to be you. My philosophy is that, you know, you did it their way for a long time. Soon, it's time for your way."

It was plain to see that Jesse wasn't really talking about my parents and me. But everything that he said resonated. It reverberated in my mind, growing louder instead of softer.

"I think you're right," I said.

"I know I'm right," he said, smiling.

"No, really. I'm going to apply to the University of Los Angeles."

"Good for you," he said.

"And you should, too," I told him. "Stop swimming if you hate it. Do something else. Something you love."

Jesse smiled. "You know, you're nothing like I imagined you'd be."

"What do you mean?" I asked him. It was hard for me to believe that Jesse had thought about me before, that he even knew I existed before tonight.

"I don't know; you're just . . . different."

"In a good way or a bad way?"

"Oh, definitely a good way," he said, nodding. "For sure."

"What did you think I was like before?" I asked, now desperate to know. How did I seem before that was bad? I needed to make sure I didn't seem like it again.

"It doesn't matter," he said.

"C'mon," I said. "Just say whatever it is."

"I don't want to, like, embarrass you or something," Jesse said.

"What? What are you talking about?"

Jesse looked at me. And then decided to just say it. "I don't know. I got the impression that maybe you might have had a crush on me."

I could feel myself move away from him. "What? No, I didn't."

He shrugged as if this was no skin off his back. "Okay, see? I was wrong."

"What made you think that?"

"Carolyn, my ex-girlfriend . . ." he said, starting to explain.

"I know who Carolyn is," I said.

"Well, she thought that you might."

"Why would she think that?"

"I don't know. Because she was always jealous when girls looked at me. And you must have looked at me once. And it made her think that."

"But, I mean, you believed her."

"Well, I mean, I hoped she was right."

"Why?"

"What do you mean, 'why'?"

"Why did you hope that she was right? Did you want me to have a crush on you?"

"Of course I did. Doesn't everyone want people to have crushes on them?"

"Did you want *me* in particular to have a crush on you?"

"Sure," Jesse said as if it were obvious.

"But why?"

"Well, it doesn't matter why, does it? Because you didn't. So it's irrelevant."

A conversational roadblock.

It was one I could only get past if I admitted the truth. I weighed the pros and cons, trying to decide if it was worth it.

"Fine—I had a crush on you once. Freshman year."

Jesse turned and smiled at me. "Oh yeah?"

"Yeah, but it's over."

"Why is it over?"

"I don't know; you were with Carolyn. I barely knew you."

"But I'm not with Carolyn and you know me now."

"What are you saying?"

"Why don't you have a thing for me now?"

"Why don't you have a thing for *me* now?" I asked.

And that's when Jesse said the thing that set my entire adult love life in motion. "I think I actually do have a thing for you. As of about an hour and a half ago."

I looked at him, stunned. Trying to find the words.

"Well, then I do, too," I finally said.

"See?" he said, smiling. "I thought so."

And then he leaned over when no one was looking and he kissed me.

That summer, I had to work triple the normal amount of shifts at the store as penance for my underage drinking. I had to listen to four separate lectures from my parents about how I had disappointed them, how they never thought I'd be the kind of daughter who got *detained*.

Marie took the assistant manager job, making her my boss

for a third of the hours I was awake. I learned that the only thing I disliked more than hanging out with her was taking orders from her.

Olive spent the summer on the Cape with her older brother, waiting tables and sunbathing.

Sam moved to Boston two weeks ahead of schedule and never said good-bye.

But I didn't mind any of that. Because that was the summer Jesse and I fell in love.

E mma, would you just turn around?"

"What?" I said.

"Just turn around, for crying out loud!"

And so I did, to find Jesse standing behind me on a sandy beach in Malibu, California. He was holding a small ruby ring. It was nine years after he kissed me that first time in the Acton Police Station.

"Jesse . . ." I said.

"Will you marry me?"

I was speechless. But not because he was asking me to marry him. We were twenty-five. We'd been together our entire adult lives. We had both moved across the country in order to attend the University of Los Angeles. We'd spent our junior year abroad in Sydney, Australia, and backpacked across Europe for five months after we graduated.

And we had built a life for ourselves in LA, far away from Blair Books and five hundred–meter freestyles. Jesse had become a production assistant on nature documentaries, his jobs taking him as far as Africa and as close to home as the Mojave Desert.

I, in a turn of events that seemed to infuriate Marie, had become a travel writer. My sophomore year of school, I found out about a class called travel literature offered by the School of Journalism. I'd heard that it wasn't an easy class to get into.

In fact, the professor only took nine students per year. But if you got in, the class subsidized a trip to a different place every year. That year was Alaska.

I'd never seen Alaska. And I knew I couldn't afford to go on my own. But I had no interest in writing.

It was Jesse who finally pushed me to apply.

The application required a thousand-word piece on any city or town in the world. I wrote an essay about Acton. I played up its rich history, its school system, its local bookstore—basically, I tried to see my hometown through my father's eyes and put it down on paper. It seemed a small price to pay to go to Alaska.

My essay was fairly awful. But there were only sixteen applications that year, and apparently, seven other essays were worse.

I thought Alaska was nice. It was my first time leaving the continental United States and I had to be honest with myself and admit it hadn't been all it was cracked up to be. But imagine everyone's surprise when I found that I loved writing about Alaska even more than I liked being there.

I became a journalism major and I worked hard at improving my interviewing techniques and imagery, as per the advice of most of my professors.

I graduated college a writer.

That's the part that I knew killed Marie.

I was the writer of the family while she was in Acton, running the bookstore.

It had taken me a couple of years to get a job that sent me out on assignments, but by the age of twenty-five, I was an assistant editor at a travel blog, with a tiny salary but with the luxury of having visited five of the seven continents.

The downside was that Jesse and I had very little money.

On the cusp of twenty-six, neither of us had health insurance and we were still eating saltines and peanut butter for dinner some nights.

But the upside was so much sweeter: Jesse and I had seen the world—both together and separately.

Jesse and I had talked about getting married. It was obvious to everyone, ourselves included, that we would have a wedding one day. We knew it was what we would do when the time was right, the way you know that once you shampoo your hair, you condition it.

So I was not shocked that Jesse wanted to marry me.

What shocked me was that there was any ring at all.

"I know it's small," he said apologetically as I put it on. "And it's not a diamond."

"I love it," I told him.

"Do you recognize it?"

I gave it another glance, trying to discern what he meant.

It had a yellow-gold band with a round red stone in the middle. It was banged up and scratched, clearly secondhand. I loved it. I loved everything about it. But I didn't recognize it.

"No?" I said.

"Are you sure?" he said, teasing me. "If you think about it for a second, I think you might."

I stared again. But the ring on my finger was much less interesting to me than the man who had given it to me.

Jesse had grown up to be even more handsome than he had been cute. His shoulders had grown wider, his back more sturdy. No longer training, he had gained weight in his torso, but it was weight that fit him fine. His cheekbones stood out in almost any light. And his smile had matured in a way that made me think he'd be handsome late into life.

I was madly in love with him and had been for as long as I could remember. We had a deep and meaningful history together. It was Jesse who had held my hand when my parents were furious to find out I'd never sent in my application to the University of Massachusetts, and in doing so, had forced their hand to send me to California. It was Jesse who supported me when they asked me to move home after we graduated, Jesse who dried my tears when my father was heartbroken that I would not come home to help run the store. And it was also Jesse who helped me remain confident that, eventually, my parents and I would see eye-to-eye again one day.

The boy that I first saw that day at the swimming pool had turned into an honorable and kind man. He opened doors for me. He bought me Diet Coke and Ben & Jerry's Chunky Monkey when I had a bad day. He took photos of all the places he'd been, all the places he and I had been together, and decorated our home with them.

And now, as we firmly settled into adulthood and the resentments of his childhood faded away, Jesse had started swimming long distance again. Not often, not regularly, but sometimes. He said he still couldn't stand the chlorine smell of the pool, but he was starting to fall in love with the salt of the ocean. I was so enamored with him for that.

"I'm sorry," I said. "I don't think I've ever seen this ring before."

Jesse laughed. "Barcelona," he said. "The night of—"

I gasped.

He smiled, knowing that he didn't need to finish the sentence.

"No . . ." I said.

He nodded.

We had just gotten into Barcelona on the Eurail from Madrid. There was a woman selling jewelry on the street. The two of us were exhausted and headed straight for our hostel. But the woman was hounding us to please take a look.

So we did.

I saw a ruby ring.

And I'd said to Jesse, "See? I don't need anything fancy like a diamond. Just a ring like this is beautiful."

And here it was, a ruby ring.

"You got me a ruby ring!" I said.

Jesse shook his head. "Not just *a* ruby ring . . ."

"This isn't *the* ruby ring," I said.

Jesse laughed. "Yes, it is! This is what I've been trying to tell you. This is *that* ring."

I looked at it, stunned. I pulled my hand away from my face, getting a better view. "Wait, are you serious? How did you do that?"

I had visions of Jesse making international phone calls and paying exorbitant shipping fees, but the truth was much simpler.

"I snuck back and bought it when you went looking for a bathroom that night," he said.

My eyes went wide. "You've had this ring for five years?"

Jesse shrugged. "I knew I was going to marry you. What was the point of waiting to buy you some diamond when I knew exactly what you wanted?"

"Oh, my God," I said. I was blushing. "I can't believe it. It fits perfectly. What are . . . what are the odds of that?"

"Well," Jesse said shyly, "actually pretty high."

I looked at him, wondering what he meant.

"I took it to a jeweler to have it resized based on another one of your rings."

I could tell he was worried this made it less romantic. But to me, it was only more so.

"Wow," I said. "Just . . . wow."

"You didn't answer my question," he said. "Will you marry me?"

It seemed like an absurd thing to ask; the answer was so obvious. It was like asking if someone liked French fries or whether rain was wet.

Standing there on the beach, with the sand underneath our feet, the Pacific Ocean in front of us, and our home just a few miles away, I wondered how I got so lucky to be given everything I ever wanted.

"Yes," I said as I wrapped my arms around his neck. "Absolutely. Of course. Definitely. Yes."

We were married Memorial Day weekend at Jesse's family's cabin in Maine.

We had talked about a destination wedding in Prague but it wasn't realistic. When we resigned ourselves to marrying in the United States, Jesse wanted to do it in Los Angeles.

But for some reason I didn't want to do it anywhere but back in New England. The impulse surprised me. I had spent so much time exploring everywhere else, had put so much emphasis on getting away.

But once I had put enough distance between myself and where I grew up, I started to see its beauty. I started to see it the way outsiders do—maybe because I had become an outsider.

So I told Jesse I thought we should get married back home, during the spring, and though he did take a bit of convincing, he agreed.

And then it became obvious that the easiest place to do it was up by Jesse's parents' cabin.

Naturally, my parents were thrilled. In some ways, I think the night I was caught by the cops and the day I called my parents and told them we were going to get married in New England shared a lot in common.

Both times, I had done something my parents thought was wildly out of character for me, and it surprised them so much that it instantly changed things between us.

Back in high school, it had made them distrust me. I suspect it had been the trouble with the police that did it more than the drinking. And the fact that I started dating the very boy with whom I'd been detained only served to compound the problem. To them, I had gone from a precious little girl to a hooligan overnight.

And with the wedding, I went from their independent, globe-trotting daughter to a bird flying home to the nest.

My mom handled a lot of the finer details, coordinating with Jesse's parents, reserving the spot by the lighthouse on the water just a mile away, and choosing the wedding cake when Jesse and I couldn't make it back for the taste test. My dad helped negotiate with the inn down the street, where we'd have our reception. Marie, married to Mike just nine months before us, lent us the place settings and table linens from their wedding.

Olive flew to Los Angeles from her home in Chicago to host my bachelorette party and my bridal shower. She got rip-roaring drunk at the former and wore a shift dress and an over-sized hat to the latter. She was the first to arrive the weekend of the wedding—always proving that Olive didn't do anything half-assed.

Our friendship had been a long-distance one since we went off to college. But I never met another woman who meant to me what she did. No one else could make me laugh like she could. So my oldest friend remained my best friend, despite however many miles kept us apart, and it was for that reason that I made her my maid of honor.

There was a brief moment when my mother and father seemed unsure whether to acknowledge that Marie and I had not chosen each other for that esteemed role. But we were bridesmaids for each other and this seemed to mollify them.

As for Jesse's side of the bridal party, those spots went to his two older brothers.

Jesse's parents didn't ever really care for me very much and I always knew that it was because they blamed me for the fact that he stopped swimming. Jesse had confronted them, had told them the full truth: that he hated training, that he was never going to pursue it on his own. But all they saw was the convenient chronology: I showed up and suddenly Jesse didn't want what they believed he'd always wanted.

But once Jesse and I became engaged—and once Francine and Joe found out we were willing to have the wedding at their cabin—they opened up a bit more. Maybe they just saw the writing on the wall—Jesse was going to marry me whether they liked me or not. But I like to think that they simply started seeing me clearly. I think they found there was a lot to like about me once they started looking. And that Jesse had grown into an impressive man regardless of whether or not he followed their dream.

Aside from a few minor breakdowns over my dress and whether we should practice for our first dance, Jesse and I had a relatively painless wedding-planning experience.

As for the actual day, the truth is I don't remember it.

I just remember glimpses.

I remember my mother pulling the dress up around me.

I remember pulling the train of it high enough as I walked to avoid getting the edges dirty.

I remember the flowers smelling more pungent than they had in the store.

I remember looking at Jesse as I walked down the open aisle—looking at the black sheen on his tux, the perfect wave of his hair—and having a sense of overwhelming peace.

I remember standing with him as we had our picture taken during the cocktail hour between the ceremony and the reception. I remember he whispered into my ear, "I want to be alone with you," just as a flash went off on the photographer's camera.

I remember saying, "I know, but there's still so much . . . wedding left."

I remember taking his hand and escaping out of sight when the photographer went to change the battery in his camera.

We rushed back to the cabin when no one was looking. It was there, alone with Jesse, that I could focus again. I could breathe easy. I felt grounded. I felt like myself for the first time all day.

"I can't believe we just snuck out of our own wedding," I said.

"Well . . ." Jesse put his arms around me. "It's our wedding. We're allowed to."

"I'm not sure that's how it works," I said.

Jesse had already started unzipping my dress. It would barely budge. So he pushed the slim skirt of it up around my thighs.

We had not made it past the kitchen. Instead, I hopped up on the kitchen counter. As Jesse pushed up against me, as I pressed my body against his, it felt different from all the other times we'd done it.

It meant more.

A half hour later, just as I was coming out of the bathroom fixing my hair, Marie knocked on the door.

Everyone wanted to know where we were.

It was time to be announced.

"I guess we have to go, then," Jesse said to me, smiling with the knowledge of what we'd been doing as we kept them waiting.

"I guess so," I said in the same spirit.

"Yeah," Marie said, none-too-amused. "I guess so."

She walked ahead of us as we made the short walk over to the inn.

"Looks like we've angered the Booksellers' Daughter," Jesse whispered.

"I think you're right," I said.

"I have something really important to tell you," he said. "Are you ready? It's really important. It's breaking news."

"Tell me."

"I'll love you forever."

"I already knew that," I said. "And I'll love you forever, too."

"Yeah?"

"Yeah," I said. "I'll love you until we're so old we can barely walk on our own and we have to get walkers and put those cut-up yellow tennis balls on them. I'll love you past that, actually. I'll love you until the end of time."

"You sure?" he said, smiling at me, pulling me toward him. Marie was just up ahead, grabbing the door to the reception hall. I could hear the din of large-scale small talk. I imagined a room full of my friends and family introducing themselves to one another. I imagined Olive already having made friends with half of my father's extended family.

When this was over, Jesse and I were leaving on a ten-day trip to India, courtesy of his parents. No living out of backpacks or sleeping in hostels. No deadlines or film shoots while we were there. Just two people in love with each other, in love with the world.

"Are you kidding?" I asked. "You are my one true love. I don't even think I'm capable of loving anyone else."

The double doors opened and Jesse and I walked through,

into the reception hall, just as I heard the DJ announce, "Introducing . . . Jesse and Emma Lerner!"

Hearing my new name felt jarring to me, for a moment. It sounded like someone else. I assumed I would get over it in time, that it would grow on me, likening this moment to the first few days of a haircut.

Besides, the name didn't matter. None of that mattered when I had the man of my dreams.

It was the happiest day of my life.

Emma and Jesse. Forever.

Three hundred and sixty-four days later, he was gone.

The last time I saw Jesse he was wearing navy blue chinos, Vans, and a heather gray T-shirt. It was his favorite. He'd done the laundry the day before just so he could wear it.

It was the day before our anniversary. I had managed to snag a freelance assignment writing up a piece on a new hotel in the Santa Ynez Valley in Southern California. Despite the fact that a work trip isn't exactly the most romantic way to spend an anniversary, Jesse was going to join me on the trip. We would celebrate one year of marriage touring the hotel, taking notes on the food, and then squeezing in a visit to a vineyard or two.

But Jesse was asked to join an old boss of his on a quick four-day shoot in the Aleutian Islands.

And unlike me, he had not yet been to Alaska.

"I want to see glaciers," Jesse said. "You've seen them but I haven't yet."

I thought about how it felt to stare at something so white it looked blue, so large that you felt small, so peaceful you forgot just what an environmental threat they posed. I understood why he wanted to go. But I also knew that if I were in his position, I'd turn down the opportunity.

Some of it was travel fatigue. He and I had spent almost ten years grabbing on to every opportunity to get on a plane or a train. I was working at a travel blog and writing freelance on the side, doing my best to get placed in loftier and loftier publications.

I was a professional at navigating security checkpoints and baggage claims. I had enough frequent-flyer miles to go absolutely anywhere I dreamed of.

And I'm not saying that travel wasn't incredible, that our life wasn't incredible. Because it was.

I had been to the Great Wall of China. I'd hiked a waterfall in Costa Rica. I'd tasted pizza in Naples, strudel in Vienna, bangers and mash in London. I'd seen the *Mona Lisa*. I'd been inside the Taj Mahal.

I had some of my most incredible experiences abroad.

But I'd also had a lot of them right in my own home. Inventing cheap at-home dinners with Jesse, walking down the street late at night to split a pint of ice cream, waking up early on Saturday mornings to the sun shining through the sliding glass door.

I had predicated my life on the idea that I wanted to see everywhere extraordinary, but I'd come to realize that extraordinary is everywhere.

And I was starting to yearn for a chance to settle in somewhere and maybe, perhaps, not need to rush to get on a plane to go somewhere else.

I had just found out that Marie was pregnant with her first child. She and Mike were buying a house a short commute from Acton. It seemed all but finalized that she would take over the store. The Booksellers' Daughter realizing her full potential.

But here is what surprised me: I had the smallest inkling that her life didn't sound quite so bad.

She wasn't always packing or unpacking. She was never jetlagged. She never had to buy a phone charger she already had because she'd forgotten the original thousands of miles away.

I had mentioned all of this to Jesse.

"Do you ever just want to go home?" I said.

"We are home," he'd said to me.

"No, *home* home. To Acton home."

Jesse looked at me suspiciously and said, "You must be an impostor. Because the real Emma would never say that."

I laughed and let it go.

But I wasn't *actually* letting it go. Case in point: If Jesse and I were going to have children, were we still going to be hopping on a quick flight to Peru? And maybe more important: Was I ready to raise children in Los Angeles?

The very moment these questions occurred to me, I started to realize that my life plans had never really extended past my twenties. I had never asked myself if I *always* wanted to be traveling, if I *always* wanted to live so far from my parents.

I began to suspect that this jet-setting Jesse and I had been living had always felt temporary to me, like something I knew I needed to do and then one day would be over.

I think that I wanted to settle down one day.

And the only thing that shocked me more than realizing it was realizing I had never realized it before.

Of course, it did not help matters that I was pretty sure Jesse hadn't been thinking any of this. I was pretty sure Jesse wasn't thinking this at all.

We had created a life of spontaneous adventure. Of seeing all the things people say one day they will see.

I couldn't very well change the entire modus operandi of our lives.

So even though I wanted him to skip Alaska and go to Southern California with me, I told him to go.

And he was right. I'd already seen a glacier. But he hadn't.

So—instead of preparing to celebrate our one-year wedding anniversary—I was driving Jesse to LAX so that he could hop on a flight to Anchorage.

"We'll celebrate our anniversary when I get home," he said. "I'm gonna go all out. Candles, wine, flowers. I'll even serenade you. And I'll call you tomorrow."

He was meeting the rest of the crew in Anchorage and then getting on a private plane, landing in Akun Island. Most of the time after that, he'd be filming aerial shots from a helicopter.

"Don't stress out about it," I said. "If you can't call, I totally get it."

"Thank you," he said as he gathered his bags and looked at me. "I love you more than anyone has ever loved anyone in the history of the world. Do you know that? Do you know that Antony didn't love Cleopatra as much as I love you? Do you know that Romeo didn't love Juliet as much as I love you?"

I laughed. "I love you, too," I said. "More than Liz Taylor loved Richard Burton."

Jesse came around the side of the car and stood at my window.

"Wow," he said, smiling. "That's a lot."

"All right. Get out of here, would you? I have errands to run."

Jesse laughed and kissed me good-bye. And then I watched him walk in front of our car through the automatic doors, into the belly of Los Angeles International Airport.

Just then, my favorite song came on the radio. I turned up the volume, sang at the top of my lungs, and pulled the car away from the curb.

As I navigated the streets back home, Jesse texted me.

I love you. I'll miss you.

He must have sent it just before he went through airport security, maybe right after. But I didn't see it until an hour or so later.

I texted him back.

I'll miss you every second of every day. Xoxo

I knew that he might not see it for a while, that I might not hear from him for a few days.

I pictured him riding in a small plane, landing on the island, hopping into a helicopter, and soon seeing a glacier so big it left him breathless.

I woke up the morning of our anniversary, sick to my stomach. I rushed to the bathroom and vomited.

I had no idea why. To this day, I don't know if I ate something bad or if, on some level, I could just sense the looming tragedy in my bones, the way that some dogs can tell a hurricane is coming.

Jesse didn't call to wish me a happy anniversary.

The commercial flight made it to Anchorage.

The Cessna made it to Akun Island.

But the first time they took the helicopter out, it never came back.

The best anyone could conclude was it went down somewhere over the North Pacific.

The four people on board were lost.

My husband, my one true love . . .

Gone.

Francine and Joe flew into LA and moved into my apartment. My own parents came and rented a hotel a few minutes' walk away but spent every waking minute with me.

Francine kept saying that she didn't understand why this wasn't a national news story, why there wasn't a nationwide search party.

Joe kept telling her that helicopters crash all the time. He said it as if it were good news, as if that meant there was a plan in place for moments like these.

"They will find him," he would say to her over and over. "If anyone can swim to safety, it's our son."

I held it together for as long as I could. I held Francine as she sobbed in my arms. I told her, just as Joe did, that it was only a matter of time until we got a call saying he was safe.

My mom made casseroles and I would cut them up and put them on plates for Francine and Joe and say things like, "We need to eat." But I never did.

I cried when no one was around and I found it hard to look in the mirror, but I kept telling everyone that we would find Jesse soon.

And then they found a propeller of the helicopter on the shore of Adak Island. With Jesse's backpack. And the body of the pilot.

The call we had been waiting for came.

But it went nothing like we expected.

Jesse had not yet been found.

He was believed to be dead.

After I hung up the phone, Francine broke down. Joe was frozen still. My parents stared at me, stunned.

I said, "That's crazy. Jesse didn't die. He wouldn't do that."

~

Francine developed such strong panic attacks that Joe flew her home and checked her into a hospital.

My mom and dad stayed on an air mattress at the foot of my bed, watching my every move. I told them I had a handle on it. I thought, for certain, that I did.

I spent three days walking around in a daze, waiting for the telephone to ring, waiting for someone *else* to call and say the first call had been wrong.

That second call never came. Instead, my phone was tied up with people checking in to see if I was OK.

And then, one day, Marie called and said she'd left Mike in charge of the store. She was flying in to be here for me.

I was far too numb to decide whether I wanted her around.

The day Marie arrived, I woke up late in the afternoon to find that my mom had gone to the store and my dad had left to pick Marie up from the airport. My first time alone in what felt like forever.

It was a clear day. I decided I didn't want to be in my house anymore. But I didn't want to leave it, either. I got dressed and asked the neighbors if I could borrow their ladder so that I could clean the gutters.

I had no intention of cleaning anything. I just wanted to stand, high up on the earth, unencumbered by the safety of walls, floors, and ceilings. I wanted to stand high enough that if I fell, it'd kill me. This is not the same thing as wanting to die.

I climbed up to the roof and stood there, with glassy bloodshot eyes. I stared straight ahead, looking at treetops and into the windows of high-rises. It didn't make me feel any better than being in the house. But it didn't make me feel any worse, either. So I stayed there. Just standing and looking. Looking at anything that didn't make me want to crawl into a ball and fade away.

And then I saw, in the sliver of a view between two buildings, so far in the distance you almost couldn't make it out . . .

The ocean.

I thought, *Maybe Jesse is out there in the water. Maybe he's swimming. Maybe he's building a raft to get home.*

The hope that I clung to in that moment didn't feel good or freeing. It felt cruel. As if the world were giving me just enough rope to hang myself.

I got down off the roof and searched through Jesse's things. I ransacked his closet, dresser, and desk before I found them.

Binoculars.

I got back up on the roof and I stood right where I could see the sliver of sea. I waited.

I was not enjoying the view. I was not relishing the peace and quiet. I was not reveling in my solitude.

I was looking for Jesse.

I saw waves cresting onto the shore. I saw a boat. I saw people under umbrellas, lying on towels, as if there wasn't important work to be done.

I heard my dad and sister enter the house and start looking around for me. I heard, "Emma?" coming from them in every room of the house. I recognized the worry as it grew in their voices, as each time they said my name they were met with more silence. Soon, my mom came home and her voice joined the chorus.

But I couldn't respond. I had to stand there and watch for Jesse. It was my duty, as his wife. I had to be the first to spot him when he made landfall.

When I noticed someone coming up to the roof, I assumed it was my dad and I thought, *Good, he can look, too.*

But it was Marie.

She stood there, looking at me, as I held the binoculars up to my face and stared at the ocean.

"Hi," she said.

"Hi."

"What are you doing?" she said as she started walking toward me.

"I'm going to find him."

I felt Marie put her arm around my shoulder. "You can't . . . that won't . . . work," she said.

"I have to be looking for him. I can't give up on him."

"Em, give me the binoculars."

I wanted to ignore her, but I needed to explain my logic. "Jesse could come back. We have to be watching."

"He isn't coming back."

"You don't know that."

"Yes. Yes, I do."

"You just can't stand that I'm no longer in your shadow," I said to her. "Because it means you aren't the center of the world anymore. Jesse is coming back, Marie. And I am going to sit here and wait until he does. Because I know my husband. I know how incredible he is. And I'm not going to allow you to make me feel like he's anything less just because you like it better when I feel small."

Marie reared her head back, as though I'd struck her.

"I have to stay here and watch for him. It's my job. As his wife."

When I saw the look on my sister's face in that moment, a mixture of compassion and fear, I realized that she thought I was crazy.

For a moment, I wondered, *Oh, my God. Am I crazy?*

"Emma, I'm so sorry," she said as she put her arms around me and held me the way a mother holds a child, as if we were of the same body. I was not used to that type of sister, the type of sister that is also a friend. I was used to having *just* a sister, the way some of your teachers are just teachers and some of your coworkers are just coworkers. "Jesse is dead," she told me. "He's not out there somewhere trying to come home. He's gone. Forever. I'm so sorry. I'm so, so sorry."

For a moment, I wondered, *What if she's right?*

"He's not dead," I said, my voice wavering and rocky. "He's out there."

"He's not out there," she said. "He's dead."

For a moment, I wondered, *Is that possible?*

And then the truth washed over me like a flood.

~

I sobbed so hard for so long that every day I would wake up with my eyes swollen shut. I didn't get dressed for three weeks.

I cried for him, and for what I'd lost, and for every day left of my life that I had left to live without him.

My mom had to force me to bathe. She stood in the shower with me, holding my naked body up to the water, carrying my entire weight in her arms because I wouldn't stand up on my own.

The world seemed so dark and bleak and meaningless. Life seemed so pointless, so cruel.

I thought of how Jesse took care of me and how he held me. I thought of how he felt when he ran his hands down my back, how his breath smelled sweet and human.

I lost hope and love and all of my kindness.

I told my mom that I wanted to die.

I said it even though I knew it would hurt her to hear it. I had to say it because of how much it hurt to feel it.

She winced and closed her eyes and then she said, "I know. But you can't. You have to live. You have to find a way to live."

Six weeks after I left Jesse at the airport, I came out of my bedroom, walked into the kitchen where my parents were talking, and I said, with a calmness and clarity of purpose that I had been lacking for weeks, "I want to go back to Acton. I don't want to stay here anymore."

My father nodded and my mom said, "Whatever you need."

I do not remember who packed up my things, who sold my car and my furniture. I do not remember getting on the plane. All I know is that, a week later, I landed at Logan Airport.

Home.

Emma and Sam
Or, how to put yourself back together

When you lose someone you love, it's hard to imagine that you'll ever feel better. That, one day, you'll manage to be in a good mood simply because the weather is nice or the barista at the coffee shop on the corner remembered your order.

But it does happen.

If you're patient and you work at it.

It starts just by breathing in the Massachusetts air again. Your soul recharges ever so slightly when you see brick walkways and brownstones in Boston, when you pull into your parents' driveway and move back into your old bedroom.

Your emotional fortitude grows stronger as you sleep in your childhood bed and eat your mother's pancakes for breakfast and hide from most of the world.

You spend all of your time watching the Travel Channel and you get so bored of it that you pick up a novel from the stack of books in your bedroom, the books that your parents have given you over the years that you refused to crack open until now.

You read all the way through to the end of one, only to find out that the husband dies. You hurl the book across the room, breaking the bedside lamp. When your mom comes home that night, you tell her what happened. You ask her for books to read where no one dies.

Two days later, you find both of your parents in the living

room with a pile of novels on the coffee table. They are skimming through them one by one, making sure every character lives to the end. That night, you have a new stack of books to read and you open up the first one, confident it won't break you down.

It is the first time in a long time that you have felt safe.

Marie finds out that she is having identical twin girls. You want to buy her a pair of matching onesies but you don't want to leave the house. You order them online to have them sent to her. When the site asks you for a gift message, you know that you should congratulate her and use a lot of exclamation points but you don't have it in you. You can't summon up enthusiasm, can't even bring yourself to type it. Instead, you type, "For my little baby nieces."

Your mom comes home with a new bedside lamp for you, made just for reading. It shoots up from the base and then hangs over your head, hovering just above the pages. You read three books from the stack that week, by the light through the window during the day and the lamplight hovering above you at night.

Your nieces are born. They are named Sophie and Ava. You hold them. They are beautiful. You wonder how it's possible Marie got everything she ever wanted and you . . . ended up here. You know this is called self-pity. You don't care.

Olive flies in from Chicago to see you. Everyone assumes she will stay at her parents' place but you feel immense relief when she says she'd rather make up a bed on the floor of your room. She doesn't ask how you are because she knows there's no answer. Instead, she tells you that she's thinking of giving up caffeine and makes you help her Facebook-stalk the man she just began seeing. You feel less alone when she's there, which is a welcome reprieve from the crushing loneliness you feel almost all the time. When she packs up to go back to Chicago, you joke about going with her, fitting in the overhead compartment. Olive says, "You probably can't see it just yet, but this place is good for you."

One day, the memories that haunt every section of your town and your house, the memories of where you and Jesse met and fell in love as teenagers, feel contained and manageable. So you venture outside.

You head to your family's bookstore.

You realize you aren't ready for a full day out of the house when you break down next to the Shel Silverstein collection Marie put up in the back corner.

You don't even know why you're breaking down. Nothing about Shel Silverstein reminds you of Jesse. Except that Shel Silverstein wrote about what it meant to be alive and you feel like you aren't alive anymore. Because Jesse isn't. You feel like you stopped living when he went missing. You feel like the rest of your days are killing time until it's time to die.

You know the only thing you can do is get in the passenger's seat of your dad's car and allow him to drive you back home and put you to bed.

But then you feel yourself growing stronger in that bed, as if you're squeezing the tears out of yourself, wringing yourself dry of pain. You imagine yourself bleeding grief, as if the water from your eyes is the pain itself. You imagine it leaving your body and being soaked up by the mattress.

You wake up one morning feeling dry and completely empty, so empty that if someone knocked on you, you'd sound hollow.

Hollow and empty are terrible ways to feel when you're used to being full of joy. But it's not so bad when you're used to feeling full of pain.

Hollow feels okay.

Empty feels like a beginning.

Which is nice, because for so long you have felt like you were at the end.

You ask your parents for a new bed. You feel childish doing it. But you don't have any money because you have not pitched a story in a very long time and you quit working at the blog.

Your parents don't understand why you're asking and you can't quite explain it to them. You just say, "This one is tainted." But what you mean is that you feel like it absorbed your suffering. You know it sounds crazy but you believe your pain is in the mattress and you don't want to absorb it back into your own body.

You know it's not that simple. But it feels like it is.

Two weeks later, you have a new mattress and box spring. You watch your dad tie the old ones to a friend's truck. You watch him drive down the street headed for the dump.

You feel better. Freer.

You realize this is called superstition.

You're OK with that.

You know that you will never truly be free of the grief. You know that it is something you must learn to live with, something you manage.

You start to understand that grief is chronic. That it's more about remission and relapse than it is about a cure. What that means to you is that you can't simply wait for it to be over. You have to move through it, like swimming in an undertow.

Toward the end of Marie's maternity leave, your parents come down with food poisoning. There is no one to open the store. You offer to do it. They tell you that you don't have to.

They say they can ask one of the sales clerks. You tell them you've got it under control.

When they say thank you, you realize that you have missed being relied upon. You remember the pride of being useful.

You wake up early and you take a shower and you get in the car. When you put the key in the door of the bookstore, you realize that Jesse is gone but maybe your life is still here. Maybe you can do something with it.

Three days before Marie is supposed to return to the store, she tells your parents that she doesn't want to come back to work. She has tears in her eyes. She says she's sorry that she's disappointing them but she just wants to stay at home with her babies. She says she can't imagine spending her days away from them. Your parents are caught off guard. They quickly become supportive.

That night, you overhear them talking about it. You hear your mother console your father, you hear her tell him that the store doesn't have to go to you or Marie. She says it's going to be fine.

The next day, they start looking for a new store manager.

You know what you need to do.

You sit them down at the kitchen table that night and you ask for the job. When they ask if you're sure that's what you want to do, you say you are but the truth is somewhere in the gray area between yes and no.

Surprised but pleased, your parents agree, saying nothing would make them prouder.

Now, you have a job.

And then, slowly, day by day, minute by minute, at such a snail's pace that you can barely register that anything is happening at all, you find a life's purpose again.

It is right there, in Blair Books, the very place you've spent your life running from. It is in the children's reading nook and the messy stockroom. It is in the curated display table at the front of the store and the bargain bin in the back. You look at the bookmarks. The ones that say "Travel the World by Reading a Book."

You have already seen the world.

Marie and Mike bring the girls over for dinner one Sunday, and right before dessert, Mike mentions that they have an appointment with a hearing specialist on Tuesday. That night, you overhear your parents saying that it's about time. You realize that you spend so little time with your nieces, so little time with your sister, that you didn't realize the twins have stopped responding to the sound of their names or to loud noises.

You resolve to call Marie after the appointment. You are going to be an attentive sister. You are going to be a good aunt.

Marie answers the phone in tears but you are able to piece together what has happened.

Your nieces are going deaf.

It has something to do with a gene called connexin 26.

You go over to Marie's house that night and bring her what you used to love on a bad day. You bring her Diet Coke and Ben & Jerry's. You find a flavor with coconut and chocolate because you know her favorite candy bar is an Almond Joy. She puts the ice cream in the freezer and leaves the Diet Coke on the counter. But she hugs you so hard you think it might leave a mark. You hold her and let her sob.

You move out of your parents' house into a studio apartment in Cambridge. You say you're moving out because you want to live in a brownstone but the truth is you're moving out because Olive agrees that it's time for you to start to meet people. Any people. New people.

Five months into your job as the manager, you sit your parents down and pitch them on selling e-books and e-readers. You outline how to do it. When they tell you that you're great at your job, you start crying and you miss Jesse. Happy moments are the worst, that's when the ache is strongest. But you wipe your eyes, get back to work, and when you put your head on the pillow that night, you consider it a good day.

An old college friend of your father's comes into the store looking for him but he's not in. The man sees that you are the manager and asks your name. You say your name is Emma Lerner and the man frowns. He says he knows Colin always wanted one of his girls to take over the store. You say that you *are* one of his girls. The man apologizes for his mistake.

Marie and Mike buy a house down the street from your parents. Mike will have to commute far to the sporting goods stores but Marie thinks it's important to be near your parents.

After she's settled in, you call her and ask her if she'd like to take a sign language class with you in Boston. You tell her you're excited to learn how to talk with your hands. She agrees and it is the only time she takes to do something out of the house, without her children. After a few weeks, you realize that you are your sister's entire social life.

One day after class, Marie asks if you'd like to stay out and get lunch. You take her to a Mongolian barbecue place and you run into Jesse's older brother Chris. You say hello and you catch up and you are surprised to find that you do not cry.

As you and Marie are walking back to the T, she asks if you're okay. As you're explaining how you feel, it hits you like a ton of bricks. For years now people have said to you, "May his memory be a blessing." You realize, finally, that's exactly what it is.

You are happier to have known him than you are sad to have lost him.

You wonder if grief is less chronic than you think. If remission can last for years.

You go to the hairdresser one day and she asks you if you've ever considered highlights. You tell her to go for it. When you walk out of the salon, you feel like a million bucks. You start scheduling future appointments.

Your parents partially retire and give you the store. You are so proud, so happy, so eager to take it over that you decide to change your name back. You are a Blair. You haven't ever been more proud to be a Blair. The day your new license comes you cry and look up to the sky, as if Jesse is there, and you say, "This doesn't mean I don't love you. This just means I love where I come from."

When Marie finds out the store is being handed over to you, she gets upset. She accuses you of taking it from her. You tell her you're just picking up the ball that she dropped. The two of you erupt. She's yelling and you're yelling. In anger, she screams, "Oh, please. We all know you're the favorite. Perfect Miss Emma who does everything exactly as Mom and Dad want."

You start laughing. Because it's so absurd.

But then you realize it's true.

You have become the person your parents always wanted you to be and you've done it almost entirely by accident.

You didn't think you wanted to work with books or live in Massachusetts or be close to your sister. But it turns out you do. That's what makes you happy.

And then you say to yourself, *Wait, no, that's not right. I can't be happy.*

Because you don't have him. He's gone. You can't be happy, can you?

And then you stop and truly ask yourself, *Am I happy?*

And you realize that you just might be.

You apologize to Marie. She apologizes to you. You spell out, "I was being an idiot," in sign language. Marie laughs.

Later, you ask her if it's a betrayal to Jesse to feel good, to like your life now. She just says, "Not at all. That's all he'd want for you. That's exactly what he'd want."

You think she might be right.

You take off your wedding ring and you put it in an envelope of your love letters and pictures. You will never let it go but you do not need to wear it.

You go back to your hairdresser and ask her if she thinks you'd look good with a pixie cut. She says you'd look great. You trust her. You go home, newly shorn, and you aren't quite sure what to make of yourself.

But then Marie sees it and tells you that you look like a movie star, and when you look at yourself in the mirror again, you sort of see what she means.

Six months later, you decide to take up the piano.

And just by walking into a music store, you set a whole second life in motion.

I could have started by trying to take piano lessons. But I decided to just leap into it. I wanted something to do with my hands at home. It was either piano or cooking and, well, cooking seemed messy.

So I found a secondhand-instruments shop in Watertown and drove over on a Sunday afternoon.

The doors chimed as I walked through them and they caught on themselves as they closed behind me. The store had a leathery scent to it. It was filled with rows of guitars. I found a magazine stand and rifled through it for a minute, unsure of what I was actually looking for.

I suddenly felt uncomfortable and completely out of my element. I didn't know what questions to ask or of whom to ask them.

Standing there surrounded by a sax, trumpets, and a series of instruments I couldn't even name, I realized I was out of my league. I was tempted to give up, to turn around and go home. I took a step away from the magazines and bumped right into two bronze drums. They made a clang as I accidentally knocked them into each other. I straightened them out and looked around to see if anyone saw me.

There was a salesman a few feet over. He looked up at me and smiled.

I timidly smiled back and then turned to the magazines again.

"Hey," the salesman said. He was now standing right next to me. "Are you a timpanist?"

I looked up at him and I saw the recognition in his eyes at the very same time it clicked in mine.

"Sam?" I said.

"Emma Blair . . ." he said, taken aback.

"Oh, my God," I said. "Sam Kemper. I don't even . . . I haven't seen you in . . ."

"Ten years or more, maybe," he said. "Wow. You . . . you look great."

"Thanks," I said. "You do, too."

"How are your parents?"

"Good," I said. "Really good."

It was quiet for a moment as I stared at him, surprised at how much he'd changed. I was trying to remember if his eyes had always been that stunning. They were a warm brown that seemed so kind and patient, as if they saw everything with compassion. Or maybe I was simply projecting what I remembered of him onto his face.

But there was no doubt that he'd grown up to be an attractive man. His face had angled out a bit, had grown some character.

I realized I was staring.

"Do you play the timpani now?" Sam said.

I looked at him as if he were speaking French. "What?" I said.

He pointed to the bronze drums behind me. "I saw you by the timpani; I thought maybe you had started to play."

"Oh," I said. "No, no. You know me. I don't play anything. I mean, except for when they made us learn 'Mary Had a Little Lamb' on the recorder, but I hardly think that counts."

Sam laughed. "It's not exactly the timpani, but I think it counts."

"We all can't play a bajillion instruments or however many it was that you play," I said. "Six, was it?"

Sam smiled shyly. "I've picked up a few since then, actually. Most of them amateur-level, though."

"And here I just have the recorder. Oh!" I said, suddenly remembering. "I also played the finger cymbals in the fourth-grade holiday concert! So there's two."

He laughed. "You're an expert, then! I should be asking you questions."

I played along with him, pretending to be a humble genius. "Well, finger cymbals are pretty basic. You mostly just want a pair of cymbals that will fit on your fingers and then you hit them together to make a clanging noise." I hit my own pointer fingers together enthusiastically to show him. "Finger cymbaling is really about confidence."

He laughed again. He always made me feel like I was the funniest person in the room.

"And from there, the sky's the limit," I said. "I know a girl who started out on the finger cymbals; now she plays the actual cymbals."

I grew slightly embarrassed, as if because he'd laughed, I'd taken that as license to perform a stand-up comedy routine. But he laughed again. A hearty laugh. And my anxiety faded away.

"Actually, all of that is a lie. I mean, I did play the finger cymbals but . . . I'm considering learning the piano. Hence, why I'm standing in the middle of this shop looking really confused."

"Ah," he said, nodding his head. "Well, if you want my opinion . . ."

"I do," I said. "Yours is exactly the opinion I want."

He smiled. "Then I think you should get one of the Yamaha PSRs in the back by the drum machines. They're only sixty-one keys and they aren't weighted, but if you're just starting out or you're not really sure you're going to make it a lifelong passion, I think it's silly to spend four hundred bucks on a keyboard. But that's just me."

"No, that's great advice. Would you mind showing me one of the ones that you're talking about?"

"Oh," he said as if he was surprised that I was actually listening to him. "Sure. I think they have one back here."

He turned around and headed toward the back of the store. I followed him. "Do you still play a lot of piano?" I asked him.

He nodded as he looked back at me slightly. "For fun, yeah," he said as he stopped at a short black keyboard on a stand. "This one would probably be great for you."

I hit a few of the keys. They were silent except for the dull *thunk* of the key physically hitting the board.

"I don't think it's plugged in . . ." he said.

"Right. That makes sense." I was legitimately embarrassed that I'd tried to play an unplugged keyboard, perhaps the most embarrassed I'd been since a few months prior when a customer told me my fly was down. "How much is it?"

"Oh, uh . . ." He bent down to look at the price tag. It was about half as much as I'd assumed I'd have to spend.

I decided to seize the day and go for it.

"OK, I'll take it."

He laughed. "Are you serious?"

"Yeah," I said. "You have to start somewhere, right?"

"I guess that's true," he said.

Quiet settled over us.

"Wow," I said. "I can't believe I ran into you."

"I know!" he said. "What are the odds of that?"

"Well, if we both live in the same city, I guess fairly high."

Sam laughed. "I just assumed you were out in California somewhere."

I nodded, unsure just how much Sam knew. "Yeah, well, you know."

Sam nodded somberly. "Yeah," he said, a dryness in his voice. "I hear you."

And now I knew that he knew it all. And my impulse was to get as far away from him as possible as quickly as I could. "Well, my parents will be so happy to hear you're doing well," I said. "Thanks for your help, Sam. It was great to see you."

I put my hand out and watched as Sam was surprised by my ending the conversation.

"Oh, yeah, sure," he said.

And then I excused myself and headed to the register.

"Did anyone help you with your purchase today?" the woman behind the counter said to me as she handed my credit card back.

"Hm?" I asked her. I took it and placed it back into its spot in my wallet.

"Did any salespeople help you decide on your purchase today?" she asked.

"Oh," I said. "Sam helped me out. He was great."

"Sam?"

"Yeah."

"There's no one that works here named Sam."

For a minute, I thought maybe I was in a ghost story.

"Sam Kemper," I said. "He just advised me on this keyboard."

The woman shook her head, unsure what I was talking about.

I turned around, shifted my gaze from left to right, then stood on my tippy toes to get a better view. But I couldn't see him anywhere. I was starting to feel like maybe I was crazy. "Like six feet tall, wearing a black shirt, a little bit of stubble . . ." The cashier looked at me like she might know who I was talking about. I pushed forward. "Really nice eyes?"

"Oh, yeah, I know who you're talking about."

"Great."

"That guy doesn't work here," she said.

"What do you mean he doesn't work here?"

"He's a customer. He comes in a lot, though."

I closed my eyes and sighed. I'd been talking to him as if he were a salesman the whole time. "My mistake," I said. "I'm an idiot."

She started laughing. "No worries." She handed me my receipt. "Do you need help bringing it out to your car?"

"Um . . ." I looked at it and decided I could do it on my own. "I think I'm good. Thanks."

I picked up the keyboard and headed for the door, looking for Sam as I went. I made it all the way to the front of the store before I saw him. He was coming down the stairs.

"Sam!" I said.

"Emma!" He said it in my exact same inflection.

"You're still here," I said. "I thought maybe you'd left."

"I was upstairs. I'm here looking at baby grands."

Admittedly, it took me a second to realize that baby grand wasn't some sort of candy bar.

"Oh, wow, you're buying a baby grand piano," I said, setting the keyboard down for a moment. "Further proof that you don't actually work here."

He smiled.

"I'm so sorry I assumed that you were a salesperson. I think I just figured because you worked at our store and . . . Anyway, I just made an ass out of myself when I went up to the register and tried to give you commission on my purchase."

Sam laughed. "You know, I suspected at the end there that you might have thought I worked here, but I wasn't sure how to clear it up without . . ."

"Making me feel dumb?"

He laughed. "Kinda."

"Well, I officially feel dumb."

"No, don't," he said. "It was my pleasure to help you. Really. It's so nice to see you again." The sincerity with which he looked at me was disarming. And I wasn't sure whether I liked that or not. I was thinking maybe I did.

"I owe you a thank-you," I said. "You were a great help."

"Do you need lessons?" Sam said. "If you wanted I could . . . teach you. I'd be happy to do it. Show you a few things, just to get you started maybe."

I looked at him, unsure how to respond.

"Or if not that, maybe I could just take you out for a drink sometime," he said.

The realization of what was happening washed over me like a wave. Not one of those small waves that runs over your feet and gets the bottom of your jeans wet as you walk along the sand, either. The kind of wave that happens when you're coming out of the water, with your back to the ocean, and it just appears out of nowhere and pummels you.

"Oh, my God," I said, stunned. "You're asking me out?"

I saw Sam's shoulders slump and I caught the disappointment pass across his face before he covered it up.

"I was trying to be casual and subtle about it. Maybe one of those dates neither of us are sure is a date," he said, and then he shook his head. "It's over ten years later and I'm just as bad at it now as I was the first time, huh?"

I felt myself blushing and my blushing made Sam start to blush.

"Sorry," he said. "I'm just getting out of a really long relationship, so I'm out of practice. You might not believe it but I used to be very good at talking to women back in college. As my dad always says, be direct but—"

Sam looked at me like he'd just revealed a terrible secret. He put his hand on his face and pinched the bridge of his nose. "Did I just admit that I ask my father for dating advice?" he said, without changing his expression.

I laughed. A quiet laugh. A "Yes, you did, but it's totally fine" laugh.

That's when I remembered how much I always liked him.

I *liked* him.

Sam was *cute*. And *sweet*. And he thought I was *funny*.

"It's fine," I said. "Look. I thought you were a salesperson. You ask your dad how to hit on women. We're like the Tweedledee and Tweedledum of social interaction."

He laughed. He looked so relieved.

I wanted to see him again. That was the truth. I wanted to spend more time with him. I wanted to be around him.

"How about this?" I said. "You can teach me 'Chopsticks' and I'll buy you a beer."

"Well, if it's just 'Chopsticks' you're after, I have a great idea."

I looked at him, willing to hear him out.

He took my keyboard and I followed him as he led me up the stairs. The rickety, tight staircase led to a room full of huge instruments. A few upright pianos, a harp, a cello. Sam led me toward a sleek black baby grand. He put my keyboard down and then sat at the piano, tapping the spot next to him on the bench. I joined him.

He looked over at me and put his hands delicately on the keys. Then leaned into it and started playing "Chopsticks."

I watched as his hands flew across the keys, the way they seemed to instinctually know what to do. He had nice hands, strong but gentle. Short, clean nails; long, lean fingers. I know women sometimes say they like men to have calluses and knobby knuckles, that they like a man whose toughness shows on his palms. But looking at Sam's hands, I decided that way of thinking was all wrong. I liked the way his hands were agile and almost elegant. I found myself looking up his wrists to his arms and shoulders.

Watching Sam play the piano, remembering how skilled he was, how talented he was, how dexterous—I found myself wondering what else he could do with his hands.

You think you know who you are, you think you have your identity down pat, signed and sealed in a box that you call "me," and then you realize you're attracted to musicians—that "dexterous" is sexy to you—and you have to rethink everything you know about yourself.

He stopped playing. "All right, now you go."

"Me?" I said. "Do that? I don't even know where to start."

He pressed down on a white key in front of me. I, dutifully, put my pointer finger on it.

"Try this finger," he said as he pulled my middle finger onto the key.

I nodded.

"Now, hit that key like this."

He hit another key in a rhythm, six times.

So I did the same with my key.

"And now hit this one," he said as he pointed to another.

I followed each of his instructions, just as he told me. I was supposed to be looking at the keys, but half the time I was looking at him. He caught me once or twice, and I turned my head back to my fingers and the keys beneath them.

I played slowly and unmelodically. My fingers hesitated and then moved too quickly, sort of panicked and squirrelly. But I could recognize a faint pattern in my own movements.

His body brushed up against mine as we sat on that bench. He kept touching my hands with his.

"All right," he said. "Think you can do that fast now? I'll play the other part as you do it."

"Sure," I said. "Yeah, I got it."

I rested my finger on the first key. He put his hand, gently, on the one just below it. "On three," he said. "One . . . two . . . three."

I hit mine.

He hit his.

And there it was.

Duh Duh Duh Duh Duh Duh *Duh Duh Duh Duh Duh Duh* Duh Duh Duh Duh *Duh Duh Duh* . . .

"Chopsticks."

We only played for a few seconds before I had hit all the notes I knew. Feeling shy, I pulled my hands back into my lap.

A part of me hoped he'd continue to play. But he didn't. He stopped his hand in place and rested it gently on the keys. He looked at me.

"So now that you know 'Chopsticks,'" he said, "let's go get a beer."

I laughed. "You're smoother than you think," I said.

"My dad says it's best to be persistent," he said, joking. He looked confident. Hopeful.

I thought about it for a minute.

I thought about how nice it would be to order a gimlet and sit and talk to someone who was both a handsome man and an old friend.

But as Sam looked at me, waiting for my response, I suddenly felt a very sharp sense of fear. True fear.

This wouldn't be dinner with an old friend.

This would be a date.

I couldn't just throw myself into something like that.

I looked at Sam's smile. It was fading as I made him wait for a response.

"It's a rain check," I said. "Is that OK?"

"Yeah," he said, shaking his head. "Totally. Of course."

"I really want to," I said, reassuring.

"No, I get it."

"I just have a thing."

"No worries."

"I'll give you my number," I said, wanting him to know that I did want to see him again, that I *was* interested. "And maybe we can go out next weekend."

Sam smiled and handed me his phone.

I called myself, so his number showed up on my phone, too. I handed his phone back.

"I should get going," I said. "But we'll talk soon?"

"Yeah," he said. "Sounds good."

"It was really nice to see you," I said.

"You, too, Emma. Seriously."

He reached out his hand and I grabbed it. We shook but then let our hands hang there for a moment. The effect was somewhere between shaking and holding.

As I drove back to my apartment that afternoon, with a keyboard in the back and Sam's number in my phone, I found myself wondering whether I could be with someone like Sam, whether Sam could mean something to me.

I had always had a tender spot for him, always cared for him. And maybe it was time that I went out on a date with a nice guy. A nice guy who had always been good to me, who I might have even said yes to back in high school if things had been different.

Good things don't wait until you're ready. Sometimes they come right before, when you're almost there.

And I figured when that happens, you can let them pass by like a bus not meant for you. Or you can *get* ready.

So I got ready.

I thought about it all night. I tossed and turned. And then, the next morning, on my way into the store, I texted Sam.

Drinks on Friday around 7:30? Somewhere in Cambridge? You pick.

It was before nine. I didn't expect him to answer.

But my phone dinged right away.

McKeon's on Avery Street?

And there it was.

I had a date.

With Sam Kemper.

I had never been so excited and so sick to my stomach at the same time.

What was I going to do if I started to have feelings for someone?

Maybe it wouldn't be Sam. Maybe it would be years in the future. But realizing you want love in your life means you have to be willing to let love *in*.

And that meant I needed to let Jesse *go*.

I could think of no other way to do it, no other way of processing it, than putting it into words. So, after work that night, I sat down on my couch, grabbed a piece of paper and a pen, and I wrote a letter.

Dear Jesse,

You've been gone for more than two years but there hasn't been a day that has gone by when I haven't thought of you.

Sometimes I remember the way you smelled salty after you'd gone for a swim in the ocean. Or I wonder whether you'd have liked the movie I just saw. Other times, I just think about your smile. I think about how your eyes would crinkle and I'd always fall a little bit more in love with you.

I think about how you would touch me. How I would touch you. I think about that a lot.

The memory of you hurt so much at first. The more I thought about your smile, your smell, the more it hurt. But I liked punishing myself. I liked the pain because the pain was you.

I don't know if there is a right and wrong way to grieve. I just know that losing you has gutted me in a way I honestly didn't think was possible. I've felt pain I didn't think was human.

At times, it has made me lose my mind. (Let's just say that I went a little crazy up on our roof.)

At times, it has nearly broken me.

And I'm happy to say that now is a time when your memory brings me so much joy that just thinking of you brings a smile to my face.

I'm also happy to say that I'm stronger than I ever knew.

I have found meaning in life that I never would have guessed.

And now I'm surprising myself once again by realizing that I am ready to move forward.

I once thought grief was chronic, that all you could do was appreciate the good days and take them along with the bad. And then I started to think that maybe the good days aren't just days; maybe the good days can be good weeks, good months, good years.

Now I wonder if grief isn't something like a shell.

You wear it for a long time and then one day you realize you've outgrown it.

So you put it down.

It doesn't mean that I want to let go of the memories of you or the love I have for you. But it does mean that I want to let go of the sadness.

I won't ever forget you, Jesse. I don't want to and I don't think I'm capable of it.

But I do think I can put the pain down. I think I can leave it on the ground and walk away, only coming back to visit every once in a while, no longer carrying it with me.

Not only do I think I can do that, but I think I need to.

I will carry you in my heart always, but I cannot carry your loss on my back anymore. If I do, I'll never find any new joy for myself. I will crumble under the weight of your memory.

I have to look forward, into a future where you cannot be. Instead of back, to a past filled with what we had.

I have to let you go and I have to ask you to let me go.

I truly believe that if I work hard, I can have the sort of life for myself that you always wanted for me. A happy life. A satisfied life. Where I am loved and I love in return.

I need your permission to find room to love someone else.

I'm so sorry that we never got the future we talked about. Our life together would have been grand.

But I'm going out into the world with an open heart now. And I'm going to go wherever life takes me.

I hope you know how beautiful and freeing it was to love you when you were here.

You were the love of my life.

Maybe it's selfish to want more; maybe it's greedy to want another love like that.

But I can't help it.

I do.

So I said yes to a date with Sam Kemper. I like to think you would like him for me, that you'd approve. But I also want you to know, in case it doesn't go without saying, that no one could ever replace you. It's just that I want more love in my life, Jesse.

And I'm asking for your blessing to go find it.

Love,
Emma

I read it over and over and over. And then I folded it, put it in an envelope, wrote his name on it, and tucked it away.

I got in bed and I fell asleep.

I slept soundly and woke as the sunlight started beaming in from my window. I felt rested and renewed, as if the earth and I were in perfect agreement about when the sun should rise.

When I showed up at the bar, Sam was wearing a dark denim button-down shirt and flat-front gray chinos. He looked like he might have put pomade in his hair, and when I leaned in to hug him hello, I noticed that he was wearing cologne.

I'd known it was a date. I'd wanted it to be a date.

But the cologne, the smell of wood and citrus, made it all crystal clear.

Sam liked me.

And I liked him.

And maybe it was that simple.

I knew it wasn't. But maybe it could be.

"You look great," Sam said.

When I got ready that evening, I'd put on a tight black skirt and a long-sleeved black-and-white-striped T-shirt that clung to the better parts of me. I took more care applying my mascara than I had in years. When it clumped, I used a safety pin to straighten my lashes, the way I'd seen my mom do when I was a child.

And then I put on pale pink ballet flats and headed toward the door.

I caught a glimpse of myself in the mirror just as I was leaving the house.

Something wasn't right. This wouldn't do. I turned around

and exchanged my flats for black heels. Suddenly, my legs looked longer than they had any right to be.

Feeling confident, I went back into the bathroom and outlined the edges of my lips in a perfect crimson line, filling it in with a lipstick that was called Russian Red. I'd only worn it once a few months ago when I took Marie out for a fancy dinner in Back Bay. But I'd liked it then. And I liked it now.

When I made my way back to the front door and once again caught a glimpse of myself in the mirror, I felt borderline indestructible.

I looked good.

I knew I looked good.

This was my good look.

"Thank you," I said to Sam there at the bar. I pressed my lips together and I sat down on the stool next to his. "You're no slouch yourself."

The bartender, a tall, formidable woman with long, dark hair, came over and asked me what I wanted to drink. I quickly perused their signature cocktails list and nothing struck a chord. It all just looked like various ways to mix fruit juice and vodka.

"Gimlet?" I said.

She nodded and turned away, starting to mix.

"What are you having?" I asked him. He was sitting in front of a pale draft beer. "I hope you haven't paid for that yet. It's supposed to be on me."

Sam looked over at me and smiled a sorrowful smile. "They made me pay when they handed over the beer," he said. "But that just means you'll have to buy my second."

"Fair enough."

The bartender put my drink in front of me and I handed her my credit card. She disappeared.

"I mean, you say that, but for my second beer, I plan on ordering the most expensive one on the menu."

We were both sitting facing forward, looking at each other with glances and side eyes.

"That's OK," I said. "It's the least I can do since you took the time to teach me this."

I started playing "Chopsticks" on the bar with my right hand as if the keys were underneath it. Sam angled his body toward me to watch.

"Very good!" he said when I was done.

"A plus?" I asked.

He thought about it while sipping his beer. "A-minus," he said as he put his beer down. "You just missed it by a hair."

"What?" I said. "Where did I go wrong?"

"You missed a note."

"No, I didn't!" I said.

"Yes, you did. You did this," he said, hitting the bar with the same fingers I'd hit it with just a few moments ago. "And it's this." He hit the bar again. It looked exactly like the first one.

"That's the same thing."

Sam laughed and shook his head. "Nope. It's not."

"Do it again."

"Which one?"

"Do what I did and then do what the real thing is."

He started to repeat mine.

"No, no," I said. "Slower. So I can spot the difference."

He started over and slowed it down.

He did mine.

And then he did his.

And there it was. Right toward the end. I'd skipped a key.

I smiled, knowing I was wrong. "Aw, man!" I said. "I did mess it up."

"That's OK. You're still very good for a beginner."

I gave him a skeptical look.

"I mean," he said, his whole body shifting away from the bar and toward me. "You play the bar beautifully."

I rolled my eyes at him.

"I'm serious, actually. If you got into it, I bet you could be really good."

"You probably say that to all the girls," I said, waving my hand at him, dismissing the compliment. I gracefully picked up my gimlet and slowly brought the filled-to-the-brim glass to my lips. It was sweet and clean. Just the littlest bit dizzying.

"Just my students," he said.

I looked at him, confused.

"Now seems like a good time to tell you I'm a music teacher," he said.

I smiled at him. "Ah, that's awesome. What a perfect job for you."

"Thanks," he said. "And what about you? Are you some big travel writer now? My mom said she saw your name in *Travel + Leisure*."

I laughed. "Oh yeah," I said. "I was. I did that for a while. But, uh . . . no, now I'm actually running the store."

"No way," Sam said, disbelieving.

"Shocking, I know," I said. "But it's true."

"Wow," he said. "Colin Blair's greatest wish. There's a Blair running Blair Books."

I laugh. "I guess dreams do come true," I said. "For my dad at least."

"But not for you?" Sam said.

"Not the dream I originally dreamt, as you know," I said. "But I'm starting to think you don't always know what your dreams are. Some of us have to run smack into one before we see it."

"Ah," Sam said. "Cheers to that." He tilted his glass toward me and I clinked mine against his. "May I change the subject ever so briefly?" he said.

"Be my guest," I said.

"You seem to get even more beautiful with time," he said.

"Oh, stop it," I said, pushing his shoulder away with my hand.

I was flirting. Me. Flirting.

It feels so good to flirt. No one ever talks about that. But in that moment, I felt like flirting was the very thing that made the world go around.

The excitement of wondering what the other person will say next. The thrill of knowing someone is looking at you, liking what they see. The rush of looking at someone and liking what you see in them. Flirting is probably just as much about falling in love with yourself as it is with someone else.

It's about seeing yourself through someone's eyes and realizing there is plenty to like about yourself, plenty of reasons someone might hang on your every word.

"So you're a music teacher," I told him. "Where do you teach?"

"Actually, not far from Blair Books. I'm just over in Concord," he said.

"Are you serious?" I said. "You've been that close by and you never stopped in to say hello?"

Sam looked at me and said, very sincerely, "If I had known you'd be there, I assure you, I'd have rushed over."

I could not stop the smile from spreading across my face. I grabbed my gimlet and took a sip. Sam's beer was almost finished.

"Why don't I get you another?" I said.

He nodded and I waved the bartender over.

"Your most expensive beer on the menu," I said to her gallantly. Sam laughed.

"That's a pretty rich stout, are you sure you want that?" the bartender asked.

I looked at Sam. He put his hands in the air as if to say, "You're in charge."

"That'll be fine," I said to her.

She left and I turned back to him. We were both quiet for a minute, unsure what to say next.

"What's your favorite song to play?" I asked him. It was a stupid question. I knew it when I asked it.

"On the piano?"

"Sure."

"What do you want to hear?" he asked.

I laughed. "I didn't mean now. There's no piano now."

"What are you talking about? We played 'Chopsticks' right here on this bar."

I laughed at him, game to play, but suddenly having a hard time remembering what songs are played on a piano. "How about 'Piano Man'?"

Sam made a face. "A little on the nose, don't you think?"

"It's all I could think of!"

"All right, all right," he said. "It's actually a good choice anyway because it has a nice bit of show-off flair at the beginning."

He straightened his posture and rolled up his sleeves, as if he were playing an actual instrument. He moved a napkin out of the way and then picked up my drink. "If you could please get this out of my way, miss," he said.

"Certainly, sir," I said.

He interlaced his fingers and stretched them out away from his chest.

"Are you ready?" he asked me.

"I was born ready."

He nodded his head dramatically and began to run his hands over the bar, as if there were a full piano right there in front of him. I watched as his fingers glided over the nonexistent keys. He was so confident as he pretended to play that I almost believed it.

"Excuse me," he said as he was playing, "but I believe the harmonica would have come in by now."

"What? I can't play the harmonica."

"Sure you can."

"I don't know the first thing."

"You must know how musicians hold harmonicas. I assume you've seen at least one blues band in your life."

"I mean, sure."

He kept his head down, looking at the bar, playing. People were starting to look at us. He didn't care. Neither did I.

"Let's hear it."

I surprised myself and I did it. I put my hands up to my mouth as if there were a harmonica between them and I ran my mouth over the space it would have occupied.

"Slower," Sam said. "You're not Neil Young."

I laughed and stopped for a minute. "I don't even know what I'm doing!"

"You're doing great! Don't stop."

So I played along.

"All right, wait for a minute; there's no harmonica in this part."

I put my fake harmonica down as he kept playing. I could tell he was going through the full song, each note. I watched how effortless it was for him, how his fingers seemed to move with the expectation they'd make a beautiful sound. And yet they were making no sound at all.

"Now!" he said. "Get that harmonica going. This is your moment."

"It is? I didn't know!" I said, desperately pulling my hands up to my face and really committing to it.

And then Sam slowed and I could tell the song was ending. I took my hands down and I watched him as he hit the last few notes. And then he was done. And he looked at me.

"Next request?" he asked.

"Have dinner with me?" I asked him.

It just popped out of my mouth. I wanted to talk more, to spend more time with him, to hear more about him. I wanted more. "We can eat here or anywhere nearby if you're in the mood for something in particular."

"Emma . . ." he said seriously.

"Yeah?"

"Can we get burritos?"

～

Dos Tacos was brightly lit with orange and yellow undertones instead of the flattering blue light of the bar. But he still looked handsome. And I still felt beautiful.

Even when I bit into my gigantic carne asada deluxe burrito.

"If I could only eat Mexican food for the rest of my life, that would be fine with me," Sam said. "Completely fine."

I wanted to tell him that food in Mexico tasted nothing like this. I wanted to tell him about the three weeks Jesse and I spent in Mexico City, where we found this tiny little restaurant that served amazing chiles rellenos.

But I didn't want to talk about the past.

"I wouldn't mind at all," I said. "Not one bit." I reached over and took a chip out of the basket in front of us at the same time that Sam did.

We collided, ever so briefly, and I liked the feel of his hand on mine. *This is what it's like to be on a date*, I thought. *This is what it's like to be normal.*

"But if we're talking about desserts," Sam said, "I don't know if I'd choose Mexican for the rest of my life. French maybe, éclairs and custards. Italian could be interesting, tiramisu and gelato."

"I don't know," I said. "Indian desserts are pretty incredible. They are all really creamy and nutty. Like rice puddings and pistachio ice cream type stuff. I might have to go with that."

"Wow, that sounds great."

I nodded. "But maybe nothing beats tres leches. Which is Mexican, I suppose. Although, almost every Latin American country you go to claims it's theirs. It's like baklava. I swear, I've spoken to at least twenty people who all claimed they know for a fact their people invented baklava."

"That's funny, because my family invented tres leches right here in the United States."

I laughed. "And I personally invented baklava."

Sam laughed and I looked around to see that everyone appeared to have cleared out and the staff behind the counter had started cleaning up.

"Oh no," I said. "I think they're closing." I pulled my phone out of my purse to check the time. It was 10:02.

"Are you saying the night is over?" Sam asked as he finished the chips sitting in between us. The way he said it, the way he smiled at me and held my gaze, told me that he didn't think the night was over, that he knew I didn't, either.

"I'd say we should go to a bar and get a drink," I said. "But we already did that."

Sam nodded. "We sort of did things in reverse, didn't we? Maybe we should go get lunch now."

"Or meet for coffee." I gathered all the trash onto my tray. "Either way, we should get out of here. I don't want to be like that guy who would always come read books ten minutes before closing. Remember that guy?"

"Remember him?" Sam said, standing up. "I still resent him."

I laughed. "Exactly."

Sam and I threw everything away, thanked the man behind the counter, and walked out onto the sidewalk. It was one of those Boston nights that almost make the winters worth it. The air was warm but fresh. The moon was full. The tall, age-old buildings that often looked dirty in the day glowed at night.

"I have a crazy idea," Sam said.

"Tell me."

"What if we went for a walk?"

My first thought was that it sounded wonderful and my second was that I wouldn't last more than ten minutes in my heels.

"Too quaint?" he asked. "Like it's the nineteen fifties and I'm asking you to split a milk shake?"

I laughed. "No!" I said. "I love the idea. I just know that my feet will start to hurt."

Up ahead, I saw one of the ubiquitous crimson red signs that litter the city—CVS.

Seven minutes later, I had my high heels in my purse and a pair of five-dollar flip-flops on my feet. Sam had a king-sized Snickers.

"Where to?" I asked him, ready to take on the city.

"I didn't really have a plan," Sam said. "But, uh . . ." He looked up and down the street. "This way?" He pointed away from the cluster of buildings.

"Great," I said. "Let's do it."

And off we went. Slowly at first, just putting one foot in front of the other, talking as we did.

The city was humming. Groups of girls out together, college kids walking around, tipsy drinkers smoking cigarettes out on the sidewalk, men and women holding hands on their way out or way home.

Sam told me about teaching eighth-grade orchestra and jazz band, about how he had recently started picking up extra money as a studio musician a few times a month.

I told him how the store was doing, how my parents were doing. I updated him on Marie, told him about Sophie and Ava, even showed him a few signs I'd learned recently. I told him about a few days before when I recognized Ava signing, "Milk, please."

Sam listened as if I was the most fascinating woman in the universe and I realized how long it had been since someone listened to me like that.

We both made fun of ourselves for living in the city and working in the same suburban area where we grew up, a reversal of the common commute.

We stepped over gum and we made way for other pedestrians and we bent down to pet dogs. We walked past Harvard dorms and Harvard Yard. Twice we walked past a T stop and I wondered if we both wouldn't gravitate toward it, using it as a way to say good-bye. But my feet didn't head in that direction and neither did Sam's. We just kept walking, slowly and peacefully, deeper into the night.

We eventually found ourselves walking along the Charles. My feet started to hurt and I asked Sam if we could sit on one of the benches along the river.

"Oh, I thought you'd never ask. I think I started forming a blister around Porter Square."

We sat down on a bench and I picked up my phone to check the time. It was one in the morning. I wasn't tired. And I didn't feel like going home.

There was so much we had already talked about. We had talked about work and music and families and books. We had talked about anything and everything—other than Jesse.

But once we sat down on that bench, it somehow became impossible to ignore.

"So I suppose you know I'm a widow," I said.

Sam looked at me and nodded. "I had heard," he said. "But I wasn't sure if I should bring it up." He reached over and grabbed my hand, gently and with tenderness. "Emma, I'm so sorry."

"Thank you," I said.

"I hope this feels okay to you," he said. "Us being out here. Together."

I nodded. "Surreal, maybe," I said. "But, yeah, it feels okay."

"I can't even imagine how hard it has been for you," he said. "How long has it been?"

"A little over two years," I said.

"Is that a long time or a short time?"

That's when I knew that Sam was sincerely listening, that he was interested in learning exactly who I was in that moment. I realized that Sam understood me, maybe had always understood me, in a way that very few people did. And that meant that he knew that two years was both forever and just a moment ago.

"It depends on the day," I said. "But right now, it feels like a long time. How about you? Who broke your heart?"

Sam sighed, as if preparing himself to rehash it all. "I was with someone for years," he said. He wasn't looking at me. He was looking out onto the water.

"What happened?" I asked.

"What always happens, I guess."

"Werewolf got her?" I asked him.

He laughed and looked at me. "Yeah, brutal. Took her right out of my arms."

I smiled and continued to listen.

"We just outgrew each other," he said finally. "It sounds so banal. But it hurt like nothing before."

I didn't know anything about growing apart. I only knew being *ripped* apart. But I imagined it felt like a tree root slowly growing so big and strong that it breaks through the sidewalk. "I'm sorry," I said. "It sounds awful."

"I just wasn't the same person at thirty that I was at twenty," he said. "And neither was she."

"I don't think anybody is," I said.

"I feel a bit jaded by it now, to be honest," he said. "Like, will I be the same person at forty? Or . . ."

"Will we outgrow this, too?" I said, completing his thought.

And then Sam said something that has stayed with me ever since.

"I think it's a good sign, though," he said, "that I was crazy about you at sixteen and I'm still crazy about you now."

I smiled at him. "It certainly seems promising," I said.

Sam shortened the distance between us and put his arm around me. My shoulder crept into the pit of his arm and he reached across the length of my back. He squeezed me just the littlest bit.

It didn't seem easy, the idea of loving someone again.

But it did seem possible.

So I sat there with him, watching the river, and allowing myself to feel hope again, to feel joy again, to feel how nice it was to be in a man's arms on a bench by the river.

I don't know how long we stayed like that.

I just know that it was four a.m. when I finally made it home.

At my front door, in the early hours of the morning, fifteen years after we met, Sam Kemper finally kissed me.

It was sweet and fresh and gentle. He smelled like morning dew, like a wonderful beginning.

"When can I see you again?" he asked as he looked at me.

I looked right back at him, no artifice between us. "I'm here," I said. "Call me."

Four and a half months into our relationship, I told Sam I loved him. He'd said it a few weeks before and told me that I didn't need to say it back, not then anyway. He said he'd been head over heels for me all through high school, carrying a torch for me since the first time he met me at the store. He told me that part of the reason he left Acton without saying good-bye the summer before college was that he knew that I had fallen in love with Jesse, that he didn't have a shot.

"What I'm saying is that loving you—even if I'm not sure you love me—it's familiar territory," he said. "I've picked it right back up like riding a bike. And I can do it for a little while longer, if that's what you need."

I was immensely grateful because it was exactly what I needed.

It wasn't that I didn't love him. I did. I knew I loved him even before he said it. But I couldn't utter the words. I wasn't prepared to acknowledge the shift that had already happened. I wasn't ready to let go of the word "wife" and grab on to the word "girlfriend."

But that night, four and a half months in, as we both lay in my bed, naked and touching, entangled in blankets and sheets, I realized that even if I wasn't ready for the truth, that didn't make it untrue.

"I love you," I said into the darkness, knowing the sound had nowhere to go but into his ears.

He grabbed my hand and squeezed it. "I thought you might," he said. I could tell he was smiling just by his tone.

"I'm sorry I couldn't say it until now."

"It's OK," he said. "I get it."

Sam always seemed to have a grasp on what was truly important. He never seemed bogged down by petty things. He prioritized the heart of the situation over the details. He paid attention to actions more than words.

I didn't like sleeping in my own bed anymore without him. I always held his hand at the movies. I waited all day to see him again just so I could kiss the soft spot by his eye, where his wrinkles were settling in.

He knew I was head over heels in love with him. So he was OK if it took me a while to say it. And that just made me love him more.

"I just . . . it's sometimes hard not to associate moving forward with forgetting the past," I said.

"If it helps . . ." Sam said as he moved closer to me. My eyes were adjusting to the darkness and I could see the glow of his skin. "I don't expect you to stop loving him just because you love me."

I probably should have smiled or kissed him. I should have told him how much I appreciated his magnanimous spirit and his selflessness. But instead, I started crying so hard I shook the bed.

He held me, kissing the top of my head, and then he said, "Is it OK if I tell you a few more things I've been thinking?"

I nodded.

"I think you and I have something that could last for a very long time, Emma. Maybe I even knew that back in high school, maybe that's why I was as infatuated with you as I was. But I feel—I have always felt—more myself with you than anyone I've ever met. And for the first time, I'm starting to see what it would mean to grow *with* someone, as opposed to merely growing beside someone, the way I did with Aisha. I'm not worried about our future, the way I thought I'd be when I fell in love again. I'm OK just being with you and seeing where it goes. I just want you to know that if what we have lasts, and one day we talk about getting married or having kids, I want you to know I'll never try to replace Jesse. I'll never ask you to stop loving him. You can love your past with him. My love for you now isn't threatened by that. I just . . . I want you to know that I'll never ask you to choose. I'll never ask you to tell me I'm your one true love. I know, for someone like you, that isn't fair. And I'll never ask it."

I was quiet for a minute as I processed what he'd said. He put his arm underneath me and held me tight. He smelled my hair. He kissed my ear. "I've just been thinking about that for a while and I wanted to tell you."

I stopped crying and I took a very deep breath in.

The room smelled of sweat and sleep. The bed beneath us felt soft and safe. I had found a man who understood who I was and accepted me entirely, who was strong enough to make peace with the tender spot in my heart for the love I used to have.

"I love you," I said to him, again. The second time, it came out of my mouth with less effort.

"I love you, too," he said. "I love everything about who you are. Always have."

I moved onto my side to face him with my hands underneath my head. He turned to meet me. We looked at each other and smiled.

"It makes me so happy to have you in my life," I said. "I don't know what I did to deserve you."

Sam smiled. "Think of all the people in the world," he said, tucking my longest hair behind my ear. "And I was lucky enough to find you twice."

"Think of all the women trying to buy a piano," I said. "And I'm the one you hit on."

Sam laughed.

"Turn around, would you?" he said. He said this when he wanted to spoon me, when he wanted to fit my body into the cradle of his. I did so happily.

"Good night, sweetheart," he said. I could smell the mint and sweetness of his breath.

"Good night," I told him, and then I said, "I don't know how I got so lucky."

I kept it at that. I didn't say the rest of the sentence that popped into my head.

I don't know how I got so lucky to have both of you. My two true loves.

Sam got us tickets to the symphony. We had been together for over a year. The two of us had just moved in to an apartment in Cambridge and adopted a pair of cats. My parents, ecstatic to have Sam back in their lives, had jokingly started to call him "son."

That night as I was walking out of Symphony Hall in an emerald green dress, Sam in a handsome dark suit, I probably should have been reflecting on the music we'd heard or asking Sam what he thought of some of the performers.

But instead, all I could think about was how hungry I was.

"You look lost in thought," Sam said as we walked through the streets of Boston, headed for the Green Line.

"I'm ravenous," I said to him. "I realize we ate dinner but I just had that tiny salad and now I feel like I could eat a full meal."

Sam laughed. "Should we stop somewhere?" he asked.

"Please," I said. "Somewhere with french fries."

Soon enough, I was eating a hamburger with the wrapper still half on as Sam and I walked down the street in black-tie attire. Sam was holding the rest of the bag in one hand—I'd already eaten the carton of french fries—and drinking a chocolate milk shake with the other.

"How are your feet feeling?" Sam asked me.

"OK," I answered. "Why?"

"What if we walked around for a bit before getting on the T?" he asked. "You look gorgeous and the weather is nice and . . . I don't know. I want to prolong the moment."

I smiled. I figured I had a few minutes of walking before my heels started to rub up against the broad bones of my feet.

"I'm in," I said, and then I took another bite of my burger. When I swallowed, it occurred to me that there was a flaw in his argument. "How are you going to try to say that this is a beautiful moment between us when I'm eating a Whopper?"

Sam laughed. "I think I just love you that much," he said. "That even standing next to you as you cram Burger King into your mouth is special to me." He took a sip of his milk shake after he said it. I watched as his cheeks sucked in to pull the ice cream up the straw while he stood on the sidewalk looking dapper in his dark suit. I knew exactly what he meant. I felt exactly what he felt.

"You look cute trying to inhale that milk shake," I told him.

"See?" he said. "That's how I know you're in love with me. You've also gone crazy."

We continued to walk along the sidewalk as I took another bite of my burger.

"I really mean it," Sam said. "I'm madly in love with you. I hope that you know how much."

I smiled at him. "I suspect I do," I said teasingly.

"I don't know if this is exactly the right time but . . . I want to make sure you know that I want to spend the rest of my life with you. I don't know if I've properly conveyed it but I am committed to this, to us. I'm in, you know? For life. I want you forever. My only concern is that I don't want to pressure you."

"I don't feel pressure," I said. I was still processing what he was saying, still beginning to understand how monumental this moment we were having truly was.

"Are you sure?" he said. "Because I have to be honest. I'm ready to cash in. I'd commit to you for the rest of our lives without a single doubt in my mind. I have never been happier than I have been during this year with you. And—the way I see it—you're it for me. You're everything."

I looked at him, listening to him. I didn't respond because I was wrapped up in how wonderful it felt to be me just then, how nice it felt to be loved the way he loved me.

Sam shifted his gaze and drank from his milk shake. And then he looked at me and said, "I guess what I'm saying is I'm ready. So now I'll just wait until you're ready, if you're ever ready. If you ever want to."

"If I ever want to . . ." I wanted to make sure I understood exactly what he was saying.

"Marry me," he said, taking another sip of his milk shake.

"Wait, are you . . ." I wanted to ask him if he was proposing but something about the word seemed so formal, so daring.

"I'm not proposing," Sam said. "But what I'm saying is that I'm not 'not proposing' because I don't want to. I want to. I just want to wait until you're ready for me to propose."

"I don't think I understood half of that sentence," I said, smiling at him.

"It wasn't the best one I've ever said," he said, laughing.

"Can you just say what you're saying clearly and succinctly?" I asked.

Sam smiled and nodded. "Emma Blair, if you ever decide that you want to marry me, please tell me. Because I would like to marry you."

I dropped the hamburger onto the street. I didn't mean to;

it just fell out of my hand, as if my brain had said to my fingers, "Stop whatever you're doing, and pay attention to what's happening." And then I took both of my free hands and wrapped them around Sam's face and kissed him with everything I felt in my heart.

When I pulled away, I didn't let him speak. I said, "Let's do it."

"What?" Sam said.

"I want to marry you."

"Wait," Sam said. "Are you sure?" I could tell that he couldn't believe what he was hearing and it made me love him even more.

"I'm absolutely positive," I said. "I want to marry you. Of course I do. I love you. So much."

"Oh, wow," Sam said, smiling so wide his eyes crinkled. "Are we . . . are we getting engaged?"

I laughed, blissful. "I think we are," I said.

Sam took stock of the moment. "No, no, no," he said, shaking his head. "This won't do. It has to be better than this. We can't get engaged while I'm holding a milk shake."

He dropped his milk shake in the trash can. I picked my hamburger off the ground and threw it away.

"OK," Sam said. "We're gonna do this right."

He got down on one knee.

"Oh, God," I said, overwhelmed and stunned. "Sam! What are you doing?"

"I just don't have a ring yet," he said. "But I know everything else. Come here." He reached for my hand and held it in his.

"Emma," he said, teary. "I want to spend the rest of my life with you. I always have. You and I . . . we fit like the gears of a machine, like interlocking pieces that join together effortlessly, turning in tandem, perfectly in sync.

"I believe in us, sweetheart. I believe that I am good for you and that I am a better man because of you. And I want to spend the rest of my life by your side. So, Emma Blair, here it is: Will you marry me?"

The first thought that popped into my head was, *This is too soon.* But then the second thought was, *I think I deserve to be happy.*

"Yes," I said quietly. I was surprised just how hard it was to project my voice in that moment, how much my astonishment had muted me. But he heard me. He knew my answer. He stood up and kissed me as if it were the first time.

I felt a welling in my eyes that I knew I stood no chance of holding back. I started bawling.

"Are you okay?" Sam asked me.

I nodded emphatically. "I'm wonderful," I said. "I'm . . ."

I wasn't sure what word I was looking for, what adjective I could possibly use to describe the chaotic elation that was running through my heart.

"I love you," I said, realizing that it was as close as I could ever get.

"I love you, too."

I was tempted to say, "I'm so grateful for you," and "I can't believe you're real," but instead I pulled him close to me and held him as tight as I possibly could.

He dried my tears as we hailed a cab. He held my hand as we rode back to our apartment. He brushed the hair out of my face as we walked in.

He helped me unzip my dress. We made love on our bed, parallel to the headboard, as if there wasn't any time to lie right. We lost ourselves in each other, the last vestige of a wall between us had been knocked down.

Afterward, Sam opened a bottle of champagne. He got his phone and held it in his hand as we called everyone on speakerphone to tell them the good news.

When we were done, we walked into the living room and played "Heart and Soul" together, half-naked, drunk, and swooning.

As I sat next to him on the piano bench, I said, "What if I'd never walked into the music store . . ."

Sam smiled gently and looked at me as he played the keys on the piano ever so softly. And then he said, "But you did."

I decided that was my answer to questions of fate. I could go around asking myself what if x hadn't happened, and the answer would always be, "But it did."

What if Jesse hadn't gotten on that helicopter?
But he did.

I decided to no longer wonder what would have happened if things had worked out differently. And instead, I would focus on what was in front of me. I would focus on reality instead of asking myself questions about fictions.

I kissed Sam's temple. "Take me to bed!" I said.

Sam laughed and took his hands off the piano. "OK, but most of the time when women say that, they mean it sexually."

I laughed. "I mean it sleep-ually," I said.

And then I let out a yelp as Sam stood up and lifted me into his arms.

"Sleep-ually it is," he said as he laid me down on my side of our bed and tucked me in. I fell asleep in the crook of his arm just as he said, "I'm going to find you the perfect diamond ring. I promise."

I was joyful that night.

I felt as if I was moving forward.

I thought that if Jesse could see me from wherever he was, he'd be smiling.

What I was not thinking was, *Jesse is alive. He'll be home in two months. Look what I've done.*

AFTER

~

Both

Or, how to put everything you love at risk

I am lying awake in bed next to Sam, staring at the ceiling. Our gray cat, Mozart, is lying on my feet. Homer, his brother, is black and white and never leaves his spot underneath the piano in the living room except to eat.

It's almost nine a.m. on Wednesday, one of my days off and the day Sam doesn't have to be at school until eleven. On these late mornings, I have illusions about the two of us going out for breakfast, but Sam always refuses to open his eyes until the very last second. This school year so far we have gone to breakfast on a Wednesday exactly zero times. Right now, Sam is sound asleep beside me.

It's been seven weeks since I found out that Jesse was alive. Our initial conversation was kept brief, and due to concerns of Jesse's well-being, contact has been limited. I have been getting most of my updates via e-mail from his mother, Francine.

All I know is that he's been at risk for refeeding syndrome and complications from hypoglycemia.

The doctors did not clear him to be released until yesterday.

That means that he is coming home tomorrow.

When I told Sam about this last night, he said, "OK. How are you feeling?"

I told him the God's honest truth. "I have no idea."

I am very confused right now. In fact, I'm so confused that I'm confused about how confused I am.

What Sam and I have . . . it's love. Pure and simple and true.

But I'm no longer feeling pure, nothing is simple, and I'm no longer sure what's true.

"What's on your mind?" Sam asks me.

I look over at him. I didn't realize he had woken up yet.

"Oh," I say, turning back to the ceiling. "Nothing. Really. Nothing and everything."

"Jesse?" he asks.

"I guess, yeah."

Sam swallows and stays silent and then he turns away from me, getting up and going into the bathroom. I can hear the faucet start and then the water splash as he brushes his teeth. I hear the familiar squeak and rumble of the shower.

My phone rings and I reach onto my bedside table to see who it is. I do not recognize the number. I should put it through to voice mail but I don't. Lately, I can't stand to miss a single call.

"Hello?"

"Is this Emma Lerner?" It is the voice of a young woman.

"It's Emma Blair," I say. "But yes, speaking."

"Mrs. . . . ." The woman stops herself. "Ms. Blair, my name is Elizabeth Ivan. I'm calling from the *Beacon*."

I close my eyes, cursing myself for answering.

"Yes?"

"We are doing a piece on the rescue of Jesse Lerner of Acton."

"Yes."

"And we wanted to give you an opportunity to comment."

I can feel myself shaking my head, as if she could pick up on any of my nonverbal clues. "I'm sorry. I don't think I'd like to publicly comment."

"Are you sure? The Lerners are contributing."

"Yeah," I say. "I hear you. I just don't think I'm comfortable, but thank you very much for the opportunity."

"Are you—"

"Thank you, Ms. Ivan. Have a great day."

I hang up the phone before she can speak again. I double-check twice that my phone is off and I throw myself back down onto my pillows, covering my face with my hands, wondering if I will ever feel only one emotion again in my life.

Because lately it's happiness *and* fear, joy *and* sorrow, guilt *and* validation.

It is not simply happiness. Simply fear. Simply joy. Simply sorrow.

The deafening silence in the room means that my ears can only focus on the sound of the water spraying from the shower in the bathroom.

I think of the steam building up.

I think of how warm it must be.

I think of the way the hot water must feel soothing and comfortable. I think of Sam. The way he looks when he's wet. I think of the hot water running down his shoulders. The shoulders that carried my obscenely large desk up four flights of stairs when we moved in together. The shoulders that brought up two boxes of books at a time as he teased me that I should stop hoarding books, knowing full well that would never happen.

Sam is my life. My new, beautiful, wonderful, magical life.

I get up out of bed and I open the bathroom door. It's just

as steamy in here as I imagined. The mirror is too fogged up to see myself as I take off my shirt and slide out of my underwear. But I know what I'd see if I could: I'd see a short, blond, pear-shaped thirtysomething woman with a pixie cut and a smattering of freckles under her right eye.

I slide the curtain open just barely and I step into the shower. Sam opens his eyes. I can tell he is relieved to see me. He puts his arms around me and holds me tight. The warmth of his skin warms me up exactly as I knew it would.

His chin is nestled into my shoulder.

"I know everything is really complicated right now," he says to me. "I'll do whatever you want. I just . . . I need to know what you're thinking."

"I love you," I say into his shoulders as the hot water hits my face and pastes my hair to my forehead. "I love you so much."

"I know," he says, and then he pulls himself away from me and turns toward the water.

He washes the shampoo out of his hair.

With his back to me, I grab the bar of soap and lather it up in my hands. I rub it across his shoulders and down his back. I reach forward and soap up his chest. As the water washes it away, I put my cheek on his back. I put my arms around him. I'd glue myself to him if I could. For the past three nights, I've had dreams of wrapping the two of us together in one rope. I've dreamed of tying it tight so neither of us can escape. I've dreamed of knots so taut they can't be undone. Rope so thick it can't be cut.

Sam puts his arms forward onto the shower wall to steady himself. And then he says, "Just . . . just do me a favor."

"Anything."

"Don't stay with me if you want to be with him," he says. "Don't do that to me."

My dreams, the rope and the knots, I know exactly what they mean.

You don't tie yourself to something unless you're scared you might float away.

The beginning of December is one of my least favorite times of year in Massachusetts. It always feels like the calm before the storm.

The air is often thin and frigid, as if it could shatter like glass. But, today at least, it's warm enough that the light precipitation is just a drizzle of rain and not the beginning of flurries. Although this is a somewhat unwelcome reminder that our first snow is looming.

I am wearing black jeans, a slouchy cream sweater, tall brown boots, and a black peacoat. I never wondered what I'd be wearing when I saw Jesse again because I never thought it would happen.

And yet here is the answer to the question I never knew to ask myself: jeans and a sweater.

There's no dress code for this sort of thing, for seeing the love of your life who has been missing since your first anniversary.

One of the loves of your life.

One of.

Sam left early this morning and didn't wake me up to say good-bye. I opened my eyes only when I heard him shutting our front door on his way out. I watched him from the bedroom window. I saw him walk to his car and get in. His face looked stoic but his posture betrayed him. Shoulders slumped, head bowed, he looked like a man at the end of his rope.

He pulled away before I could call out to him, and when I dialed his number, he didn't answer.

Meanwhile, Jesse lands at three. Which means I have the whole morning and most of the afternoon to get through as if this isn't the most unbelievable day of my life.

Just before nine, I pull into the parking lot behind Blair Books and make my way inside, turning on all the lights and bringing it to life—the way I do almost every morning.

My parents are officially retiring next year. But at this point, they have retired all but in name. I run the store. I am in charge. The clerks report to my assistant manager, Tina, who reports to me.

My dad still oversees the bookkeeping. My mom comes in on Saturday afternoons and works the floor—she wants to know what people are reading and she likes to keep in touch with the same customers she's grown to care for over the past twenty years.

Everything else is me.

Blair Books is the one thing in my life right now that I am unequivocally proud of.

I may be a bit overwhelmed and sometimes feel like I'm in over my head, but I am good at running this store.

Sales are staying solid in light of the changes in the industry. Not many people can say that. Just being able to keep the lights on at a time when even big-box chain stores have closed is, obviously, the most important thing. But the truth is that's only a fraction of where my pride lies. I am, more than anything, incredibly excited about how we are engaging readers.

We have author events at least twice a month. We have signed copies of best-selling books. We have eleven different reading groups and a writers workshop that each meet here once a month. We have a thriving online business. We have exceptional customer service. We have free doughnuts once a week.

I am especially proud of the free doughnuts.

When I'm done tidying up the store this morning, I head to my office and sit down at my desk to check my e-mail. I see a message from my mother at the top of my in-box.

The subject line says *Did You See This?* The body of the e-mail is a link to the article in the *Beacon* about Jesse. It must have gone live this morning. Underneath the link, my mother wrote, *Call me anytime today if you need to talk. I'm thinking of you.*

I'm not sure that I want to read the article but I can't stop myself from clicking.

Missing Local Man Surfaces on Pacific Island
BY ELIZABETH IVAN

Jesse Lerner, 31, from Acton, has been found after having gone missing three and a half years ago.

Lerner had been involved in a fatal helicopter crash that killed the other three passengers on board. The team was on their way to film in the Aleutian Islands when the helicopter experienced a critical engine failure. Lerner, then 28, was presumed dead. Seven weeks ago, he was discovered at sea by a ship heading to Midway Atoll.

Midway is a former naval air facility and is currently

managed by the United States Fish and Wildlife Service. Though it is far out into the Pacific, a third of the way between Honolulu and Japan, there are anywhere from thirty to sixty FWS members stationed there at any given time.

Lerner is believed to have spent the majority of his time stranded on an islet within a thousand kilometers of Midway. There has been no official word on how he made his way to safety.

Hospitalized shortly after rescue, Lerner has recently been cleared for travel and will arrive back in Massachusetts sometime this week, most likely by way of Hanscom Field. His parents, Joseph Lerner and Francine Lerner of Acton, eagerly await his arrival. "We cannot tell you the depth of the pain of losing a child. And we cannot begin to describe the relief in finding out he's coming home," said the Lerners in a joint statement.

Over a decade ago, Lerner made headlines when he beat the high school state record for the five hundred-meter freestyle. A year before he went missing, Lerner married local woman Emma Blair. When contacted, Blair had no comment.

I finish reading the article and I read it again. And then again. And then again. I snap out of it only when Tina calls my name.

"Good mornin', Emma," she says to me as she comes in through the back just before ten. With her thick Boston accent, my name sounds more like "Emmer" than "Emma."

She pronounces "library" as "libry," calls water fountains "bubblahs," and leaves work on time so she's not late for "suppah."

Boston accents are warm and cozy and wonderful to me.

When I hear people make fun of them on TV, I always wonder if they've ever been here. So many people in Massachusetts don't even speak with a Boston accent, and the ones who do would never *pahk they-ah cah in Hahvahd Yahd*.

There's nowhere to park in Harvard Yard.

"Good morning, Tina," I say.

Tina is the sort of employee you search high and low for. She's an empty-nested stay-at-home mom who loves books more than anyone I've ever met. She is sweet to everyone, but firm with people who are unkind. She misses her kids, who are all in college, and works here to busy her mind. I don't think she or her husband needs the money she makes. It's not that I've asked, it's just that she uses at least a quarter of her paycheck every week to buy books with her discount.

When I start to get overwhelmed by all that there is to do running this store, it is Tina who I count on.

The other thing that I like about her is that she has absolutely no interest in being my friend. We work together. I am her boss. We are kind to each other and occasionally share a laugh in the stockroom. That's the beginning and the end of it.

When I first started managing people, I had a hard time setting boundaries and expectations. I wanted everyone to like me. I wanted the people here to feel like they were part of a family—because that is what this store has always been to me. Family. But business doesn't work like that. And I don't need my employees to like me. I need them to respect me and do their jobs well.

I've learned that lesson the hard way a few times, but at least I can say I've learned it. Now, I have a group of employees who might sometimes go home and complain about me but take pride in their jobs and run a great bookstore.

Today I am especially grateful that my employees are not my friends. I know that Tina reads the *Beacon*. I'm sure she read the article. But I know she will not ask me a single thing.

When the Acton Ladies Reading Society comes in at eleven to start their book group, I begin to get anxious.

Jesse's plane lands in four hours.

Jesse, my Jesse, will be home today.

I dropped him off at LAX three years and seven months ago and I will be at the airfield this afternoon when he lands.

I am not good at my job for the hours between noon and two. I am scatterbrained, unfocused, and impatient.

I ring up a woman for $16.87 and when she hands me a twenty-dollar bill, I give her $16.87 back.

A man calls asking if we have any copies of *Extremely Loud & Incredibly Close* and I tell him, "Yes, we carry all of Jonathan Lethem's books."

When I see Mark, the only one of my employees whom I would say classifies as a book snob, come to relieve me, I am the very definition of relieved.

It's time to go.

I can go.

I can get out of here.

As I gather my things and take a look at myself in the bathroom mirror, I regret, for a moment, that I'm not better friends with Tina. It would be nice to look at someone and say, "OK, how do I look?" And have them say, "You look great. It's all gonna be fine."

I consider calling Marie when I get to my car. She might be the perfect person to give me whatever sort of pep talk a person needs before they go meet their long-lost husband. But when I pick up my phone, I'm sidetracked by a text from Sam.

I love you.

It's the sort of thing we text to each other every day, but seeing it now, it is both life-affirming and heartbreaking.

I stare out the windshield, stunned at what is happening to my quiet and stable life.

I have a husband and a fiancé.

I turn the ignition, start my car, and head out of the parking lot.

After years without him, the man I lost is coming home.

I pull into the airfield to see that the parking lot is empty. I check the time. I'm eighteen minutes early.

I fidget in the car, unsure how to contain all of the nervous energy in my body. And then my phone erupts with the sound of my ringtone and I see Olive's face on my screen.

I answer.

"How are you doing?" she asks, even before saying hello.

"I don't know," I say.

"Is he home yet?"

"He will be soon. He's supposed to land in fifteen minutes."

"Jesus," she says.

"Tell me about it."

"What can I do?"

This is Olive's go-to mode of function. *What can I do?* It's a wonderful quality in a friend. It means that she is always the one that is clearing the plates when she's staying at your house. She is always the one sending thoughtful gifts and checking in on you at opportune moments. But in a situation like this, she's not in her element.

Because there is nothing for her to do.

There is nothing to be done.

All of this just . . . *is*.

"Can I at least send you flowers?" she says.

I smile. "I don't think flowers are going to help me deal with the fact that I have a husband and a fiancé at the same time," I tell her.

"What you're describing is completely absurd," she says. "Flowers help with everything."

I laugh. "Thank you," I say, "for managing to be funny right now."

"And thank you for thinking that joking about intense things is appropriate," Olive says. "Tracey does not agree."

Tracey is Olive's girlfriend. I have to say that their pairing makes absolutely no sense to me. Tracey is serious and erudite and corrects other people's grammar. She's regal, thin, and gorgeous. Whereas the best part of Olive, to me, has always been that she says whatever pops into her brain, eats whatever is in front of her, and will try anything you propose.

Sam easily explains it away by saying that opposites attract, but I'm still digging for some piece that I'm missing. Sam must say to me, "Do we really have to keep talking about Olive and Tracey?" at least once a month.

"Do you think he is OK?" Olive says. "I mean, I know he's alive and they say he's healthy enough, but do you think he's going to show up and have gone mad? I mean, wouldn't you? Three years alone? He was probably living off of coconuts and talking to volleyballs."

"This isn't helping," I tell her. "This is the opposite of helping."

"Sorry. I'll shut up."

"No," I say. "Don't shut up. Just stop talking about how my husband is probably mentally unstable. Talk about something else. I have time to kill until everyone gets here and I'm afraid if I have to kill it alone, I'll be the one that's mentally unstable."

Olive laughs. "Like I said, you keep a good sense of humor in a crisis."

"I wasn't joking," I tell her.

And then we both start laughing because that's the funniest thing of all, isn't it? How serious this is, how unfunny it is.

Just as I'm laughing my hardest, I see a white SUV pull into the parking lot and I know, even before seeing the driver, that it is Jesse's parents.

"Ah," I say to her. "I have to go. Francine and Joe are here."

"Oh, my God," Olive says. "This all sounds so uncomfortable."

"A bit, yeah," I say as I turn off the car.

"I mean, when was the last time you talked to them?"

"I basically haven't since he disappeared," I tell her. The three of us kept up the pretense of family for a few months, calling one another on holidays and birthdays. But that faded quickly. To be honest, I think it was too painful for all of us. For the past few years, we've lived in the same town and not seen each other except for the occasional run-in at the grocery store.

"All right, wish me luck dealing with this. I gotta go."

Olive has a very bad habit that I never noticed until we moved away from each other and had to conduct our entire relationship over the phone. When you say you have to go, she says OK and then talks for another half hour.

"OK," she says. "Good luck. I'm here for you. Is Sam okay? How's he doing?"

"Sam is . . ." I don't know how to finish the sentence and I don't have time to. "I don't know. I really have to go," I say. "Thank you for calling. I don't know how I would do this without you."

"I'm here anytime, you know that," Olive says. "If there is anything I can do, please let me know."

"I will," I say. "I promise. All right, I'll talk to you soon."

"Talk to you soon. Are you and Sam definitely going through with the wedding? I mean, at this point everything is up in the air, right?"

"Olive!" I say, losing my patience.

"Sorry," she says, realizing what she's doing. "I'm being such an Olive right now."

I laugh. "You kind of are," I say.

"OK, I'm going. I love you. I'm here for you. I won't even ask how Sophie and Ava are because I know you don't have time."

"Great. Thank you. I love you. Good-bye."

"Bye."

When she hangs up the phone, I realize how alone I am. For a moment, I thought the problem was just that I needed to get Olive off the phone. Now, I remember what the real challenge is.

I get out of my car. Francine waves as she sees me.

I wave back and start walking over to them.

Francine is wearing a fitted burgundy dress with a navy pea-coat. Her wavy dark brown hair just grazes her shoulders.

She hugs me, firmly and passionately, as if she's missed me all these years. I pull away from her just as Joe puts his arms around me. He looks like he's dressed for church. Gray slacks, light blue button-down, navy blue blazer. I notice that he has started losing his hair. His face has low valleys in places that used to be plains.

"Hi, sweetheart," he says to me.

"Emma," Francine says, putting a scarf around her neck. "It's like a breath of fresh air to see you."

"Thanks," I say back to her. "You, too." I don't know what to call her. When I was a teenager, I called her "Mrs. Lerner." When I was married to her son, I called her "Franny."

"Look at your hair!" she says, moving her hand toward my short hair but not actually touching it. "It's so different."

I am stronger than when I knew them. I stand straighter. I am more patient. I hold fewer grudges. I am more thankful for what I have, less resentful for what I don't. I am less restless. I read a lot more books. I play the piano. I'm engaged.

But, of course, she can't see all that.

The only change she can see is my short, blond hair.

"It's very gamine."

"Thanks," I say back as if I am confident this is a compliment but, by the way Francine says it, I'm not.

"How are you?" she says.

"Um," I say. "Good. You?"

"Us, too," she says. "Us, too. The Lord works in mysterious ways but I am stunned, humbled really, at what a gift today is."

Jesse wasn't raised with any religious instruction and in high school I once heard Francine say she didn't "care what you think God wants" to a proselytizing Mormon who rang their doorbell. Now I'm wondering if that's changed. If losing Jesse made her a born-again Christian and if getting him back serves as all the proof she needs that she's on the right track.

Joe looks at me briefly and then looks away. I can't tell what he's thinking. But he appears to be much more conflicted about everything. Francine seems to think that life is going to be perfect again, just as soon as Jesse gets off that plane. But I think Joe understands that everything is going to be a lot more complex.

"All right," Francine says. "Shall we head in there? I can't believe he lands soon. Look at this, the three of us on our way to see our boy."

She pulls out her phone and checks it.

"Looks like Chris, Tricia, and the boys will be here with Danny and Marlene in a minute."

I knew Chris and Tricia had kids not because anyone told me but because I saw Tricia in T.J. Maxx last year, many months pregnant with a toddler at her side.

I don't actually know who Marlene is. I can only assume she's Danny's girlfriend, fiancée, or wife.

The simple fact is that I know almost nothing about the Lerners anymore and they know almost nothing about me. I don't even know if they know about Sam.

Joe and I follow Francine as she walks confidently in the direction of the terminal.

"It is hard to predict how he'll be feeling," Francine says as we walk. "From what I've heard and the advice that I've been given by professionals, our job right now is to make him feel safe."

"Of course," I say.

Right before we get to the door, Francine turns and looks at me. "In that vein, we have chosen not to tell him you've moved on."

So they do know. Of course they do.

"OK," I say, unsure how else to respond other than to acknowledge that I've heard her.

The wind picks up and I find myself wishing I had brought a warmer coat. The air here is sharper than I expected. I button up tighter and I watch as Joe does the same.

"You can tell him if you want," Francine says. "I just don't know if he can handle finding out you are already engaged to someone else."

It is the "already" that bothers me. The "already" nested firmly in the sentence, as if it's right at home between "you are" and "engaged."

I resolve to stay quiet. I tell myself the best response is sto-icism. But then, before I realize I've done it, I've let the feelings in my chest become words out of my mouth.

"You don't need to make me feel guilty," I tell her. "I feel plenty guilty all on my own."

Even though I know she hears me, she pretends she's heard nothing. It doesn't matter; even if she did acknowledge it, I know there's no way she could possibly understand what I mean.

I feel awful for giving up on Jesse. For thinking he was dead. For moving on. For falling in love with someone else. I'm actu-ally furious at myself for that.

But I'm also really angry at myself for not being loyal to Sam, for not remaining steadfast and true in my devotion, like I have promised him I would be. I am mad at myself for being unsure, for not being the sort of woman who can tell him he's the only one, for not giving him the kind of love he deserves.

I'm mad at myself for a lot of things.

So much so that I barely have time to consider what anyone else thinks of me.

"OK," Joe says abruptly. "Let's go. Jesse's going to land any minute."

I watch through the plate-glass window in front of me as a plane flies low in the sky and lands on the runway.

My heart starts beating so hard in my chest that I am afraid I am having a heart attack.

A man on the ground wheels out a staircase. A door opens. A pilot walks out.

And then there is Jesse.

Worse for wear and yet, somehow, never more beautiful to me than right now.

Pictures never did his smile justice. I remember that now.

He's also thin and frail, as if his body is made only of muscle and bone. His once-gentle face is sleek, hard edges where soft cheeks used to be. His hair is longer, shaggier. His skin is mottled light brown and pink, looking very much like a three-year sunburn.

But his mannerisms are the same. His smile is the same. His eyes, the same.

I stare at him as he gets off the plane. I stare at him as he hugs Francine and Joe. I stare at him as he comes closer to me, as he looks me in the eye with purpose. I notice that the pinkie on his right hand stops at the first knuckle. He lost a finger somewhere along the way.

"Hi," he says.

Just hearing that one word makes me feel as though I have gone back in time, to a part of my life when things made sense, when the world was fair.

"Hi."

"You are a sight for sore eyes."

I smile. I bury my face in my hands. He grabs me, holding me. I can feel my pulse beat erratically, as if it isn't sure whether to speed up or slow down.

I wonder if this is all real.

But when I open my eyes again, he's still there. He's right here in front of me, surrounding me.

I grieved him as if he were dead. But here he is.

It's almost terrifying, how much it defies logic and reason. What else do we know about the world that isn't true?

"You're home," I say.

"I'm here."

You know how every once in a while you look back on your life and you wonder how so much time has passed? You wonder how each moment bled into the next and created the days, months, and years that now all feel like seconds?

That's how I feel.

Right now.

In this moment.

It feels like our entire past together spans eons and the time I've spent without him is an insignificant little flash.

I have loved Jesse since the day I saw him at that swim meet.

And I'm having a hard time remembering how I lived without him, how I could bear to look at a world that I thought he wasn't in, and why I thought I could ever love anyone the way I love him.

Because it has been him.

My whole life.

It has always, always been him.

How have I spent all of my time forgetting who I am and who I love?

The last couple of hours have been a daze. I've stood by, saying barely anything, as the whole family embraced Jesse's return home. I watched as Francine cried her eyes out and prayed to God at the sight of him, as Chris and Tricia introduced him to their son, Trevor, and their baby girl, Ginnie. As Danny introduced him to his new wife, Marlene.

My phone has rung a number of times but I have yet to bring myself to even look at the caller ID. I can't handle real life right now. I can barely handle what's happening right in front of me.

And I can't even begin to reconcile what is happening right in front of me to my real life.

There is so much for Jesse to process. You can tell there is a great deal that his family wants to say, so much they want to do. I find myself wanting to tell him every thought I've had while he's been gone, wanting to describe every moment I've spent without him, every feeling I have right now. I want to plug my heart into his and upload the past three and a half years right into his soul.

I can only imagine that everyone else here wants to do that same thing.

It must be so overwhelming to be him, to be the person everyone is staring at, the person everyone wants to see with their very own eyes and hold in their own hands.

As I watch Jesse interact with his family, I feel suddenly like I don't belong here.

Jesse is holding his niece, Ginnie, for the first time, trying to remain calm. But I know him. I know what the downturn of the corners of his eyes means. I know why he pulls his ears back, why his neck looks rigid and stiff.

He's uncomfortable. He's confused. This is all so much for him. Too much.

I catch his eye. He smiles.

And I realize it's everyone else who doesn't belong here. There may be twenty people in this room but there are only two people in the whole world to Jesse and me and they are Jesse and me.

When his family has calmed down, they all start discussing how they will make their way back to Francine and Joe's house. I watch Jesse pull apart from the pack and then I feel his arm on me, pulling me aside.

"Is your car here?" he says.

"Yeah. Just right outside."

I can't believe I'm talking to him. He's right in front of me. Talking to me. Jesse Lerner. My Jesse Lerner. Is alive and talking to me. Nothing has ever been so *impossible* and yet *happening*.

"All right, great. Let's get out of here soon, then."

"OK," I say, stone-faced.

"Are you OK?" he asks me. "You look like you've seen a ghost." The moment he hears it come out of his mouth, he closes his eyes. When he opens them back up, he says, "I'm sorry. You are seeing a ghost. Aren't you?"

I look at him and I am hit with a wave of exhaustion.

Do you know how tiring it is to see a dead man in front of

you? To have to remind your brain every half second that your eyes aren't lying?

I'm overwhelmed by the stunning incredibility of the truth. That I can, right this very second, reach out and touch him. That I can ask him any of the questions I've spent years of my life wishing I'd asked him. That I can tell him I love him.

The desire to tell him, and the belief that he would never hear me, has gutted me year after year after year.

And now I can tell him. I can just open my mouth and say it and he will hear it and he will know.

"I love you," I say. I say it because I mean it right now, but I also say it for every single time I couldn't say it then.

He looks at me and he smiles a deep and peaceful smile. "I love you, too."

It all hurts so bad and feels so good that I'd swear my heart is bleeding.

There is such immense relief of an ache so deep that I fall to pieces, as if I hadn't realized until now how much effort it was taking to seem normal, to stand up straight.

My legs can't hold me. My lungs can't sustain me. My eyes stare ahead but don't see a thing.

Jesse catches me before I fall to the ground. Everyone is looking but I barely care.

Jesse supports my weight and leads me around the corner, into the bathroom. When the door shuts, he puts his arms around me, tightly, holding me so close that there's no air between us. For years there were immeasurable miles separating us and now, not even oxygen.

"I know," he says, "I know."

He is the only person who can understand my pain, my astonishment, my joy.

"I'm going to tell my family we need some time, OK?"

I nod vehemently into his chest. He kisses the top of my head. "I'll be right back. Stay here."

I stand against the bathroom wall and watch him walk out the door.

I look at myself in the mirror. My eyes are glassy and bloodshot. The skin around them is blotched red. The diamond ring on my finger catches the dingy yellow light.

I could have taken it off before I came here. I could have slipped it off my finger and left it in my car. But I didn't. I didn't because I didn't want to lie.

But right now, I cannot for the life of me understand why I thought wearing it was better than tossing it in my jewelry box and replacing it with my little ruby ring.

Both of them are only half the truth.

I close my eyes. And I remember the man I woke up next to this morning.

Jesse is back.

"OK," he says. "Let's go."

He grabs my hand and leads me out through a back door. He walks toward the parking lot. His family is still inside. The wind blows through our hair as we run toward the bank of cars.

"Which one is yours?" he asks. I point to my sedan at the corner of the lot. We get into the car. I turn on the ignition, put the car in reverse, and then I put the car right back into neutral.

"I need a minute," I say.

Sometimes I think this is a dream that I'm going to wake up from and I don't know whether that would be good or bad.

"I get it," Jesse says. "Take all the time you need."

I look at him, trying to fully process what is happening. I find myself staring at the space where the rest of his pinkie used to be.

It will take us days, maybe weeks, months, or years, to truly understand what each other has gone through, to understand who we are to each other now.

Somehow that makes me feel calmer. There's no rush for us to make sense of all of this. It will take as long as it takes.

"All right," I say. "I'm good."

I pull out of the spot and toward the road. When I get to the main drive, I take a right.

"Where are we going?" he says.

"I don't know," I tell him.

"I want to talk to you. I want to talk to you forever."

I look at him, briefly taking my eyes off the road.

I don't know where I'm driving; I just drive. And then I turn on the heat and I feel it blaze out of the vents and onto my hands and feet. I can feel the smothering warmth on my cheeks.

We hit a red light and I come to a stop.

I look over at him and he's looking out the window, deep in thought. No doubt this is even more bewildering for him than it is for me. He must have his own set of questions, his own conflicted feelings. Maybe he loved someone out there in the world while he was gone. Maybe he did unspeakable things to survive, to get back here. Maybe he stopped loving me somewhere along the way, gave up on me.

I have always thought of Jesse as my other half, as a person that I know as well as I know myself, but the truth is he's a stranger to me now.

Where has he been and what has he seen?

The light turns green and the sky is getting darker by the minute. The weather forecast said it might hail tonight.

Tonight.

I'm supposed to go home to Sam tonight.

When the winding back roads we are traveling get windier, I realize I'm not headed anywhere in particular. I pull over onto a well-worn patch on the side of the road. I put the car in neutral and pull up the hand brake, but I keep the heat on. I unbuckle my seat belt and I turn to look at him.

"Tell me everything," I say. He's hard for me to look at, even though he's all I want to see.

Wherever he was, whatever he was doing, has weathered him. His skin has a leatheriness that it didn't have when he left. His face has wrinkled in the overused spots. I wonder if the lines around his eyes are from squinting off in the distance, looking for someone to save him. I wonder if his pinkie isn't the only wound, if there are more beneath his clothes. I know there must be a great deal beneath the surface.

"What do you want to know?" he asks me.

"Where were you? What happened?"

Jesse blows air out of his mouth, a telltale sign that these are all questions he doesn't really want to answer.

"How about just the short version?" I say.

"How about we talk about something else? Absolutely anything else?"

"Please?" I say to him. "I need to know."

Jesse looks out the window and then back to me. "I'll tell you now, and then will you promise that you won't ask about it again? Nothing more?"

I smile and offer him a handshake. "You've got yourself a deal."

Jesse takes my hand, holds it. He feels warm to the touch. I have to stop myself from touching more of him. And then Jesse opens his mouth and says, "Here it goes."

When the helicopter went down, he knew he was the only survivor. He declines to tell me how he knew that; he doesn't want to talk about the crash. All he'll say is that there was an inflatable raft with emergency supplies, including drinking water and rations, that saved his life and got him through the weeks it took to find land.

Land is a generous description for where he ended up. It was a rock formation in the middle of the sea. Five hundred paces from one end to the other. It was not really even an islet, let alone an island, but it had a gradual enough slope on one side to give it a small shore. Jesse knew he'd traveled far from Alaska because the water was mild and the sun was relentless. Initially, he planned to stay there only long enough to rest, to feel earth under his feet. But soon, he realized that the raft had been punctured along the rocks. It was almost entirely deflated. He was stuck.

He was almost out of water and running low on food bars. He used the old water containers to collect rainwater. He searched the rocks for any signs of plants or animals but found only sand and stone. So he figured out how to fish.

There were some missteps along the way. He ate a few fish that made him vomit. He drank the water faster than it replenished. But he also found oysters and mussels growing on the shoreline and during a particularly relentless rainstorm managed to store over a week's worth of water—getting him ahead of the game. During the scorching sun of midday, he hung the deflated raft between two rocks and slept in the shade. Soon, he figured out a fairly reliable routine.

Jesse was eating raw fish, barnacles, and food bars, drinking rainwater, and hiding from the sun. He felt stable. He felt like he could make that work for as long as he needed to until we found him.

But then, after a few weeks, he realized we were never going to find him.

He says he had a breakdown and then, after, an epiphany.

That's when Jesse started training.

He knew that he couldn't spend the rest of his life living alone on a small patch of rocks in the Pacific. He knew his only way out was the very thing he had been raised to do.

He trained to swim a race.

He counted his strokes and each day swam out farther than he had the day before.

He started out slow, frailer and more fatigued than he'd ever been.

But after a few months, he was able to make it far out into the ocean. He felt confident that one day he'd be strong enough to swim the open water as long as he had to.

It took him almost two years to work up the stamina and the guts to do it. He had setbacks both minor (a jellyfish sting) and major (he saw a shark circling the rocks on and off for a few weeks). And when he finally set out for good, it wasn't because he believed that he could make it.

It was because he knew he'd die if he didn't.

He had run out of food bars long ago and the oysters had dried up. Half of the raft had been torn and lost to the wind. He feared that he was not growing stronger but weaker.

There was a rainstorm that brought him days' worth of water. He drank as much as he could and managed to strap a few bottles on his back using pieces of the raft.

And then he got in the water.

Ready to find help or die trying.

He does not know exactly how long he was out in the open sea and he lost count of the strokes. He says he knows it was less than two days when he saw a ship.

"And that's when I knew it was all over," he says. "That I would be OK. That I was coming home to you."

He never mentions his finger. In the whole story, in his telling me everything, he never mentioned that he lost half of his finger. And I don't know what to do because I agreed not to ask anything more. I start to open my mouth, to ask what I know I'm not supposed to. But he cuts me off and I get the message. We're done talking about that now.

"I thought of you every day," he says. "I have missed you for all these years."

I start to say it back and then realize I'm not sure if it's true. I thought of him always—until one day I thought of him less. And then I thought of him often but . . . that's not really the same thing.

"You were always in my heart," I finally say. Because I know that's true. That's absolutely true.

No matter how much history Jesse and I have shared, no matter how much we may feel like we understand the other, I'm not sure I can ever understand the pain of living alone in the middle of the ocean. I don't know if I can ever truly appreciate the courage it takes to swim the open water.

And while I'm in no way comparing the two, I don't think Jesse can understand what it feels like to believe the love of your life is dead. And then to be sitting across from him in your car off the side of the road.

"Now you go," he says.

"Now I go?"

"Tell me everything," he says. The minute he says it, I know that he knows I'm engaged. He knows everything. Between the acute awareness of his voice and the sense of "here it comes" that lives in his focused eyes and tight lips, I can tell he figured it out on his own.

Or he noticed my diamond ring.

"I'm engaged," I say.

Then, suddenly, Jesse starts laughing. He looks relieved.

"What? Why are you laughing? Why is this funny?"

"Because," he says, smiling, "I thought you were already married."

I feel a smile erupt across my face even though I can't tell you where, exactly, it comes from.

And then I start laughing and playfully hit him. "It's practically the same thing!" I say to him.

"Oh, no, it's not," he says. "No, it absolutely is not."

"I'm planning to marry someone else."

"But you haven't yet."

"So?" I say.

It's so easy to talk to him. It was always easy to talk to him. Or maybe it's just that I've always been good at it.

"I'm saying that I have spent the last three and a half years of my life hoping with everything I have in me to see you again. And if you think that you being engaged to someone else is going to stop me from putting our life back together, you've lost your goddamn mind."

I look at him, and at first the smile is still spread wide across my face, but soon, reality starts to set in and the smile fades. I put my head in my hands.

I am going to hurt everyone.

The car becomes so quiet all I can hear is the roll of the cars whizzing past us on the road.

"It's more complicated than you realize," I say finally.

"Emma, look, I get it. You had to move on. I know everybody did. I know that you thought I was . . ."

"Dead. I thought you were dead."

"I know!" he says, moving toward me, grabbing my hands. "I can't imagine how hard that must have been for you. I don't want to imagine it. All these years, I knew you were alive, I knew I had you to go back to. And I know you didn't have that. I'm so sorry, Emma."

I look up at him and I can see there are tears in his eyes to match the ones forming in mine.

"I'm so sorry. You have no idea how sorry. I should never have done it. I should never have left you. Nothing on this earth, no experience I could ever have, would be worth losing you or hurting you the way that I did. I used to lay awake at night and worry about you. I would spend hours and hours, days, really, worried about how much you must be hurting. Worried about how you and my mother and my whole family must be aching. And it nearly killed me. To know that the people I loved, that you, you, Emma, were grieving for me. I am so sorry that I put you through that.

"But I'm home now. And what drove me to get home, what kept me going, was you. Was coming home to you. Was coming back to the life that we had planned. I want that life back. And I'm not going to let the decisions that you made when you thought I was gone affect how I feel about you now. I love you, Emma. I've always loved you. I never stopped loving you. I'm incapable of it. I'm incapable of loving anyone but you. So I absolve you of anything that happened while I was gone and it's now our time. Our time to put everything back together the way it was."

It's now so hot in the car that I feel like I have a fever. I turn down the heat and I try to wrestle out of my jacket. It's hard, in the small space of the driver's seat, to wiggle left and right just enough to get my arms out. Jesse, wordlessly, takes hold of one of the sleeves and pulls for me, helping me finally free myself.

I look at him, and if I push away the shock and the confusion and the bittersweetness, what I'm left with is extreme comfort. Opening my eyes and seeing his face staring back is more like home than anything I can remember. Right here in this car is the best part of my teenage years, the best part of my twenties. The best part of me. The whole beginning of my life is this man.

The years he's been gone have done nothing to erase the warmth and comfort we have from the years we spent in each other's lives.

"You were the love of my life," I say.

"I *am* the love of your life," Jesse says. "Nothing's changed."

"Everything has changed!"

"Not between us, it hasn't," he says. "You're still the girl with the freckles under her eye. And I'm still the guy that kissed you in the police station."

"What about Sam?"

It is the first time I see sadness and anger flash over Jesse's face. "Don't say his name," he says, moving away from me. The sharpness of his tone disarms me. "Let's talk about something else. For now."

"What else could we possibly talk about?"

Jesse looks out the window for a moment. I can see his jaw

tense, his eyes fixate on a point. And then he relaxes and turns back to me. He smiles. "Seen any good movies?"

Despite myself, I'm laughing and soon he is, too. That's how it's always been with us. I smile because he's smiling. He laughs because I am laughing.

"This is really hard," I say when I catch my breath. "Everything about this is so . . ."

"It doesn't have to be," he says. "I love you. And you love me. You're my wife."

"I don't even think that's true. When you were declared dead, it . . . I mean, I don't even know if we're still married."

"I don't care about a piece of paper," he says. "You're the woman I've spent my entire life loving. I know that you had to move on. I don't blame you. But I'm home now. I'm here *now*. Everything can be the way it's supposed to be. The way it should be."

I shake my head and wipe my eyes with the back of my hand. "I don't know," I say to Jesse. "I don't know."

"*I* know."

Jesse leans forward and wipes away the tears that have fallen down my neck.

"You're Emma," he says as if that's the key to all of this, as if the problem is that I don't know who I am. "And I'm Jesse."

I look at him, half smiling. I try to feel better the way he wants me to. I try to believe that things are as simple as he is telling me they are. I can almost believe him. Almost.

"Jesse—"

"It's going to be OK, OK?" he says. "It's all going to be fine."

"It is?"

"Of course it is."

I love him. I love this man. No one knows me the way he knows me, no one loves me the way he loves me.

There is other love out there for me. But it's different. It isn't this. It isn't this exact love. It's better and it's worse. But I guess that's sort of the point of love between two people—you can't re-create it. Every time you love, everyone you love, the love is different. You're different in it.

Right now, I want nothing but to revel in *this* love.

This love with Jesse.

I throw myself into his arms and he holds me tight. Our mouths are now close together, our lips just a few inches from touching. Jesse moves the littlest bit closer.

But he doesn't kiss me.

Something about that strikes me as the most gentlemanly thing he has ever done.

"Here is what we are going to do," he says. "How about you drop me off at my parents'? It's getting late and my family is probably wondering where I am. I can't . . . I can't keep them wondering where I am . . ."

"OK," I say.

"And then you head home. To wherever you live," he says. "Where do you live?"

"In Cambridge," I tell him.

"OK, so you go home to Cambridge," he says.

"OK."

"Where do you work? Are you at a magazine or freelance?" Jesse asks expectantly.

I'm almost hesitant to disappoint him. "I'm at the bookstore."

"What are you talking about?" he says.

"Blair Books."

"You work at Blair Books?"

"I moved back here after you . . ." I drift off and go another route. "I started working there. And now I really like it. Now it's mine."

"It's yours?"

"Yeah, I run it. My parents are in and out, sort of. Mostly retired."

Jesse looks at me as if he can't compute it. And then he changes his face entirely. "Wow," he says. "I did not expect that."

"I know," I say. "But it's good. It's a good thing."

"All right," he says. "Then I'd imagine you'll be at the bookstore tomorrow?"

"I usually get in around nine. Open at ten."

"Can I see you for breakfast?"

"Breakfast?"

"You can't expect me to wait until lunch to see you . . ." he says. "Breakfast is already too long."

I think about it. I think about Sam. With guilt weighing me down, I start to speak.

Before I can respond, Jesse adds, "C'mon, Emma. You can have breakfast with me."

I nod. "Yeah, OK, yeah," I say. "Seven thirty?"

"Great," he says. "It's a date."

It is just after eight when I pull into the parking lot of my apartment. I tighten my coat as I step out. The wind is starting to pick up, the temperature dropped as the sun went down, and I can feel the rough breeze and the cold air on my shoulders and neck. I rush into my building.

I walk into the elevator. I press the button for the fifth floor. I watch the elevator close and as it does, I close my eyes.

When he asks me what happened today, what do I say?

How do I tell the truth when I don't know what it is?

I'm so lost in my own thoughts that I jump when the elevator dings and the doors open.

Standing in the hallway, right at our front door, is Sam.

Beautiful, kind, fractured, heartbroken Sam.

"You're back!" he says to me. "I thought I saw your car pull up in front just now when I was taking out the trash but I wasn't sure. I . . . I called you earlier, a few times actually, but I never heard from you, so I wasn't sure when you were coming home."

He wasn't sure *if* I was coming home.

His eyes are glassy. He's been crying. He seems to think that if he's peppy enough I won't notice.

"I'm sorry." I put my arms around him and feel him lean into me. His relief is palpable. "I lost track of time."

We head back into our apartment. The moment the door is

open, I can smell tomato soup. Sam makes the most incredible tomato soup. It is spicy, light, and sweet.

I come around the corner into the kitchen and I can see that he has ingredients out to make grilled cheese, including vegan cheddar because I'm convinced I'm growing lactose intolerant.

"Oh, my God," I say to him. "You're making tomato soup and grilled cheese for dinner?"

"Yeah," he says, trying to act cool, putting in considerable effort to make his voice sound carefree. "I thought it might be nice since it's so cold today."

He moves toward the cutting board and starts assembling sandwiches as I put my bag on the table and sit down at the counter. I watch him, carefully grating cheese, softly buttering the bread, as I unzip my boots and put them by the door. Sam's hands are shaking ever so slightly. His face looks pained, as if it's working overtime just to remain even.

It aches to look at him, to know that he's trying so hard to be OK right now, that he's trying to be understanding and patient and secure, when he's anything but. He is standing there, putting a frying pan down over a medium flame, trying to pretend that the fact that I saw my (former?) husband today isn't tearing him up inside.

I can't put him through this any longer.

"We can talk about it," I say to him.

He looks up at me.

Mozart walks into the kitchen and then turns around, as if he knows he doesn't want to be here for this. I watch as he joins Homer under the piano.

I grab Sam's hand. "We can talk about anything that is on your mind; you can ask me anything you want. This is your life, too."

Sam looks away from me and then nods.

He turns off the flame.

"Go ahead. Whatever you want to know. Just ask me. It's OK. We're gonna be honest and we're gonna be OK." I don't actually know what I mean by that, about us being OK.

He turns to me. "How was he?" Sam asks.

"Oh," I say, surprised that Sam's first question is about Jesse's well-being.

"He's OK. He's good. He seems . . . like he's adjusting." I don't mention that he seems almost bizarrely unflappable, that he is singularly focused on restoring our marriage.

"How are you?"

"I'm OK, too," I say. "I'm a little stunned by everything. It's very weird to see him. I'm not sure what to make of it." I'm choosing vague words because I'm afraid to narrow anything down. I'm afraid to commit to any particular feeling more than another. I honestly don't know what words I'd choose even if I was committed to specifics.

Sam nods, listening. And then he breathes in and asks what he really wants to know. It's clear the first two questions were warm-ups and this is game time. "Did you kiss him?"

It's funny, isn't it? So often men see betrayal in what you've done instead of how you feel.

"No," I say, shaking my head.

Sam is instantly relieved but I feel worse. I'm getting by on a technicality. Jesse didn't even try to kiss me, so I don't know if I would have let him, or if I would have kissed him back. But I still get credit as if I'd resisted. I don't feel great about that.

"I'd understand if you did kiss him," Sam says. "I know that . . . I guess what I'm saying is . . ."

I wait for him to finish his sentence but he doesn't finish it.

He just gives up, as if it's too overwhelming to try to choose words for his thoughts.

I know how he feels.

He turns the burner on again and goes back to making sandwiches.

"You're in an impossible situation," I tell him. I want him to know that I understand what he's going through. But I could never really understand it, could I? I have no idea what it's like to be him right now.

"You are, too," he says.

We're both playing the same game with each other. We want to understand, we want to make the other person feel understood, but the truth is we're on opposite sides of the street right now, looking over at each other and imagining what life must be like.

I watch him as his eyes narrow and his shoulders broaden from the tension in his body. I watch as he puts butter on a piece of bread.

Maybe I understand him more than I think.

Sam is making his fiancée a grilled cheese sandwich while worrying that she might leave him.

He's scared he's about to lose the person he loves. There's not a fear on this earth more common than that.

"Let's make these together," I say, stepping toward the pan and taking the spatula out of his hand.

I'm great at flipping things with a spatula.

I'm not great at choosing what to add to a lackluster soup and I have no idea what cheese to pair with anything. But show me a half-baked omelet and I will flip it with the ease of a born chef.

"You keep buttering; I'll flip," I tell him.

He smiles and it's honestly just as striking as watching the sun shine through the clouds.

"All right," he says. He puts more energy into swiping butter across the sliced bread. It's so yellow, the butter.

Before I met Sam, I kept sticks of cheap butter in the refrigerator and when I needed it for toast, I chopped it off in tiny chucks and futilely tried to spread the cold mess over the hot toast like a woman in a faded dramatization of an infomercial.

When Sam and I moved in together, he had this small little porcelain container that he put on the counter and when I opened it up, it looked like an upside-down cup of butter sitting in a puddle of water.

"What the hell is this?" I'd asked him as I was plugging in the toaster. Sam was putting glasses away in the cupboards, and when I said it, he laughed at me.

"It's a French butter dish," he said as he got off the step stool he'd been using and flattened the box the glasses had been in. "You keep the butter in the top part, put cold water in the bottom, and it keeps it chilled but spreadable." He said it as if everyone knew this, as if I was the crazy one.

"I have been all over France," I said to him, "and I have never seen one of these. Why is this butter so yellow? Is this some sort of fancy organic butter?"

"It's just butter," he said as he grabbed another box and started unloading its contents into the silverware drawer.

"This is not just butter!" I held the top cup part out to show him, as if he'd lost his mind. "Butter butter is pale yellow. This butter is yellow yellow."

"All I just heard was, 'Butter butter yellow butter yellow yellow.'"

I laughed.

"I think we're both saying the same thing," he said. "Butter is yellow."

"Admit there is something up with this butter," I said, pretending to interrogate him. "Admit it right now."

"It's not Land O'Lakes, if that's what you're asking."

I laughed at him. "Land O'Lakes! What are we, Bill and Melinda Gates? I buy store-brand butter. The name on my butter is exactly equal to the name of the store I bought it from."

Sam sighed, realizing he'd been caught. He confessed. "It's all-natural, organic, hormone-free, grass-fed butter."

"Wow," I said, acting as if this was a great shock. "You think you know a person . . ."

He took the butter from me and proudly put it on the counter, as if to say that it was officially a member of our home. "It *might* cost almost twice as much as regular butter. But once you try it, you will never be able to eat normal butter again. And *this* will become your normal butter."

After we had fully unpacked the kitchen, Sam opened the bread and took out two slices. He put them in the newly plugged-in toaster. When they were done, I watched how easy it was for him to spread butter on the slices. And then my eyes rolled back into my head when I took a bite.

"Wow," I said.

"See?" Sam had said. "I'm right about some stuff. Next, I'm going to convince you we should get a pet."

It was one of many moments in my life since Jesse left that I wasn't thinking about Jesse. I was very much in love with Sam. I loved the piano and I loved that butter. A few months later, we adopted our cats. Sam was changing my life for the better and I was curious to see what else he would teach me. I was reveling in how bright our future felt together.

Now, watching him place evenly buttered bread onto the pan in front of me, I desperately want to simply love him—unequivocally and without reservation—the way I did back then, the way I felt until I found out Jesse was coming home.

We were so happy together when there was nothing to muddy the waters, when the part of myself that loved Jesse was happily and naturally repressed, kept neatly contained in a box in my heart.

Sam moves the slices of bread around the sizzling pan and I propose something impossible.

"Do you think, maybe just for tonight, that we could put a pin in all of this? That we could pretend I had a normal day at the bookstore and you had a normal day teaching and everything could be the way it was before?"

I'm expecting Sam to tell me that life doesn't work like that, that what I'm proposing is naive or selfish or misguided. But he doesn't.

He just smiles and then he nods. It's a small nod. It's not an emphatic nod or a relieved nod. His nod isn't saying anything along the lines of "I thought you'd never ask," or even "Sure, that sounds good," but rather, "I can see why you'd want to try that. And I'll go along with it." Then he gathers himself and—in an instant—seems to be ready to pretend with me.

"All right, Emma Blair, get ready to flip," he says as he puts the top slices on the sandwiches.

"Ready and willing," I tell him. I have the spatula in position.

"Go!" he says.

And with two flicks of the wrist, I have flipped our dinner.

Sam turns the heat up on the soup to get it ready.

He grabs two bowls and two plates.

He grabs himself a beer from the fridge and offers me one. I take him up on it. The cool crispness of it sounds good, and for some reason, I have it in my head that having a beer helps to make this seem like just another night.

Soon, the two of us are sitting down to eat. Our dining room table has benches instead of chairs and that allows Sam to sit as close to me as physically possible, our thighs and arms touching.

"Thank you for making dinner," I say. I kiss him on the cheek, right by his ear. He has a freckle in that spot and I once told him I considered it a target. It is what I aim for. Normally when I kiss him there, he reciprocates by kissing me underneath my eye. Freckles for freckle. But this time he doesn't.

"Thank you for flipping," he says. "Nobody flips like you."

The sandwich is gooey in the center and crunchy on the outside. The soup is sweet with just a little bit of spice.

"I honestly don't know which I love more, this or your fried chicken," I say.

"You're being ridiculous. No tomato soup has ever been as good as any fried chicken."

"I don't know!" I tell him, dunking my sandwich. "This stuff is really outstanding. So cozy and comforting. And this grilled cheese is toasted to—"

Sam drops his spoon into his soup. It splashes onto the table. He drops his hands and looks at me.

"How am I supposed to pretend everything is OK right now?" Sam says. "I'd love to pretend things were different. I would love for things to *be* different but . . . they aren't."

I grab his hand.

"I can't talk about soup and cheese and . . ." He closes his eyes. "You're the love of my life, Emma. I've never loved anyone the way I love you."

"I know," I tell him.

"And it's OK if, you know, I'm not that for you. I mean, it's not. It's not at all OK. But I know that I have to be OK if that's what ends up being the truth. Does that make sense?"

I nod and start to speak but he keeps going.

"I just . . . I feel . . ." He closes his eyes again and then covers his face with his hands, the way people do when they are exhausted.

"Just say it," I tell him. "Whatever it is. Just let it out. Tell me."

"I feel naked. Like I'm raw. Or like I'm . . ." The way he's trying to find the words to describe how he feels makes him look like he wants to jump out of his skin. He's jittery and chaotic in his movements. And then he stops. "I feel like my entire body is an open wound and I'm standing next to someone that may or may not pour salt all over me."

I look at him, look into his eyes, and I know that whatever pain he's admitting to is a drop in the bucket compared to how he feels.

I'm not sure that emotional love can be separated from physical love. Or maybe I'm just a very tactile person. Either way, it's not enough for me to say, "I love you." The words feel so small compared to everything that's in me. I have to show him. I have to make sure that it's felt as much as heard.

I lean into him. I kiss him. I pull him close to me. I press my body against his and I let him run his hands up and down my back. I push the bench back slightly, to make room for me to fit, straddling his lap. And I rock, back and forth, ever so gently, as I hold him and whisper into his ear, "I need you."

Sam kisses me aggressively, like he's desperate for me.

We don't make it to the bed or to the couch. We clumsily move only as far as the kitchen floor. Our heads bang against the hardwood, our elbows bump against the low cupboards. My pants come off. His shirt comes off. My bra rests underneath the fridge, next to Sam's socks.

As Sam and I moan and gasp, we keep our eyes closed tightly except for the fleeting moments when we are looking directly into each other's eyes. And it is in these moments that I know he understands what I am trying to tell him.

Which is the whole point, our only reason for doing what we are doing.

We don't really care about pleasure. We are aching to be felt by the other, aching to feel each other. We move to tell each other what's in our souls, to say what words can't. We are touching each other in an attempt to listen.

Toward the end, I find myself pressing my heart into his, as if the problem is that we are two separate people, as if I could fuse us together and when I did, the pain would be gone.

When it's over, Sam collapses on top of me.

I hold him close, my arms and legs wrapped around him. He moves and I hold him tighter, my limbs asking him to stay.

I don't know how long we lie like that.

I swear I'm almost asleep when Sam knocks me back into reality by pulling himself off me and rolling onto the floor between me and the dishwasher.

I roll over onto his shoulder and put my head down, hoping that this reprieve from reality isn't over.

But I can tell that it is.

He puts his clothes back on.

"He's your husband," he says. His voice is quiet and stoic, as if it's all hitting him right now. I find that this happens a lot with shocking things; it seems to hit you all at once even though you could have sworn it hit you all at once an hour ago. "He is your *husband*, Emma."

"He *was*," I say, even though I'm not sure that's exactly true. "It's semantics, really, isn't it?"

I grab my shirt and throw it over myself, but I don't respond. I don't have anything comforting to say. It *is* semantics. I think I'm heading into a time in my life where words and labels will lose their meaning. It will only be the intent behind them that will matter.

"I'm so miserable. I feel torn apart," he says. "But it's not about me, right? He's the one that spent three years lost at sea or wherever he was. And you're the one that lived as a widow. And I'm just the asshole."

"You're not an asshole."

"Yes, I am," Sam says. "I'm the asshole who's standing in the way of you two being reunited."

I am, again, at a loss for words. Because if you replace the word "asshole" with "man"—"I'm the *man* who's standing in the way of you two being reunited"—then, yeah. He's right.

If I hadn't run into Sam that day at the music store, if I hadn't fallen in love with him, this would have been the greatest time in my life.

Instead of the most confusing.

For a moment, I let myself think of what my life would be like right now if all of that had never happened, if I'd never allowed myself to move on.

I could have done it. I could have shut myself off to life and to love. I could have pinned Jesse's name to my heart and lived every day in honor of him, in remembrance of him. In some ways, that would have been a lot easier.

Instead of writing that letter telling him that I needed to let him go and find a new life, I could have spent my days waiting for him to return from a place I thought he could never come back from. I could have dreamt of the impossible.

And my dream would be coming true right now.

But I gave up on that dream and went out and found a new one.

And in doing so, I'm ruining all of us.

You can't be loyal to two people.

You can't yearn for two dreams.

So, in a lot of ways, Sam is right.

He is the wild card.

In this terrible-wonderful nightmare-dream come true.

"It's like I'm eighteen all over again," he says. "I love you and I have you and now I'm terrified I'm going to lose you to Jesse for the second time."

"Sam," I say. "You don't—"

"I know this isn't your fault," Sam says, interrupting me. His mouth turns down and his chin shakes. I hate watching him try not to cry. "You loved him and then you lost him and you loved me and now he's back and you didn't do anything wrong but . . . I'm so mad at you."

I look at him. I try not to cry.

"I'm so angry. Just at everything. At you and at him and at myself. The way I told you . . ." he says, shaking his head. He looks away. He tries to calm down. "I told you that I didn't need you to stop loving him. I told you that you could love us both. That I would never try to replace him. And I really thought that I meant what I said. But now, I mean, it's like the minute I find out he's back, everything's changed. I'm so mad at myself for saying those things back then because . . ." He stops talking. He rests his back against the dishwasher, his arms over his knees. "Because I think I was kidding myself," he says, looking at his hands as he picks at his nails.

"I think it was just this thing that I said because I knew it was theoretical. It wasn't real. I wanted to give you the comfort of knowing that I wasn't trying to replace him because I knew that I *was* replacing him. He wasn't a threat because he was gone and he was never coming back. And he was never going to be able to take you away from me. He couldn't give you what I could. So I said all of that stuff about how I didn't expect you to stop loving him and how we could both fit into your life. But I only meant it in theory. Because ever since I heard he was back, I haven't been happy for you. Or even really that happy for him. I've been heartsick. For me."

He looks at me, finally, when he says this. And between the look on his face and the way his voice breaks when the words escape from his mouth, I know that he hates himself for feeling the way he does.

"Shhh," I say to him, trying to calm him down, trying to hold him and comfort him. "I love you."

I wish I didn't say it so often. I wish that my love for Sam wasn't so casual and pervasive—so that I could save that phrase for moments like this. But that's not very realistic, is it? When you love someone, it seeps out of everything you do, it bleeds into everything you say, it becomes so ever-present, that eventually it becomes ordinary to hear, no matter how extraordinary it is to feel.

"I know you do," he says. "But I'm not the only one you love. And you can only have one. And it might not be me."

"Don't say that," I tell him. "I don't want to leave you. I couldn't do that. It's not fair to you. It's not right. With everything that we've been through and how much you've done for me, how you've stood by me, and how you've been there for me, I couldn't . . ." I stop talking when I see that Sam is already shaking his head at me as if I don't get it. "What?" I ask him.

"I don't want your pity and I don't want your loyalty. I want you to be with me because you want to be with me."

"I do want to be with you."

"You know what I mean."

My gaze falls off of his eyes, down to his hands, and I watch him fiddle with the beds of his nails—his own version of wringing his hands.

"I think we should call off the wedding," he says.

"Sam . . ."

"I've thought about it a lot for the past few days and I thought, for sure, you were going to pull the trigger. But you haven't. So I'm doing it."

"Sam, c'mon."

He looks up at me, with just a little hint of anger. "Are you ready to commit to me?" Sam says. "Can you honestly say that no matter what happens from this moment on, we are ready to spend our lives together?"

I can't bear to see the look in his eyes when I shake my head. So I look away as I do it. Like every coward in the history of the world.

"I have to let you go," Sam says. "If we have any chance of surviving this and one day having a healthy, loving marriage."

I look up at him when I realize what's happening.

He's leaving me. At least for now. Sam is leaving me.

"I have to let you go and I have to hope that you come back to me."

"But how can—"

"I love you," he says. "I love you so much. I love waking up with you on Sunday mornings when we don't have any plans. And I love coming home to you at night, seeing you reading a book, bundled up in a sweater and huge socks even though you have the heat up to eighty-eight degrees. I want that for the rest of my life. I want you to be my wife. That's what I want."

I want to tell him that I want that, too. Ever since I met him I've wanted that, too. But now everything is different, everything has changed. And I'm not sure what I want at all.

"But I don't want you to share those things with me because you have to, because you feel it's right to honor a promise we made months ago. I want us to share all of that together because it's what makes you happy, because you wake up every day glad that you're with me, because you have the freedom to choose the life you want, and you choose our life together. That's what I want. If I don't give you the chance to leave right now, then I don't know," he says, shrugging. "I just don't think I'll ever feel comfortable again."

"What are we saying here?" I ask him. "What exactly are you suggesting?"

"I'm saying that I'm calling off the wedding. For now, at least. And I think one of us should stay somewhere else."

"Sam . . ."

"Then you'll be free. To see if you love him the way you love me, to see what's left between you. You should be free to do that. And you can't do that if I'm with you or if I'm pleading for you to stay. Which I don't trust myself not to do. If I'm with you, I will try to get you to choose me. I know that I will. And I don't want to do that. So . . . go. Figure out what you want. I'm telling you it's OK."

My instinct is to grab on to him tightly, to never let go, to put my hand over his mouth in order to stop him from saying all of this.

But I know that even if I can stop the words from coming out of his mouth, that won't make them any less true.

So I grab Sam by the neck and pull his head close to mine. I am, not for the first time, deeply grateful to be loved by him, to be loved the way he loves.

"I don't deserve you," I say. Our foreheads are pushed so close together neither of us can see the other. I am looking down at his knees. "How can you be so selfless? So *good*?"

Sam shakes his head slowly, without peeling away from me. "It's not selfless," he says. "I don't want to be with a woman who wants to be with someone else."

Sam cracks his knuckles, and when I hear the sound of it, I notice that my own hands feel tight and cramped. I open and close them, trying to stretch out my fingers.

"I want to be with someone who lives for me. I want to be with someone who considers me the love of her life. I deserve that."

I get it. I get it now. Sam is pulling his heart out of his chest and handing it to me, saying, "If you're going to break it, break it now."

I want to tell him that I'll never break his heart, that there is nothing to worry about.

But that's not true, is it?

I pull away from him.

"I should be the one to go," I say. I say it just as I can't believe I'm saying it. "It's not fair to make you leave. I can stay with my parents for a while."

This is where everything starts to shift. This is where it feels like the room is getting darker and the world is getting scarier, even though nothing outside of our hearts has changed.

Sam considers and then nods, agreeing with me.

And just like that, we have transitioned from two people considering something to two people having made a decision.

"I guess I'll pack up some stuff," I say.

"OK," he says.

I don't move for a moment, still stunned that it's happening. But then I realize that staying still doesn't actually pause time, it's still passing, life is still happening. You have to keep moving.

I stand up and head to my closet to gather my clothes. I make it to our bedroom before I start crying.

I should be thinking of outfits to pack, things to wear to work. I should be calling my parents to tell them I'm going to be sleeping at their house. But instead, I just start throwing things into a duffel bag, with little attention paid to whether the clothes match or what I might need.

The only thing I take on purpose is the envelope I have of keepsakes from Jesse. I don't want Sam to look through them. I don't want him hurting himself by reading love letters I once wrote to the boy I chose all those years ago.

I walk back into the kitchen, saying good-bye to Mozart and Homer on the way.

Sam is in the exact same position I left him.

He stands up to say good-bye to me.

I can't help but kiss him. I'm relieved that he lets me.

As we stand there, still close to each other, Sam finally allows himself to lose his composure. When he cries, his eyes bloom and the tears fall down his cheeks so slowly that I can catch every one before they reach his chin.

It breaks my heart to be loved like this, to be loved so purely that I'm capable of breaking a heart.

It is not something I take lightly. In fact, I think it might be the most important thing in the world.

"What am I gonna do?" I ask him.

I mean, what am I going to do *right now*? And, what am I going to do *without him*? And, what am I going to do *with my life*? And, *how* am I going to do this?

"You'll do whatever you want," he says, brushing the side of his knuckle under his eye and taking a step back from me. "That's what it means to be free."

By the time I pull into my parents' driveway, it's almost two a.m. Their front light is on, as if they've been waiting for me, but I know that they leave it on every night. My father thinks it wards off burglars.

I don't want to wake them up. So I'm planning on tiptoeing into the house and saying hello in the morning.

I turn the car off and grab my things. I realize as I step out onto the driveway that I didn't bring any shoes other than the boots on my feet. I guess I'll be wearing these indefinitely. I remind myself that "indefinitely" doesn't mean forever.

I slowly shut the car door, not so much closing it as tucking it gently into place. I sneak around to the rear of the house, onto the back deck. My parents never lock the back door and I know that it doesn't squeak like the front door does.

There is a small click as I turn the knob and a swish as I move the door out of my way. Then I'm in.

Home.

Free.

I walk over to the breakfast table and grab a pen and a piece of paper. I leave my parents a note telling them that I am here. When I'm done, I take off my boots so they don't clang against the hard kitchen floor. I leave them by the back door.

I tiptoe across the kitchen and dining room, down the hall.

I stand outside my bedroom door and slowly, gently turn the knob.

I don't dare turn on the light in my bedroom. I've made it this far and I'm not going to throw it all away now.

I sit down on the bottom edge of the bed and take off my pants and shirt. I feel around in my bag for something to wear as pajamas. I grab a shirt and a pair of shorts and put them on.

I pad over to the bathroom that my room has always shared with Marie's. I feel around for the faucet and turn the water on to a trickle. As I brush my teeth, I start to question whether I should have just woken up my parents by calling or ringing the front door. But by the time I'm running water over my face, I realize that I didn't want to wake them because I don't want to talk about any of this. Sneaking in was my only option. If your daughter shows up at two in the morning the night that her long-lost husband comes home, you're going to want to *talk about it*.

I walk back to my bedroom, ready to fall asleep. But as soon as I go to turn the blankets down, I hit my head against the overhanging lamp on the nightstand.

"Ow!" I say instinctually, and then I roll my eyes at myself. I know that goddamn lamp is there. I worry for a moment that I've blown my cover, but it remains quiet in the house.

I rub my head and slip into the covers, avoiding the lamp the way I now remember you have to.

I look out the window and I can see a few windows of Marie's house down the street. All of the lights in her house are off and I imagine that she, Mike, Sophie, and Ava are sound asleep.

I'm shaken out of it by blinding light and the sight of my father in his underwear with a baseball bat.

"Oh, my God!" I scream, scrambling to the farther corners of the bed, as far away from him as possible.

"Oh," my dad says, slowly putting down the bat. "It's just you."

"Of course it's just me!" I say to him. "What were you going to do with that?"

"I was going to beat the ever-living crap out of the thief who had broken into my home! That's what I was going to do!"

My mother comes rushing in in plaid pajama bottoms and a T-shirt that says, "Read a Mother F&#king Book." There is no way that that shirt is not a gift from my father that my mother refuses to wear out of the house.

"Emma, what are you doing here?" she says. "You scared us half to death."

"I left a note on the kitchen table!"

"Oh," my dad says, falsely assuaged, and looking at my mother. "Never mind, Ash; looks like this is our fault."

I give him a sarcastic look that I swear I haven't given since I was seventeen.

"Emma, our apologies. The next time we fear we are being attacked in the night, we will first check the kitchen table for a note."

I'm about to apologize, realizing the full extent of the absurdity of breaking into my parents' house and then blaming them for their surprise. But my mom steps in first.

"Honey, are you OK? Why aren't you with Sam?" I swear, and maybe I'm just being sensitive, but I swear there's a small pause in between "with" and "Sam" because she is unsure whom I'm supposed to be with.

I breathe in, allowing all of the formerly tensed muscles in my shoulders and back to relax. "We might not be getting married. I think I have a date with Jesse tomorrow. I don't know. I honestly . . . I don't know."

My dad puts the bat down. My mom pushes past him to sit down on the bed next to me. I move toward her, resting my head on her shoulder. She rubs my back. Why does it feel better when your parents hold you? I'm thirty-one years old.

"I should put on pants, shouldn't I?" my father asks.

My mother and I look up, as one unit, and nod to him.

He's gone in a flash.

"Tell me everything about how today went," she says. "All the parts you need to get off your chest."

As I do, my father comes back into the room, in sweats, and sits on the other side of me. He grabs my hand.

They listen.

At the end of it, when I've said everything that's left in me, when I get out every piece I have, my mom says, "If you want my two cents, you have the unique ability to love with your whole heart even after it's been broken. That's a good thing. Don't feel guilty about that."

"You're a fighter," my dad says. "You get back up after you've been knocked down. That is my favorite part about you."

I laugh and say, in a jovial tone, "Not that I run the bookstore?"

I'm joking but *I'm not joking.*

"Not even close. There are so many things to love about you that, honestly, that's not even in the top ten."

I put my head on his shoulder and rest there for a moment. I watch my mom's eyes droop. I hear my dad's breathing slow down.

"OK, go back to bed," I tell them. "I'll be OK. Thank you. Sorry again about scaring you."

They each give me a hug and then go.

I lie on my old mattress and I try to fall asleep, but I was a fool to ever think that sleep would come.

Just before six a.m., I see a light come on in Marie's house.

I take off my engagement ring and put it in my purse. And then I throw on some pants, grab my boots, and walk right out the front door.

M arie is with Ava in the bathroom with the door open. Ava is sitting on the toilet and Marie is coaxing her to relax. The twins are potty trained, but as of a few weeks ago, Ava has started backsliding. She will only go if Marie is with her. I have decided to hang back and stand by the door, as is my right as an aunt.

"You can go ahead and take a seat," Marie says to me as she sits down on the slate gray tile of the bathroom floor. "We're gonna be here a while."

The girls' cochlear implants mean that they have learned to talk only a few months behind other children. And Marie and Mike both use sign language to communicate with them, too. My nieces, whom we were all so worried about, may just end up speaking two languages. And that is in large part because Marie is a phenomenal, attentive, unstoppable motherly force.

At this point, she knows more about American Sign Language, the Deaf community, hearing aids, cochlear implants, and the inner working of the ear than possibly anything else, including all of the things she used to love, things like literature, poetry, and figuring out what authors use what pseudonyms.

But she's also exhausted. It's six thirty in the morning and she's both talking and signing to her daughter to please "go pee in the potty for Mommy."

The bags under her eyes look like the pocket on a kangaroo.

When Ava is finally done, Marie brings her to Mike, who is lying in bed with Sophie. As I'm standing in the hallway, I get a glimpse of Mike under the covers, half asleep, holding Sophie's hand. For a moment, I get a flash of what sort of man I'd want to be the father of my own children and I'm embarrassed to say that the figure is only vague and blurry.

Marie comes back out of the bedroom and we head toward the kitchen.

"Tea?" she says as I sit down at her island.

I'm not much of a tea drinker, but it's cold in here and something warm sounds nice. I'd ask for coffee, but I know that Marie doesn't keep coffee in the house. "Sure, that sounds great," I say.

Marie smiles and nods. She starts the kettle. Marie's kitchen island is bigger than my dining room table. Our dining room table. Mine and Sam's.

I am, instantaneously, overcome with certainty.

I don't want to leave Sam. I don't want to lose the life I've built. Not again. I love Sam. I love him. I don't want to leave him. I want to sit down together at the piano and play "Chopsticks."

That's what I want to do.

Then I remember that way Jesse looked when he got off that plane. All of my certainty disappears.

"Ugh," I say, slouching my body forward, resting my head in the nest I've made with my arms. "Marie, what am I going to do?"

She doesn't stop pulling various teas out of the cupboard. She pulls them all out and puts them in front of me.

"I don't know," she says. "I can't imagine being in your shoes. I feel like maybe both options are equally right *and* wrong.

That's probably not the answer you were looking for. But I just don't know."

"I don't know, either."

"Does it help to ask what your gut tells you?" she says. "Like, if you close your eyes, what do you see? Your life with Sam? Or your life with Jesse?"

I indulge her game, hoping that something as simple as closing my eyes might tell me what I want to do. But it doesn't. Of course it doesn't. I open my eyes to see Marie watching me. "That didn't work."

The kettle starts to whistle and Marie turns toward the stove to grab it. "You know, all you can do is just put one foot in front of the other," she says. "This is exactly the sort of thing people are talking about when they say you have to take things one step at a time." She pours hot water into the white mug she's set out for me. I look up at her.

"Earl Grey?" she asks.

"English Breakfast?" I ask in return and then I start laughing and say, "I'm just messing with you. I have no idea what tea names mean."

She laughs and picks up an English Breakfast packet, tearing off the top and pulling out a tea bag. "Here, now you'll know what English Breakfast tastes like for next time." She puts it in my mug and hands it to me. "Splenda?" she offers.

I shake my head. I stopped drinking artificial sweeteners six months ago and I feel entirely the same but I'm still convinced it's for a good cause. "I'm off the sauce," I say.

Marie rolls her eyes and puts two packets in her tea.

I laugh and look down toward my cup. I watch as the tea begins to bleed out of the bag into the water. I watch as it swirls, slowly. I can already smell the earthiness of it. I put my hands on the hot mug, letting it warm them up. I start absent-mindedly fiddling with the string.

"Do you think you can love two people at the same time?" I ask her. "That's what I keep wondering. I feel like I love them both. Differently and equally. Is that possible? Am I kidding myself?"

She dips her tea bag in and out of the water. "I'm honestly not sure," she says. "But the problem isn't who you love or if you love both, I don't think. I think the problem is that you aren't sure who you are. You're a different person now than you were before you lost Jesse. It changed you, fundamentally."

Marie thinks, staring down at the counter, and then tentatively starts talking again. "I don't think you're trying to figure out if you love Sam more or Jesse more. I think you're trying to figure out if you want to be the person you are with Jesse or you want to be the person you are with Sam."

It's like someone cracked me in half and found the rotten cancer in the deepest, most hidden part of my body. I don't say anything back. I don't look up. I watch as a tear falls from my face and lands right in my mug. And even though I was the one who cried it out, and I saw it fall, I have no idea what it means.

I look up.

"I think you're probably right," I say.

Marie nods and then looks directly at me. "I'm sorry," she says. "It's important to me that you know that. That you know I regret what I did."

"Regret what? What are you talking about?"

"For that day on the roof. The day that I found you looking out . . ." It feels like yesterday and one hundred years ago all at once: the binoculars, the roof, the grave anxiety of believing I could save him just by watching the shore. "I'm sorry for convincing you Jesse was dead," Marie says. "You knew he wasn't . . ."

Marie isn't much of a crier. She isn't one to show how she feels on her face. It's her voice that tells me just how deep her remorse is, the way some of the syllables bubble up and burst.

"I was the wrong person to be up there that day. I hadn't supported you, at all, really, in any of the years prior. And suddenly, I was the one telling you the worst had happened? I just . . . I thought he was gone. And I thought that I was doing you a kindness by making you face reality." She shakes her head as if disappointed in her old self. "But instead, what I did was take away your hope. Hope that you had every reason to hold on to. And I . . . I'm just very sorry. I'm deeply sorry. You have no idea how much I regret taking that away from you."

"No," I say. "That's not what happened. Not at all. I was crazy up on that roof. I'd gone absolutely crazy, Marie. It was irrational to think that he was alive, let alone that I could save him, that I could spot him up there, looking at that tiny piece of the shore. That was madness.

"Anyone thinking clearly would have made the assumption that he was dead. I needed to understand that the rational conclusion was that he was gone. You helped me understand that. You kept me sane."

For the first time, I find myself wondering if facing the truth and being sane aren't the same thing, if they are just two things that tend to go together. I'm starting to understand that they might be correlational rather than synonyms.

And then I realize that if I don't blame Marie for thinking he was dead—if I don't see her belief that he died as a sign she gave up on him—then I shouldn't be blaming myself for doing the same thing.

"Please don't give it another thought," I say to her. "What you did on the roof that day . . . you saved me."

Marie looks down at her tea and then nods. "Thank you for saying that."

"Thank you for what you did. And I'm glad it was you. I don't know if you and I would be as close . . . I mean, I think we would have just gone on . . ."

"I know what you mean," Marie said. "I know."

After all of our shared experiences and our parents' cajoling, it has been our hardships that have softened us to each other. Losing my husband and the challenges of raising Marie's twins are the things that have brought us together.

"I'm just glad that things between us are the way they are now," Marie says. "I'm very, very glad."

"Me, too," I say.

Instinctively, I grab Marie's hand and hold it for a moment and then we break away.

It is hard to be so honest, so vulnerable, so exposed. But I find that it always leads you someplace freer. I feel the smallest shift between my sister and me, something almost impercep-tible but nevertheless real. We are closer now than we were just three minutes ago.

"I've been thinking about writing again," Marie says, chang-ing the subject.

"Oh yeah?" I ask. "Writing what?"

She shrugs. "That's the part I'm not sure about. I just need to do something, you know? Anything that is not revolving around my kids. I need to get back to me, a little bit. Anyway, it might be a dumb idea because I say that I want to start writing again but I can't find anything I want to write *about*. I'm not inspired. I'm just . . . well, bored."

"You'll find something," I say. "And when you do, it will be great. Just don't make it a murder mystery where you pin the murders on a character that is clearly supposed to be me, like you did back then," I say, teasing.

She laughs, shaking her head at me. "No one ever believed me that it wasn't supposed to be you," she says.

"You named her Emily."

"It's a common name," Marie says, pretending to defend herself. "But, yeah, OK. I'm mature enough now to admit that might not have come from a totally innocent place."

"Thank you," I say magnanimously.

"I was just so annoyed that you were always copying me."

"What?" I say. "I was never copying you. I was basically the opposite of you."

Marie shakes her head. "Sorry, but no. Remember when I got really into TLC? And suddenly, you started telling everyone you loved 'Waterfalls'? Or when I had a crush on Keanu Reeves? And then suddenly, you had his picture up over your bed?"

"Oh, my God," I say, realizing she's totally right.

"And then, of course, you went and started dating the captain of the swim team. Just like me."

"Whoa," I say. "That honestly never occurred to me. But you're totally right. You and Graham. And then me and Jesse."

Marie smiles, half laughing at me. "See?"

"I must have really wanted to be like you," I say. "Because I thought Graham was so lame. And then I went and *also dated the captain of the swim team.*"

Marie lifts her tea to her mouth, smiling. "So, I think we can agree that on some level, you've always wanted to be me."

I laugh. "You know what? If being you means having just the one man in your life, I'll take it."

"Boohoo," she says. "Two men love you."

"Oh, shut up," I say as I find a dish towel and throw it at her.

Our laughter is interrupted by Mike coming down the stairs with Sophie behind him and Ava on his hip.

"Breakfast!" he says to the girls, and I see Marie reanimate, opening up the refrigerator, ready for the day.

I know when to excuse myself.

"I'm around if you need anything today," Marie says as I gather my things. "Seriously. Just call. Or stop by. I'm here for you."

"OK," I say. "Thank you."

She gives me a hug and then picks up Sophie into her arms. I head out the door.

On the way back to my parents', my phone dings. I'm not sure who I thought would be contacting me but I definitely wasn't expecting a text message from Francine.

So excited to see you again that I didn't sleep all night. This is Jesse, btw. Not my mom. Pretty weird if my mom couldn't wait to see you.

When I'm done reading it, I notice that my feet walk faster toward the door to my parents' house.

I rush my warm shower. I rush the shampoo through my hair, rush the soap over my body.

I rush putting on clothes and getting out the door.

I rush all of it, every second. There is a kick in my step and a smile on my face.

I am happy. In this brief moment of time. I am happy.

When I pull my car into the parking lot of Julie's Place a little before seven thirty, Jesse is standing right in front. He's even earlier than I am.

He looks just like he used to, even if he does look totally different.

I open my car door, step out into the cold, and I realize just why this morning feels a little bit better than the others recently.

It's finally OK to love him.

It's OK to love Jesse.

I have been given the freedom to do that.

Sam did that for me.

W hat else did you miss?" I ask Jesse as the waitress brings us our breakfasts. He's been listing everything he missed about home.

I was number one.

The sweet-and-sour chicken at the tacky Chinese restaurant in the middle of town was number two.

"I mean, there are so many people and places, but right now, honestly, all I can think about is the food."

I laugh. "So tell me, then; tell me all the food."

"All right," he says, looking down at his plate. He has barely touched his meal and I can't blame him. I can't focus on actually eating right now, either. My stomach is in knots, flooded with butterflies, twisting and turning to try to keep up with the flutter in my heart.

"Oh, God. There are just too many to name. How can I choose? I mean, there's the pizza at Sorrentos, the Snickers sundae from Friendly's, the sandwiches at Savory Lane . . ."

"Savory Lane closed," I tell him. "Actually, Friendly's did, too."

He looks at me, focused on my eyes, trying to figure out if I'm messing with him. When he sees that I'm serious, a flash of sorrow wipes across his face. He quickly replaces it with a smile, but I wonder if maybe it's all the evidence he needs that the world went on without him, that we couldn't even keep Savory Lane going as a courtesy.

"Friendly's is now a Johnny Rockets," I tell him. "It's good, though. Plus, you know, once Kimball's opens in the spring, you're not going to be thinking about a Snickers sundae. You're gonna be thinking about two scoops of black raspberry ice cream in a waffle cone."

Jesse smiles and then looks away from me, shifting his body toward the counter and away from our table, repositioning his legs. "What about Erickson's? Is that still open? Or have they forsaken me, too?"

The way he says it, the word "forsaken," and the fact that he doesn't look at me, it all adds up to make me think Jesse's angrier than he's letting on. That he does resent me for moving on. He says he understands, but maybe he doesn't really understand at all.

"They are still open, yeah," I say, nodding, trying to please him. "Most stuff is still open. Most stuff is still the same."

"Most stuff," he says, and then he changes his tone. "And Blair Books? Is Blair Books the same? I mean, clearly there's new management."

"Yeah," I say, smiling, proud of myself. "Although I've kept it mostly the same. And my parents are still involved a bit. It's not like I've gone rogue. I do things pretty much the way they did them."

"Do you even put out those little 'Travel the World by Reading a Book' bookmarks?"

"Yes!" I say. "Of course I do."

"What? No way!"

"Yeah, totally."

I have pushed the food around my plate. He's pushed his around his. Neither one of us has taken so much as a bite. When the waitress comes over, she frowns.

"Looks like you aren't very hungry," she says as she pours more water in my glass.

"It's delicious," I say. "But we're just . . ."

"We have a lot of catching up to do," Jesse says. "Can we get it to go?"

"Sure thing, sweetheart," she says, taking both of our plates with her.

When she leaves, we have no food to play with and nothing to look at but each other.

"You used to hate those bookmarks," Jesse says.

"I know," I say. I find myself embarrassed about how much I've changed. I am tempted to lie, to rewind, to remember exactly who I was before he left and try to be that version of myself again.

The Emma he knew wanted a different life. She wanted adventure. She ached with wanderlust. She used to think you couldn't find joy in simple things, that they had to be big and bold and wild. That you couldn't feel amazed at how good it feels to wake up in a nice bed, that you could only feel amazed by petting elephants and visiting the Louvre.

But I don't know if I was totally that person when he left.

And I'm definitely not that person now.

The future is so hard to predict. If I had a time machine, would it even make a difference to try to go back there and explain to my young self what was ahead?

"I guess I did say that," I tell him. "But I like them now."

"You never cease to surprise," Jesse says, smiling. Maybe it's OK with him if I'm not exactly the way I was when he left.

The waitress comes back with our meals in boxes and the check. Jesse hands her cash before I can grab my wallet.

"Thank you," I say. "That was very nice of you."

"It's my pleasure."

I check my phone and see that it's eight fifty. The time has flown by so quickly.

"I have to head to work," I tell him. "I'm running late as is."

"No . . ." he says. "C'mon. Stay with me."

"I can't," I say, smiling at him. "I have a store to open."

Jesse walks me to my car and pulls a set of keys out of his pocket, unlocking, from afar, a gray sedan a few spaces down.

"Wait a minute," I say to Jesse, as something is occurring to me. "You don't have a license. You can't be driving."

Jesse laughs. "I had a license before I left," he says. "I'm approved to drive a car."

"Yeah," I say, opening my door. "But didn't it expire?"

Jesse smiles mischievously and it slays me. "Expired, schmexpired. It's harmless."

"You just always have to push things, don't you?" I say, teasing him. "Why do you think that is?"

"I don't know," he says, shrugging. "But you can admit you find it charming."

I laugh. "Who said I find it charming?"

"Will you get in the car with me?" he says.

"In your car?"

"Or yours," he says.

"I have to go to work."

"I know. I'm not asking you to go anywhere with me. I just want to be in the car with you. It's cold outside."

I should tell him good-bye. I'm already running later than I want to be.

"OK," I say. I click both doors open and watch as Jesse sits in my passenger seat. I sit in the driver's seat next to him. When

I shut my car door, the outside world mutes, as if we can keep it at bay.

I watch as his eye line settles on my now-bare ring finger. He smiles. We both know what the empty space on my left hand means. But I get the impression there is a strange code of silence between us, indicative of the two things we don't talk about. We won't talk about what happened to my finger, just like we don't talk about what happened to his.

"I missed you, Emma. I missed us. I missed your stupid eyes and your awful lips and that super-annoying thing you do when you look at me like I'm the only person that's ever mattered in the history of the world. I missed your very un-adorable freckles."

I laugh and I can feel myself blushing. "I missed you, too."

"You did?" he says, as if this is news, as if he wasn't sure.

"Wait, are you kidding?"

"I don't know," he says. His voice is teasing. "It's hard to know what happened while I was gone."

"I was more heartbroken than I've ever been or I think I will ever be again."

He looks at me, and then out the windshield, and then out the window on the other side of him.

"We have so much to talk about and I don't even know where to start," he says.

"I know, but even if we did know where to start, I can't now. I have to go to work. I should have been there fifteen minutes ago." Tina won't be in until the afternoon. If I'm not there, the store doesn't open.

"Emma," he says, looking at me like I'm a fool. "You're not going to be at work on time, that's clear. So what's a few more minutes? What's an hour more?"

I look at him and find myself considering it. And then I feel his lips on mine. They are just as bold and surprising as they were almost fifteen years ago, kissing me for the first time.

I close my eyes and reach for him. I kiss him again. And again and again and again. I am soothed and invigorated all at once. Never before has something felt so exciting and yet so familiar.

I lose myself in him, in the way he feels, the way he smells, the way he moves.

Can you ever put things back the way they were? Can you chalk the intervening years up as a mistake and pick up as if you never left each other?

I feel Jesse's hand slide down my arm and then I hear myself accidentally hit the horn with my elbow.

I snap out of it. I pull myself away from him and look forward, out the windshield. Two of the servers at Julie's Place, including the woman who waited on us, are staring at us through the window. When they see that I see them, they start to turn away.

I look down at my phone. It's almost a quarter of ten. The store is supposed to be open in less than twenty minutes.

"I have to go!" I say, shocked that I could be running this late.

"OK, OK," Jesse says, but he doesn't move.

"Get out of my car," I say, laughing.

"OK," he says, putting his hand on the door handle. "There's just one thing I wanted to talk to you about."

"Jesse! I have to go!"

"Come to Maine with me," he says as he gets out of the car.

"What?"

"Come to my family's cabin in Maine with me for a few days. We can leave tonight. Just the two of us."

"I have a store to run."

"Your parents can manage it. For a little while. It's their store."

"It's my store," I say.

"Emma, we need time. And not stolen moments before you go to work. Real time. Please."

I look at him, considering.

He knows I'm considering it. Which is why he already starts smiling. "Is that a yes?" he says.

I know my parents will step in and I'm late and I don't have time for this.

"OK, a couple of days."

"Three," he says. "Three days."

"OK," I tell him. "Three."

"We'll leave tonight?"

"Sure. Now I have to go!"

Jesse smiles at me and then shuts the door behind him so I can finally leave. He waves at me through the window. I find myself grinning as I drive away from him, leaving him there in the parking lot.

I make my way to the road and wait for a clear opening to take a left. I watch as Jesse gestures for me to roll down my window from the other side of the lot. I roll my eyes but I do it.

He cups his hands over his mouth and yells, "I'm sorry I made you late! I love you!"

I have no choice but to scream, "I love you, too!"

I bang a left onto the main road and fly through town. I get to the parking lot of Blair Books at ten eleven and I can already see there is a customer waiting at the door.

I jump out of the car, open the back door, and run through the store turning on all the lights.

I gather myself and calmly walk to the front door and unlock it.

"Hi," I say to the woman waiting.

"Your store says that you're open from ten to seven. It's ten fifteen."

"My apologies," I say.

But when the woman heads right to the bestseller section and is no longer in my line of sight, I can't stop a smile from erupting, pulling my cheeks as wide as my ears.

Jesse.

My dad comes into the store around eleven. He is here to grab some books that he ordered for my mom, but I pull him aside to discuss the idea of my leaving for Maine.

"What do you mean you're going to Maine with Jesse?"

"Uh . . ." I say, unsure which part my dad is confused about. "I think I mean that I am going to Maine with Jesse?"

"Are you sure this is a good idea?"

"Why wouldn't it be?"

That is such a stupid thing to say. There are about twenty thousand reasons why it might not be.

"Emma, I just . . ." He stops there and doesn't finish his sentence. I see him rethink his entire train of thought. "I read you loud and clear. Of course Mom and I can cover. We'd love to, actually. I'm bored stiff at home now that I have finished watching all five seasons of *Friday Night Lights*."

"Great!" I say. "Thank you."

"Certainly," he says. "My pleasure. Will we see you tonight, then? To get your things?"

"Yeah," I say, nodding. "I'll come by to get some clothes and stuff."

"OK, great," he says.

And then he heads out. "Mom's making BLTs for lunch and you know I can't miss that."

"I know," I say.

My mom makes him BLTs multiple times a week and he loves them so much you'd think he would learn to make them himself. He's tried, a number of times. I've tried for him and Marie's tried for him. He swears it tastes different when she makes them. Something about the bacon being hot and the lettuce being sweet. I honestly have no idea. All I know is that my parents have always made love seem easy and sometimes I wish they'd prepared me for how truly complicated it can be.

Later on in the afternoon, as I'm picking up a very late lunch, I get a text message from Sam.

You forgot your allergy meds and phone charger. I left them on your desk.

The first thing I think when I see the message isn't how sweet he is or that I'm glad to be able to charge my phone. My first thought is that there's a chance he's still at the store. So I rush to my car, sandwich in hand, hoping that I can get back to the parking lot before he leaves.

I hit absolutely no red lights and I turn right into the parking lot just as Sam is in his car with his blinker ready to turn left. I wave him down.

I don't know what I'm doing, what good I think will come of this. I just know that there is nothing like thinking that you might lose your fiancé to make you realize how much you ache to see your fiancé. That remains true even if you think it's you who might be leaving, you who might be messing it all up.

Sam backs up and rolls down his window. I park my car and walk over to him.

"Hi," I say.

"Hi."

He is wearing his black wool coat with a white oxford button-down and a navy chambray tie. I bought him that tie.

He liked the tiny anchors printed on it and I said I wanted to treat him to something he'd get excited to wear at work.

"Thank you for my meds," I say. "And the charger. That was really nice of you."

Sam nods. "Yeah, well . . ."

I wait for him to finish and then realize that he's not going to.

"How are you?" I ask.

"Been better," he responds. He looks sad but also distant. It feels as if the two of us can't reach each other. I find myself moving physically closer to him, trying to connect. "I will be fine. It's just weird sleeping in our bed alone," he says. "I miss you."

"I miss you, too," I say, and then—I don't know what possesses me—before I know it, I have bent down and kissed him. He kisses me back but then pulls away. I wonder if it's because he can tell I've kissed someone else.

"Sorry," I say. "Force of habit."

"It's OK," he says.

"How were the cats this morning?" I ask. I love talking to Sam about our cats. I love inventing silly names for them and making up stories about what they do when we're not around.

"Homer slept in the bathtub," Sam says.

Before I had a cat, before I loved those two little furballs, I would have thought someone saying, "Homer slept in the bathtub," was boring enough to put me to sleep. But now it's as fascinating as if you'd told me he'd landed on Mars.

"He wasn't under the piano?"

Sam shakes his head. "Nope, he won't leave the bathroom. When I tried to take a shower this morning, I had to pick him up and lock him out of the room."

I should be back in that house. I should be with Sam and

Mozart and Homer. I don't know why Homer's in the bathtub or what it means. But I know it wouldn't happen if I was there.

Good Lord.

There is so much guilt lying around here, just waiting for me to pick it up and carry it with me. There is so much I can torture myself about.

Maybe I deserve to.

But I resolve, right now, to leave it waiting. I'm not taking it on. Even if I should. It does no one any good, least of all me, to have it clawing at my back.

"I love you," I tell him. It just slips out. I don't know what I mean by it. I just know that it's true.

"I know," he says. "I have never once doubted that."

We are quiet for a moment and I fear that he might leave. "Will you play 'Piano Man'?" I ask him.

"What?" he says.

"Will you play 'Piano Man'? On the steering wheel? And I can do the harmonica?"

I always ask him to do it when I want to fall a little bit more in love with him. I like remembering the first time he did it. I love watching how skilled he truly is. Now, it's become so familiar that I can hear the notes when he plays it, even though he's always playing in silence.

But instead of pushing up his sleeves and positioning his fingers like he has always done in the past, he shakes his head. "I'm not gonna do that."

"You always do it."

"I'm not going to perform for you," he says. "I hope you change your mind and realize that you love me and that we should be together for the rest of our lives, but . . . I'm not going to audition for the part."

It's one thing to break a heart. It's an entirely different thing to break someone's pride.

And I think I have done both to him.

"You're right," I say. "I'm sorry."

"Listen, you've been through something I can't even imagine. I know it's shaken you to your core. I love you enough to wait for a little while until you figure it out."

I grab his hand and squeeze it—as though if I could just squeeze enough, hold it the right way, the gratitude I feel in my heart might run through my arms, out my hands, and straight into his soul. But it doesn't work that way. I know it doesn't.

"Thank you," I say. "I don't know how to thank you. But thank you."

Sam takes his hand away. "But you can't have both of us," he continues. "I can't pretend things are OK until they're actually OK. OK?"

"OK," I say, nodding my head.

He smiles. "That was a lot of 'OKs' at one time, huh?"

I laugh.

"I'm gonna go," Sam says, putting his car in drive. "Otherwise, I'll be late for rehearsal. And then, you know, I suppose I'll just go home, eat some dinner, and watch ESPN Classic. A rousing good time."

"Sounds like quite a night," I say.

"I'm sure you've got big plans, too," he says, and then I watch as his face freezes. It's clear he wasn't thinking when he spoke. He doesn't want to know what I'm doing tonight. But now that he's said it, I can't get out of this without in some way acknowledging whether I do have plans. "I just meant . . . uh, you know what? Just don't say anything."

"Yeah, OK," I say. "Not saying anything."

But not saying anything is saying something, isn't it? Because if there truly was nothing for him to worry about, I would have just said, "No, Sam, seriously, don't worry."

I didn't say that. And we both know it.

Sam looks at me. And I can tell that he has reached his limit. He cannot do this anymore. "Bye, Emma," he says, starting to turn the wheel. He stops himself and starts talking again. "You know what? I'm going to keep the ball in my court."

"What do you mean?" I ask.

"I'll call you when I'm ready. But . . . don't call me. I know it probably makes the most sense for you to tell me what you've chosen after you've chosen but . . . I'd rather you tell me once I'm ready to hear it."

"I can't call you at all?"

Sam shakes his head somberly. "I'm asking you not to."

This is the smallest amount of control he can claim over his own fate. I know that I have to give it to him.

"Whatever you want," I say. "Anything."

"Well, that's what I want," he says, nodding, and then he puts his foot on the gas and drives away.

Gone.

I realize just how cold I am, how frigid it is outside, and I race back into the store. I remember that I left my sandwich on the front seat of my car and I don't even bother to go get it. I'm not hungry.

I didn't eat breakfast, either. It appears my appetite had been the first thing to go.

Tina is ringing up a pair of books for two older ladies when I walk in. "Hey, Emma," she says. "Do you remember when we are getting more copies of the new Ann Patchett?"

"It should be next Tuesday," I say as if today is any normal day, as if I can think straight. "Ladies, if you give your contact info to Tina, she or I will call you when the copies are in."

I smile and then briskly walk into the back of the store. I sit down at my desk. I put my head in my hands and I breathe.

My mind races from Sam to Jesse and back.

I keep saying that I feel like I don't know what I'm doing. But the truth is, I know exactly what I'm doing.

It's one thing to play coy with them, I suppose. But what I have to do is stop playing coy with myself.

I am going to choose one of them.

I just don't know which one it is.

Love and Maine

Or, how to turn back time

The store closed about forty-five minutes ago. The register has been tallied. The sales floor is clean. Tina went home. I'm done. I can get in the car and go. But I'm just standing in the dark stockroom. Thinking about Sam.

My phone rings and I pick it up to see that it's Jesse. Just like that, Sam flies out of my head, replaced by the man he replaced.

"Hey," Jesse says when I answer. "I thought I'd meet you at the store."

"Oh," I say, surprised. I just assumed I'd meet him at my parents' house once I'd grabbed my things.

"Is that cool?"

"Sure," I say, shrugging. "Yeah. That's good. I'm still here."

"Well, that's good," he says. "Because I'm outside the front door."

I start to laugh as I head toward the front.

"Are you serious?" I say, but he doesn't need to answer because as I step onto the sales floor from the stockroom, I see him through the glass doors.

He is silhouetted by the streetlights in the parking lot. His body, in a heavy jacket and relaxed pants, fills the glass.

I unlock the door and let him in.

He grabs me, not just with his arms, but with his whole

body, as if he needs all of me, as if he can't bear another minute apart.

And then he kisses me.

If loving them both makes me a bad person, I think I'm just a bad person then.

"So . . . Maine?" I say, smiling.

"Maine," Jesse says, nodding once in agreement.

"All right," I say. "Let me just grab my purse. Actually, we can both go out this way. My car's in the back."

"It's OK, I'll drive us."

I give him a skeptical look. Jesse waves me off. "C'mon. Grab your stuff. I'll meet you in the car."

I go back and get my purse, then lock up the store and get into his car. All despite the fact that he shouldn't be driving.

Sometimes I worry Jesse could lead me into hell and I'd follow along, naively saying things like, "Is it getting hot to you?" and believing him when he told me it was fine.

"We have to stop at my parents'," I say when we're on the road. "I need to get some clothes."

"Of course," Jesse says. "Next stop, the Blairs'."

When we pull into their driveway, I can tell just by what lights are on that everyone is over at Marie and Mike's.

Jesse and I head into my parents' house to grab my things, and I warn him we'll have to say good-bye to everyone over at Marie's.

"That's fine," he says as I unlock the front door. "How far away is Marie's?"

"No, that's Marie's," I say, pointing to her house.

Jesse laughs. "Wow," he says. I watch as he looks at the distance between Marie's house and my parents'. "The Booksellers' Daughter strikes again."

It has been so long since someone called her that. It's become moot, for a lot of reasons.

Jesse turns and looks at me. "But I guess you're more of a Booksellers' Daughter than we thought, huh?"

I smile, unsure if he means this kindly or not. "A bit more, maybe," I say.

Once we're in the house, I bound up the stairs heading to my old room, but when I turn around behind me, I notice Jesse is still in the entryway, staring.

"You OK?" I ask.

He snaps out of it, shaking his head. "Yeah, totally. Sorry. I'll wait here while you get your stuff."

I get my bag and gather the things I've left on the bathroom sink.

When I come back down, Jesse is again lost in thought. "It's weird to see that some things look exactly the same way they did before."

"I bet," I say as I make my way to his side.

"It's like some things went on without me and other things paused the moment I left," he says as we head out the front door. "I mean, I know that's not true. But all your family got was a new TV. Everything else looks exactly the same. Even that weird cat painting. It's in the exact same place."

Sam and I picked out Mozart because he looks exactly like the gray cat in the painting above one of my parents' love seats.

I never would have even considered getting a cat without Sam. But now I'm a cat person. A few weeks ago, Sam sent me a picture of a cat sitting on a peanut butter and jelly sandwich and I laughed for, like, fifteen minutes.

I put my things in Jesse's car and then the two of us start walking over to Marie's.

"You sure you're ready to see my family again?" I ask him.

"Of course," he says with a smile on his face. "They're my family, too."

I knock on Marie's door and I hear commotion.

And then Mike answers the door.

"Emma," he says, giving me a hug and then moving out of the way for us to come in. "Two times in one day. What a treat. Jesse, nice to see you again," he says, and puts his hand out. Jesse shakes it. "Pleasure's mine," Jesse says.

Jesse and Mike hung out at family gatherings, but there was never a reason to confide in each other anything more than "How've you been?" They weren't close because Marie and I weren't close. When I think back on it now, it seems best likened to boxing coaches, with Marie and I as the fighters, our husbands pouring water into our mouths and psyching us up to go back in there.

We walk into the dining room to see Marie and my parents. Sophie and Ava have gone to sleep. The moment everyone sees Jesse, they stand up to greet him.

My dad shakes Jesse's hand heartily and then pulls him in for a hug. "Son, you don't know how good it feels to set my eyes on you."

Jesse nods, clearly a bit overwhelmed.

My mom hugs him and then pulls away, holding him out at the end of her arms and squeezing him on the shoulders, and then she shakes her head. "Never been so happy to see a person."

Marie gives him a sincere and kind hug, catching Jesse off guard.

I watch as Jesse smiles and tries to politely extricate himself from the situation. He is uncomfortable and desperately trying to hide it.

"We just wanted to stop in and say good-bye. We should probably be on our way," I say.

"Where are you going?" Marie asks. I assumed my dad would fill everyone in, but apparently not. I'm surprised just how slow gossip travels in my family.

"Jesse and I are headed up to Maine for a few days," I say. I say it as if it's perfectly natural. As if I don't have a fiancé. Actually, maybe I don't have a fiancé. I really don't know what I have anymore.

"Oh, OK," Marie says, her tone matching my own. "Well, I hope you two have a nice time." She holds my gaze for just a little too long, looks at me just a little too intently. The message is clear. She wants details soon. No doubt because she cares about me but also, I'm going to guess, because this is starting to get juicy.

"Thanks," I say, and the way I look at her out of the side of my eye makes it clear I will make sure she is the first to know anything there is to know.

And then Sophie and Ava come bounding down the stairs together, holding hands. Sophie is in a set of sea green thermal pajamas, desperate to see what all the fuss is about. Ava is in mismatched yellow and orange, being dragged along.

They get about three stairs from the bottom when they stop. Ava plops down. Sophie has one hand shielding her eyes from the light and she's squinting ever so slightly.

"Hey," Marie says gently. "You two know you're not supposed to be up." I look at Jesse as he watches Marie sign every word she's saying.

My father stands up. "I'll put them back to bed," he says. "I'd like to spend some time with my grandbabies."

Jesse watches as my dad signs the words "bed" and "children." My dad then scoops up Ava and takes Sophie's hand and disappears up the stairs.

"All right," I say. "We will see you all later."

Jesse waves good-bye to everyone as I take his other hand and lead him out. But when our feet hit the street, Jesse appears lost in his own thoughts.

"Everything OK?" I ask.

Jesse snaps out of it. "What?" he says. "Yeah. Totally."

"What's on your mind?"

I assume he's going to ask about the sign language or their cochlear implants. But he doesn't. He doesn't even mention the fact that they are hearing impaired. Instead he says, "I don't know . . . it's just that . . . wow."

"What?"

"Those are my nieces."

My appetite came back just before we hit the Massachusetts border. Jesse and I drove through a fast-food place and now we're pulled over on the side of the road.

I'm eating a hamburger and french fries.

Jesse ordered a bacon cheeseburger and a Coke but he hasn't had much of either.

"I think we've actually stopped here before," Jesse says.

"At this exact one?" I ask him.

Jesse nods. "After the senior prom."

I laugh. The prom feels like a lifetime ago. We told our parents we were staying over at friends' houses but escaped early and drove up to the very cabin we're leaving for now. Olive and I had gone to Victoria's Secret the week before. She was trying to find a bra to fit under her dress but I ventured toward the more adult lingerie and bought a black strappy G-string, saving it for prom night. It was the first time I had really *tried* to be sexy. Jesse didn't even notice it that night. All he cared about was that we were alone, no one to hear us or stop us.

"Sometimes when I think about what I wore to prom, I wonder why you and Olive didn't try to stop me. Remember I had those temporary butterfly tattoos all over my body?"

He laughs. "Honestly, I thought that was hot as hell. Remember, I was eighteen."

"I don't think you're remembering just how trashy I looked."

"I remember it like it was yesterday," he says. "You were the hottest girl there."

I shake my head and finish my hamburger, balling up the wrapper and throwing it into the bag.

"Hold on," I say. "I think I have a picture. I need you to truly remember what I'm talking about. I need you to admit that I looked incredibly cheesy."

Jesse laughs while I turn around and grab the duffel bag I put in the backseat. I pull it onto my lap and shuffle through it, grabbing the envelope I took from my apartment and searching for the picture I'm talking about. I can't find it at first, even though I know it's there.

I toss the bag back into the backseat and dump the contents of the envelope onto my lap.

"Whoa," Jesse says. "What is all of this?"

"Just stuff of yours, ours," I say. "That I kept."

Jesse looks touched. "Wow," he says.

"I never forgot about you," I say. "I could never forget about you."

He looks at me briefly and then down at my lap, to the photos and papers I've saved.

He doesn't acknowledge what I've said. Instead, he grabs a picture from the pile. "Is this from New Year's Eve in Amsterdam?" he asks me.

I nod my head.

That night, we kissed other people at midnight because we were in a fight. At 12:07 a.m., we made up in the bathroom of a dingy bar in De Wallen and made out sitting on top of the sink. The photo is a selfie from the wee hours of the morning, when he and I were sitting out on a bench by the river.

Jesse picks up a candid photo of us on top of a mountain in Costa Rica and a picture of him on a beach in Sydney. You can tell I am the one taking the picture. You can tell, just from the smile on his face, how much he loves me.

"God, look at us," he says.

"I know," I say.

"Do you remember when this photo was taken?" Jesse says, showing me the one of him on the beach.

"Of course I do," I say.

"That was the day we decided we were never going to make a backup plan, so that we had to pursue our dreams," he says. "Remember? We were going to take jobs that allowed us to see the world."

"I remember."

I riffle through a few more pictures until I find another envelope inside. It's addressed to him in my handwriting. It is the letter I wrote him before I went out on my date with Sam. I push it aside, allowing it to make its way, without being noticed, back into the larger envelope it came from.

And then I find the photo I'm looking for. Our prom. Me with my butterflies.

"All right," I say. "Look at this picture and tell me the truth."

We are standing in front of a large glass window, overlooking Boston. You can see city lights in the background. Jesse is in a cheap tux with a wayward boutonniere that I pinned on him in my front yard as all of our parents watched. I'm right beside him, turned slightly to the side but looking at the camera. I am standing in a bright red dress, with way too many clips in my hair and a series of already-faded and splotchy fake butterfly tattoos down my back.

A victim of early-2000s fashion.

Jesse immediately starts laughing.

"Oh, my God," he says. "You look like you have some sort of skin condition."

I start laughing. "Nope, just fake butterflies."

"I remember thinking that those butterflies were the sexiest thing I'd ever seen."

"Oh, I remember thinking I was the coolest girl at the prom," I say. "Just goes to show things aren't always the way we remember them."

Jesse looks up at me, trying to see if I meant anything by that. I decide to ignore how much it resonates.

"But you," I say. "You nailed it. Handsome then. Handsome now."

Jesse smiles and then turns back toward the steering wheel, getting ready to get on the road.

I gather the rest of the contents of the envelope and try to put them all back. But, of course, some fall to the floor and others get caught on the edge, unwilling to be crammed in.

I pick up what's fallen, including my ruby ring, put it all back in the envelope, and then throw it in the backseat. Only then do I see that I've left something on the center console between us.

It's an almost four-year-old article from the *Beacon*.

"Local Man Jesse Lerner Missing."

Next to the headline is an old photo of him standing in his parents' yard, waving, his right hand perfectly intact.

I was still in LA when the article was published, but a copy of it made its way to me shortly after I got back to Massachusetts. I almost threw it away. But I couldn't. I couldn't bring myself to get rid of anything with his picture on it, anything that bore his name. I had so little of him left.

I grab it and fold it back in two, the way it has lived in the envelope for years.

Jesse watches my hands as I do it.

I know that he saw it.

I put it in the backseat, with the envelope. When I turn back around, I open my mouth to tell Jesse about it, to acknowledge it, but he looks away and starts the car.

He doesn't want to talk about it.

Do you ever get over loss? Or do you just find a box within yourself, big enough to hold it? Do you just stuff it in there, push it down, and snap the lid on it? Do you just work, every day, to keep the box shut?

I thought that maybe if I shoved the pain in there hard enough and I kept the box shut tight enough that the pain would evaporate on its own, that I'd open the box one day to find it was empty and all of the pain I thought I'd been carrying with me was gone.

But I'm sitting in this car right now and I'm starting to think that the box has been full for the past three and a half years. I'm pretty sure that the lid is about to come off and I'm scared to see what's inside.

After all, Jesse has a box, too.

And his is packed tighter than mine.

J esse's family cabin.

I never thought I'd see this place again.

But here I am.

It's about two in the morning. The roads to get here were so quiet, you'd think it was a ghost town.

The cabin, an oddly shaped house that resembles more of an oversized chalet, is warm and inviting—wood siding, big windows, a wraparound deck. It has the slightly mismatched sense that it used to be a tiny home but has weathered a number of additions.

There's not a single lit lamp on the property, so Jesse leaves the high beams on in order for us to get our stuff.

I grab my bag. Jesse grabs a few things from the trunk. We head toward the front door.

"You chilly?" he says as he fiddles with the key. "I'll get a fire going after we get in."

"That sounds great," I say.

The key turns and clicks, but the door sticks. Jesse has to lean into it to push through.

When it finally gives, the first thing that grabs me is the familiar woodlike musk.

Jesse walks through and turns on all the lights and the heat before I've even had a chance to put my things down.

"Settle in, I'm going to go turn off the lights in the car."

I nod and rub my hands together, trying to warm them. I look around at the stone fireplace and the cabin furniture, the afghan blankets that cover most of the chairs. The bar is stocked with half-empty bottles of liquor. The wood plank stairs are so old you can tell they creak just by looking at them.

There's not a single thing about this place that surprises me, not a single thing that feels out of place in comparison with my memory, except that I am a different person than I was the last time I was here.

I think I understand a little of how Jesse must feel coming back. I can see now what he meant back at my parents' house, how it is equally weird how much things don't change as how much they do.

Jesse comes in and shuts the door.

"This place should heat up in a few minutes, I think," he says. "Although it goes without saying that I haven't been here in years."

"The last time we were here was—"

"Our wedding," Jesse says, finishing my sentence.

I smile, remembering. Jesse smiles, too. After the reception, we spent the night at the inn so, in fact, the last time we were here was when we had sex—he in his tux, me in my wedding dress—on the kitchen counter that is currently just off to my left. I remember how romantic it seemed. Now, I find myself sort of cringing that we had sex on the counter. That's where people prepare food! What were we thinking?

"So how about this fire?" I say.

"On it!" he says as he walks over to the fireplace. It's dusty and bare, with a stack of old wood next to it.

I watch him as he moves. I watch as he selects the pieces of wood. I watch him stack them. I watch him strike a match.

"Are you tired?" he asks me. "Do you want to go to bed?"

"No," I say, shaking my head. "I'm oddly awake. You?"

He waves me off. "I'm not exactly on Eastern Standard Time."

"Right," I say.

Jesse steps to the bar. "Wine, then?"

"Gin?" I say.

"Oh, wow," he says. "All right."

He pours me a glass of Hendrick's. He pours another one for himself. I sit down and grab the afghan that's hanging on the back of the couch.

Jesse ducks underneath the bar and grabs a tray of ice from the freezer. He has to hit it against the counter in order for any of the ice to pop out.

"It might have been months, maybe years, since someone made a cocktail in this place," Jesse says. "This ice isn't exactly grade-A material."

I laugh. "It's fine, honestly."

He brings me my glass and puts his down. He moves toward the fire and stabs at it with the poker. It starts to build into a gentle roar. I straighten my posture and grab my glass. I gesture for Jesse to get his.

"To you," I say.

"To us."

I smile and we toast. I shoot back a quarter of the glass. Jesse tries to do the same and winces. "Sorry," he says, shaking his head. "It's actually been quite a long time since I had liquor."

"Don't worry," I say, throwing the rest of the contents of the glass into my mouth. "I'll get you caught up."

Soon, the fire is warming up the whole room. Our some-times stilted conversation grows more uproarious and loqua-cious as the alcohol hits our system. In no time, the two of us are reminiscing about how bad the cake tasted at our wedding and I've had three glasses of Hendrick's.

Jesse is sitting at one end of the couch with his feet on the coffee table. I'm sitting on the other end with my feet under-neath me. My shoes are off; my sweater is on the floor.

"So tell me," he says. "What stamps have you acquired on your passport?"

I am sorry to disappoint him. "Uh, none actually. None since you left."

Jesse is clearly surprised. "Not even to Southern Italy?" he asks. "You were up for that piece about Puglia."

"I know," I say. "I just . . . you know, life sent me in another direction."

We are quiet for a minute and then Jesse sits forward, his torso leaning toward me.

"I'm sorry I took that job," he says. "I'm sorry I left you. What was I thinking? Leaving the day before our anniver-sary?"

"It's OK," I say back. I want to add, "I'm sorry I got engaged to someone else," but I can't bring myself to say it. The apol-ogy would only draw attention to the most vulnerable and insecure parts of me, like a teenager wearing a bikini to a pool party.

"Do you have any idea what it's like to wish for someone every day and then finally see yourself sitting next to them?" he asks me.

"Lately, it feels like that's all I know," I tell him. "I still have trouble believing that all of this is real. That you're here."

"I know. Me, too," Jesse says. He grabs my hand and holds it in his and then he says, "You cut your hair."

I find my hand moving to the back of my head, along the nape of my neck where my hairline ends. I do it as if I'm too shy to have hair so bold. Something about the way I move irritates me. It's as if I'm not entirely myself, as if I'm performing a role. "Yeah," I say. I can hear there is an edge to my voice. I soften it. "A few years ago."

"And it's blonder," he says. "Your hair wasn't really blond before."

"I know," I say. "But I like it."

"I almost didn't recognize you," he says. "At the airport."

"I recognized you the moment you stepped out of that plane."

"You are so different," he says, moving closer. "But you're also everything I dreamt of for all of those years. And you're right in front of me." He puts his hand to my face and looks into my eyes. He leans in to me and presses his lips against mine. My brain gives way to my heart as I sink into him.

He pulls away. "I think we should sleep together," he says. He looks me in the eye and doesn't shy away.

I know that if I say yes, there is no turning back.

It will change things between Sam and me forever.

But I also know that what we're talking about is inevitable. I will sleep with him, whether it's this second or tomorrow or in two weeks. It will happen.

I want to know what Jesse feels like now—a desire that is only heightened by the memories I have of what he felt like then.

I know the consequences. I know what this might cost me.

I'm going to do it anyway.

"I think so, too," I say.

Jesse smiles and then laughs. "Then what the hell are we doing down here?" he says. He stands up and puts his hand out for me, like a gentleman.

I laugh and take it. But the moment I'm on my feet, Jesse has lifted me right back off of them, swooping me up into his arms.

"When was the last time you did it in a twin-size bed?" he asks. It is a joke. And I know better than to answer. But I'm starting to wonder if it's not such a good sign how often I'm cherry-picking the truth.

Jesse rushes us out of the living room to the stairs.

"Oh, my God!" I cry out, stunned at how easily he can move about the house with me in his arms. "You're gonna drop me!"

He doesn't listen. Instead, he bounds up the stairs, taking them two at a time. He pushes open the door to the room that was once considered his. Jesse throws me onto the bed and lands on top of me.

Nothing I've ever done has felt as much like home as this, being underneath him, feeling his lips on mine, his hands running down my body.

He unbuttons my shirt and opens it wide.

My body has changed since he left, the somewhat natural process of time. But I don't feel shy or embarrassed. I feel invigorated. As if I want to be as naked as possible, as quickly as possible—as if I want to show him all of me.

I watch as he takes his own shirt off, as he puts his arms over his head and pulls. I am surprised to see that he's even skinnier than I imagined and that there is a tangle of faded puce scars running down the left half of his torso. They look like lightning bolts tied up in knots. He wears so much of his pain and hardships on his body.

"All those years that I missed you," he says as he runs his nose gently down my collarbone, "I missed your face and your voice and your laugh."

My body is hot, my face is flush. His hands feel so much better than I remember. His body fits into the corners of mine effortlessly, like our limbs were formed around each other, ebbing and flowing in relation to the other.

He tears the button of my jeans open with a flick of his wrist. "But more than anything I missed the feel of you," he says as he pulls my jeans off of me, struggling at first to get them around my hips and then flinging them across the room. He wordlessly takes off his own. He lies back down and presses his whole body onto mine.

"I missed the way your hands feel on my back," he says. "And the way your legs feel around me."

I move slightly, inviting him.

And then I am lost.

I am no longer anyone but the Emma that loves Jesse Lerner, the Emma I've been for so much of my life.

And when we are moving together, breathing together, aching together, I hear him whisper, "Emma."

And I whisper back, "Jesse."

~

We are lying in bed.

We are naked.

We are tangled in sheets, covered in sweat.

We lie in each other's arms and I am reminded of all of the other times we lay next to each other, catching our breath side by side, limbs intertwined. We learned how to do this together, explored ourselves with each other. We loved and desired each other when we were bad at it, and we grew good at it together, in tandem.

Now, we are great at it. The best we have ever been. Even though we are done, I roll over to Jesse and we begin once more.

He reciprocates easily, pressing into me and moaning.

His breath has gone sour. His hair smells dirty. It is my favorite form of him.

"Again," he says. It is neither a question nor a command. Rather a simple fact, observed. We will do this again. We have to be closer again. Here we are again.

And this time, the passion is no longer akin to a house burning down, but instead feels like a steady burning flame, hot and warm.

Neither of us is in a rush. Neither of us could rush even if we wanted to.

We are slow and we are purposeful.

More than anything, I relish the feel of his skin against mine, the feeling of our chests touching ever so briefly before pulling away again.

Right now, in this moment, I am stunned that I am even capable of having sex with anyone else. That the world wouldn't—didn't—stop me. Before I lost him, sex always seemed like something we invented together. Now that he's back, now that he's again here with me, I wonder how I ever went crazy enough to think it could be this good with anyone else.

What I am feeling, what we are doing, is sending signals all throughout my body, like a shot of caffeine, the rush of sugar, the burn of liquor. I can feel my brain rewiring.

This is what I want.
This is what I've always wanted.
I will always want this.

We fall asleep sometime around six in the morning, just as the sun is waking up the rest of the world.

I wake up to the creak of the front door closing and the thud of two shoes hitting the interior floor. I open my hungover eyes to find that there is no one in bed beside me.

I slowly roll out of the sheets, find my underwear, and slip it on along with Jesse's shirt from yesterday. I head down the stairs as I start to smell coffee.

"There she is," Jesse says from the kitchen. He walks closer and grabs me, lifting me up. I wrap my legs around him. I kiss him. He tastes like mint and it reminds me just how awful my morning breath is. I look at the clock on the microwave. It's almost two p.m. Afternoon breath, I guess.

I haven't slept this late since we were in college. I wasn't hammered last night, but ever since the age of twenty-nine or so, my body can't shrug off a drink like it used to.

I pull away from Jesse and he puts me down.

"I should probably brush my teeth," I say.

"You noticed that, too, huh?" Jesse says, teasing me.

"Hey!"

I lightly hit him on the torso and find myself wondering if I've hit the scar that runs down his body, wondering if it's sensitive, if I've hurt him. I want to know what those scars are. I want to know if his teeth are OK after years without dental care or whether he's suffering from vitamin deficiencies. And then, of course, there's his finger.

I also know that I can't ask. I promised not to ask.

But he has to talk about it eventually. If not with me, then with someone else. I know that he is pretending to be OK, but no one would be OK after what he's been through. He can't pretend forever.

"I'm kidding," he says soothingly. "I have waited years to smell your morning breath. Everything about you, morning breath, stray hairs . . . I love it all."

When he disappeared, I kept his hairbrush for months. I didn't want to throw away something that had any of him on it.

"I love you, Emma," he says. "I want to be with you for the rest of my life."

"I love you, too," I say.

Jesse smiles. Toast pops out of the toaster with a swish and a ding.

"All right," Jesse says. "Coffee, orange juice, toast and jam, and I got us microwaveable bacon. I will be honest, this stuns me. Microwaveable bacon. Am I crazy or did they not have that a few years ago?"

I laugh as I move into the kitchen. "I think it's relatively new, yeah."

"I thought so. OK, sit down at the counter and I'll make you a plate."

"Wow," I say, impressed.

I sit down as I watch Jesse move around the small kitchen as if his life depends on it. He pours two glasses of orange juice. He pulls the toast out of the toaster. He gets the strawberry jam and searches for a knife. And then he opens the bacon and puts it on a plate and into the microwave.

"Are you ready for this? Apparently, this is going to be perfectly crisp bacon in a matter of seconds."

"I'm ready," I say. "Dazzle me."

Jesse laughs and then grabs two mugs for coffee. He pours the coffee and hands it to me. I take a sip just as the microwave beeps.

Jesse moves around the kitchen and then he's right next to me, putting two full plates of food on the counter, complete with perfectly crisp bacon.

He sits down and puts his hand on my bare leg. There was once a time when I wasn't sure where I ended and Jesse began. When we were so intertwined, so very much one being in two bodies, that my nerve endings barely lit up when he touched me.

Now is not that time.

Instead, my skin warms underneath his touch. His hand absently moves just slightly higher up my thigh and it gets hotter, brighter. And then he takes it back to eat his toast.

"Breakfast for lunch," I say. "Very charming."

"What can I say? I'm a charming guy. I also, while I was out, got you a twelve-pack of Diet Coke because I know Emma Lerner, and Emma Lerner needs a steady supply of Diet Coke in the house."

My name is not Emma Lerner and I don't drink Diet Coke anymore and I'm not sure how to respond to any of it, so I don't.

"What else did you get?" I ask him.

"Actually, not much else," he says. "I figured we could go into town for dinner."

"Oh, awesome," I say. "That sounds great."

"I'm thinking me, you, a bottle of wine, maybe lobster." I look at him, surprised. "We are in Maine," he adds, explaining himself.

"I didn't know that you ate shellfish," I say. But the minute I say it, I realize how stupid that is to say.

"Don't worry about it," he says. "Lobster will be good."

"Well, then, great. Maine lobsters and wine it is. And what's on the docket for this afternoon?"

"Anything you want," Jesse says, finishing the last of the toast and giving me the rest of his bacon. I greedily chomp it down. I want even more than what's on my plate.

"Anything?" I say.

"Anything."

It's been such a long time since I had a day where I could do anything. "What about a walk to the lighthouse?" I say.

Jesse nods. "That's a great idea. I mean, it's really cold outside, but assuming we can stand it . . ."

I laugh. "We'll bundle up," I tell him. "It will be great."

"I'm in," he says. "Let's go."

I grab his hand and pull him upstairs. I put on thick pants and a sweater. I grab my coat and a scarf. Jesse already has on jeans and a shirt but I insist he wear something warmer. I look through the closets for an old sweatshirt. I find a sweater in the back of the closet in the master bedroom. It's cream and hunter green with a reindeer on it. It obviously once belonged to his dad.

"Here," I say as I hand it to him.

He takes it from me and looks at it. He brings it up to his nose. "I am not kidding when I say this smells like mothballs and death."

I laugh. "Just put it on! Otherwise, you'll just have a jacket and a T-shirt."

He begrudgingly lifts it up over his head and pulls it down around his chest. When it's fitted on him, he claps his hands together. "To the lighthouse!"

We head out onto the front porch, wrapped tightly in our coats, scarves, and boots. It is even colder than I was expecting. The air is whipping against my ears. I can feel it sharply in the vulnerable spots between my scarf and my neck. It is one of the only things I miss about having long hair. In the summer, you feel nice and cool. But in moments like this, you're exposed.

"Onward?" Jesse asks.

"Onward," I say.

Jesse and I talk about his family. We talk about college, about high school, about our months in Europe, our honeymoon in India. I feel like my old self with him, the carefree version of me that died when I thought he did. But it would be a lie to say that I am so entranced with our conversation that I forget the cold. The cold is impossible to forget.

We can see it as our breath hits the air. We can feel it in our bones. Our lips feel cracked, our cheeks blistered, our shoulders are hunched around our necks.

We huddle close to warm each other. We hold hands inside the warmth of Jesse's coat pocket. We find a spot in the sun and we stand in it, letting the subtle heat save us.

"Come here," Jesse says, even though I am already right next to him. He takes me closer, pulling me into his chest. He rubs my back and shoulders, runs his hands up and down my arms, trying to warm me up.

It occurs to me that my memory of him was a poor substitute for the real thing.

They say that when you remember something, you are

really remembering the last time you remembered it. Each time you recollect a memory, you change it, ever so slightly, shading it with new information, new feelings. Over the past years without him, my memories of Jesse have become a copy of a copy of a copy. Without meaning to, I have highlighted the parts of him that stood out to me, and the rest have faded away.

In the copy of a copy, what stood out to me about him was how much I loved him. What faded into the background was how much he loved me.

But I remember it now, how it feels to be the recipient of this much love, this type of dedication.

I wonder what stood out to him when he remembered me. I wonder what faded to gray.

"All right," Jesse says. "We can't stand right here in the sun forever. I say we start running to the lighthouse, to warm up."

"OK," I say. "You got it."

"On the count of three."

"One . . . two . . ."

"Three!"

He takes off like a cheetah. I pump my legs as fast as I can to keep up.

As I run, the wind grows worse on my face but soon I start to heat up in my chest, in my arms, in my legs.

Jesse turns his head back and checks in on me as we're running. And then we come around the bend.

Even though it's still a bit in the distance, the lighthouse and the ocean are in plain view. The stark white of the tower against the dark blue-gray of the water is just as beautiful today as it was when we were married here. Back when I still believed that love was simple, that marriage was forever, that the world was safe to live in.

Can we start again, from this very spot?

"I'll race you to the fence," I say, even though I know that I have no shot of winning.

Jesse gets to the fence and turns around, claiming his victory. I slow down, giving up once I've lost. I walk toward him.

As I gulp the cold air into my lungs, it cuts like a knife. I take it slower; I calm my body down. There is a faint line of sweat on my skin, but it cools down and disappears in an instant.

"You won," I say as I stand next to Jesse and put my head on his shoulder. He puts his arm around me.

We stand next to the lighthouse, catching our breath, looking out onto the rocky ocean. That's the thing about Maine. The water splashes onto rocks more than sand, onto the side of cliffs more than beaches.

I can't imagine living for years on rocks and sand, using an inflatable raft as shade from the sun. There is no way that Jesse can be adjusting as simply as he's presenting.

I want to believe him. I want, so badly, to believe that he is *this* OK. I mean, I have to let him do this all at his own pace, don't I?

It's just so nice to think that things can be as beautiful as they once were.

"That was the happiest day of my life," Jesse says. "Here with everyone, marrying you."

"Mine, too," I say.

Jesse looks at me and smiles. "You look so cold you might shatter."

"I'm pretty freezing," I say. "Should we head back?"

Jesse nods. "In sixty seconds."

"OK," I say. "Sixty seconds. Fifty-nine . . . fifty-eight . . ."

But then I stop counting. I just enjoy the view and the company, a sight I never thought I'd see again with a man I thought I'd lost.

Candles on the table. Pinot Gris in our glasses. Warm bread that I've managed to crumb all over the cream-colored tablecloth.

And one small, very expensive lobster on the table. Because December is not exactly the high season.

"What are we doing?" Jesse says to me. He's sitting across the table, wearing a long-sleeve black shirt and gray chinos. I'm in a red sweater and black jeans. Neither one of us brought nice enough clothes to dine here. The maître d' was clearly hesitant to even seat us.

"I don't know," I say. "It seemed like a nice idea, but I just think . . ."

Jesse stands up and puts his napkin on the table. "C'mon," he says.

"Now?" I'm standing up.

I watch as Jesse pulls out a few bills from his pocket, counts out a reasonable figure, and puts it on the table, nestled under his glass. He doesn't have credit cards or a bank account or any sort of identification. I bet Francine gave him cash and told him she'd take care of getting him everything he needed.

"Yeah," Jesse says. "Now. Life is too short to be sitting in some restaurant drinking wine we don't care for, eating a lobster we don't like."

That is absolutely true.

We run to the car and I hop in the passenger seat, quickly shutting the door behind me. I rub my hands together. I stomp my feet. None of it warms me up.

"The wind is nuts out there!" Jesse says as he starts the car. I have offered to drive every time I've been in the car with him and he keeps turning me down.

"I'm still hungry," I say to him.

"And the night is young."

"Should we head down to the Italian place and grab some subs or a salad to go?"

Jesse nods and heads out of the parking lot. "Sounds good."

The roads are dark and winding and you can tell by the way the trees sway that the wind isn't letting up. Jesse slowly pulls into the makeshift parking lot of the restaurant. He parks and turns off the ignition, leaving the heat on.

"You stay here," he says. "I'll be back soon." He's out the door before I have time to respond.

In the quiet dark of the car, I have a moment to myself.

I use it to check my phone.

Work e-mails. Coupons. Texts from Marie and Olive asking how I'm doing. I open up a few of the work e-mails and find myself overwhelmed by one from Tina.

Dear Colin, Ashley, and Emma,

It is with a heavy heart that I have to render my resignation. My husband and I have decided to sell our home and buy a condo outside of Central Square.

Unfortunately, this means I will be leaving Blair Books. Of course, I can stay on board for the standard two weeks.

Thank you so much for the opportunity to work at your wonderful store. It has meant a lot to me.

Sincerely,

Tina

There were assistant managers before Tina and I always knew there would be assistant managers after her. But I'm having a hard time imagining it all running smoothly when she leaves. My parents are also taking a step back in the coming months and that means that everything really will rest on me— and only me—in the future. On any other day, I think I'd probably have some perspective on this, but for right now, all I can do is ignore it. I archive the e-mail and am taken to the next message in my in-box. I quickly realize it is from my wedding venue.

Dear Ms. Blair,

Our records indicate that you have inquired about the cancellation fee for your event scheduled for October nineteenth of next year. As discussed in your initial consultation, we reserve the right to hold the entire deposit.

However, as we also discussed at the time, that weekend is a popular one. Seeing as how a number of couples have expressed interest in your date, our owner has agreed to release half of your deposit if you cancel before the end of the month.

I hope this answers your question.

Sincerely,

Dawn

I didn't contact Dawn. Which means there's only one explanation.

Sam's really prepared to leave me.

I'm truly on the verge of losing him.

This isn't how my life is meant to go. This isn't what my inbox is meant to look like.

I am supposed to have love notes. I am supposed to have cat pictures and e-mails about caterers and invitations.

Not messages from the Carriage House telling me that my fiancé is a few clicks away from canceling our wedding, that I could lose him, lose a wonderful man, because of my own confusion, my own conflicted heart.

What am I doing here in Maine?

Have I lost my goddamn mind?

I am suddenly overwhelmed by the desire to get in the driver's seat and drive home to Sam right now. But if I did, if I went back to him right now, could I honestly say that I wouldn't think about Jesse anymore?

If I go home to Sam, it needs to be with the confidence that I will never leave him. I owe him that much. I mean, I owe him everything. But taking him seriously and not toying with him is the absolute least I can do. And I'm aware that even then it might not be enough.

By loving the two of them, I am no longer sure about either. And by being unsure, I might just lose them both.

Romantic love is a beautiful thing under the right circumstances. But those circumstances are so specific and rare, aren't they?

It's rare that you love the person who loves you, that you love *only* the person who loves *only* you. Otherwise, somebody's heartbroken.

But I guess that's why true love is so alluring in the first place. It's hard to find and hold on to, like all beautiful things. Like gold, saffron, or an aurora borealis.

"The guys inside said it's going to snow tonight," Jesse says as he gets back in the car. He has a pizza in his hand. "I got us a pepperoni and pineapple pizza, your favorite." He puts the pizza in my lap.

I feel myself feigning a surprised smile. I can't eat cheese. "Great!" I say.

And then we're off, heading back to the cabin over the same snowy streets. Jesse takes the turns confidently now, like a man who knows his way around.

But the roads are winding and they curve unpredictably. I find myself grabbing on to the handle above my head not once but twice.

"Maybe slow down?" I offer after the second time.

I glance at the speedometer. He's going fifty in a thirty-five-mile zone.

"It's fine," he says. "I've got it." And then he looks at me briefly and smiles. "Live a little."

I find myself relaxing even though we're going just as fast. In fact, I become so at ease within the car that I am actually surprised when I hear the whoop of a cop car stopping us.

Jesse pulls over, slowly but immediately.

My heart starts racing.

He's driving with no license at all.

None.

"Jesse . . ." I say, my voice somewhere between a panicked whisper and a breathy scream.

"It's going to be fine," he says. He's so confident about everything. He always has been. He's always the one who believes everything is going to be fine.

But he's wrong, isn't he? Everything isn't always fine. Terrible things happen in this world. Awful things. You have to do your best to prevent them.

A middle-aged man in a police uniform comes up to Jesse's window and bends over. "Evening, sir," he says.

He has a no-nonsense haircut and a stoic stance. He's got a short frame, a clean-shaven face, and hard edges. His hair, even his eyebrows, are starting to gray.

"Good evening, Officer," Jesse says. "How can I help you?"

"You need to take these turns a bit more cautiously in this weather, son," the man says.

"Yes, sir."

"License and registration."

This is my nightmare. This is a nightmare I am having.

Jesse barely shows a moment's hesitation. He leans forward into the glove box and grabs a few papers. He hands them over to the officer.

"We're in the beginning of a storm. You can't be driving like it's the middle of June," the cop says as he takes the documents from Jesse and looks them over.

"Understood."

"And your license?" The officer looks down, staring at Jesse directly. I look away. I can't stand this.

"I don't have it," Jesse says.

"Excuse me?"

"I don't have it, sir," Jesse says. This time I can hear in his voice that he is struggling to maintain his composure.

"What do you mean you don't have it?"

I just sort of snap. My arms start moving on their own. I grab the envelope I left in the car when we drove up here.

"Officer, he's just come back from being lost at sea."

The officer looks at me, stunned. Not because he believes me, but because he can't seem to believe someone would try a lie this elaborate.

"She's . . ." Jesse tries to explain, but what's he going to say? I'm telling the truth.

"I can prove it to you," I say as I look through the envelope and pull out the article from years ago about Jesse being missing. His picture is right there, in the middle of the clipping. I hand it over to the cop.

I'm not sure why he humors me enough to take it, but he does. And then he looks at the picture, and then at Jesse. And I can see that while he's still not convinced, he's not entirely sure I'm lying, either.

"Sir," Jesse starts, but the cop stops him.

"Let me read this."

And so we wait.

The cop looks it over. His eyes go from left to right. He looks at the picture and then once again at Jesse.

"Say I believe this . . ." the cop says.

"He got back a couple of days ago," I say. "He's still waiting on a license, credit cards, really any sort of ID."

"So he shouldn't be driving."

"No," I say. I can't deny that. "He shouldn't. But after being lost for almost four years, all he wants is to be able to drive a car for a few minutes."

The cop closes his eyes for a moment and when he opens them back up, he's made his decision.

"Son, get out of the driver's seat and let this young woman drive."

"Yes, sir," Jesse says, but neither of us move.

"Now," the officer says.

Jesse immediately opens up the door and stands as I get out of the car on my side and switch places with him. I walk past the officer and I can tell he's not exactly entertained by all of this. I get in the driver's seat and the officer closes the door for me.

"It's cold as hell out here and I don't feel like standing on the side of the road trying to figure out if you two are pulling something over on me. I'm deciding to err on the side of . . . gullibility."

He bends down farther to look right at Jesse. "If I catch you driving a car without a license in this town again, I will have you arrested. Is that clear?"

"Absolutely," Jesse says.

"All right," the cop says, and then he turns back. "Actually, I'd like to see your license, miss."

"Oh, of course," I say, turning toward my purse. It's at Jesse's feet. Jesse leans forward and grabs my wallet from it, pulling my license out.

"I don't have all night," the cop says.

I take it from Jesse and hand it over to the cop. He looks at it and then at me. He hands it back.

"Let's stick to the speed limit, Ms. Blair," he says.

"Certainly," I say.

And then he's gone.

I roll up the window and the car is once again dark and starting to warm. I hand my license back to Jesse.

I watch the cop pull onto the road and drive away. I put on my blinker.

I look over at Jesse.

He's staring at my driver's license.

"You changed your name back?"

"What?"

He shows me my own ID. He points to my name. My younger face smiling back at me.

"You changed your name," he says again. This time it's more of a statement than a question.

"Yeah," I say. "I did."

He's quiet for a moment.

"Are you OK?" I ask.

He puts the license back in my wallet and gets hold of himself. "Yeah," he says. "Totally. You thought I was dead, right? You thought I was gone forever."

"Right."

I don't mention that I'm not sure I was ever really comfortable changing my name to Emma Lerner in the first place, that I am and have always been Emma Blair.

"OK," he says. "I get it. It's weird to see, but I get it."

"OK," I say. "Cool."

I pull onto the road and I drive us back to the cabin. It's silent inside of the car.

We both know why the other one isn't talking.

I'm mad at him for getting pulled over.

He's mad at me for changing my name.

It isn't until I pull up in front of the cabin, and the tires crunch over the gravel, that either of us speaks up.

"What do you say we call it even?" Jesse says with a smirk on his face.

I laugh and reach for him. "I'd love to," I say. "Even-steven." I kiss him firmly on the lips.

Jesse grabs the pizza and the two of us run out of the car, heading straight to the cabin.

We shut the door behind us, keeping out the cold and the wind and the cops and the fancy restaurants where we don't like the wine.

It's warm in here. Safe.

"You know, you saved my ass out there," Jesse says.

"Yes!" I say. "I did! You'd be halfway to jail by now if it wasn't for me."

He kisses me against the door. I sink into him.

"Emma Blair, my hero," he says, a slightly sarcastic edge in his voice.

I'm still a little mad at him and now I know he's still mad at me, too.

But he pushes into me and I open myself up to him.

He runs his hands along my stomach, underneath my shirt. I gently bite his ear.

"You know where I think we should do this?" he says as he kisses me.

"No, where?"

He smiles, pointing to the kitchen counter.

I smile and shake my head.

"Remember?" he says.

"Of course I remember."

He pulls me over there and stands up against it, the way he did that day. "I couldn't get your dress off, so I had to push the bottom of it up around your . . ."

"Stop," I say, but not emphatically. I say it the way you say, "Don't be silly" or "Give me a break."

"Stop what?"

"I'm not going to have sex with you on the kitchen counter."

"Why not?" he asks.

"Because it's gross."

"It's not gross."

"It is gross. We ate there this afternoon."

"So we won't eat there again."

That's all it takes. A very simple, very misconceived idea—and I'm doing what just thirty seconds ago I said I wouldn't.

We are loud and we are fast, as if there's a time limit, as if there's a race to the finish. When we are done, Jesse pulls away from me and I hop down. I see a line of sweat on the counter.

What is the matter with me?

What am I doing?

Run-ins with the police aren't as thrilling at thirty-one as they were at seventeen. It's one of those things that was charming *once*. Ditto having sex in the kitchen and speeding. I mean, c'mon, I'm talking cops out of tickets and doing it next to a box of microwaveable bacon? This isn't me. I'm not this person.

"We forgot to eat the pizza," Jesse says as he gets up and walks to pick it up off the table by the door. He puts it on the dining table. I get dressed, eager now to be covered. Jesse opens the box.

I stare right at the pepperoni and pineapple pizza. If I eat it as is, my stomach is going to hurt. But if I pull the cheese off, I'll just be eating gummy tomato bread.

"You know what?" I say. "You go for it. I'm not feeling pizza at the moment."

"No?"

"I don't really eat cheese anymore. It doesn't sit well with me."

"Oh," he says.

It occurs to me that there are a few more things he should know, things I should be clear about.

"I changed my name back to Emma Blair because Blair Books is my store. I love it. And I've built a life around it. I am a Blair."

"OK," he says. A noncommittal word, said noncommittally.

"And I know I used to be the sort of person who always wanted to bounce around from place to place but . . . I'm happy being settled in Massachusetts. I want to run the store until I retire—maybe even hand it over to my own children one day."

Jesse looks at me but doesn't say anything. The two of us look at each other. An impasse.

"Let's go to bed," Jesse says. "Let's not worry about pizza and last names and the bookstore. I want to just lie down next to you, hold you."

"Sure," I say. "Yeah."

Jesse leaves the pizza behind as he leads me up the stairs to the bed. He lies down and holds the blanket open for me. I back into him, my thighs and butt nestled into the curve of his legs. He puts his chin in the crook of my neck, his lips by my ear. The wind is howling now. I can see, through the top of the window, that it is starting to snow.

"Everything is going to be OK," he says to me before I fall asleep.

But I'm not sure I believe him anymore.

I wake well after the sun has come up. The snow has stopped falling. The wind has retreated. For a moment after I open my eyes, everything seems peaceful and quiet.

"Not sure if you can tell from the view out the window but I think we're snowed in," Jesse says. He is standing in the doorway of the bedroom in a T-shirt and sweatpants. He is smiling. "You look adorable," he adds. "I guess those are the big highlights of the morning. We're snowed in, you're as cute as ever."

I smile. "How snowed in is snowed in?"

"We're as snowed in as you are adorable."

"Oh, God," I say, slowly sitting up and gathering myself. "We'll be stuck here for years, then."

Jesse moves toward the bed and gets in next to me. "Worse fates."

I lean into him and quickly realize that both of us could stand to bathe.

"I think I might hop in the shower," I say.

"Great idea. My parents told me they put in a walk-in sauna in the master. Last one there has to make breakfast." And off we go.

The water is warm but the air is damp and humid. The steam fogs the glass doors. There are more showerheads than I care to count, two coming from the ceiling and a number of jets coming from the walls of the shower. It is hot and muggy in here. My hair is flattened and smoothed back across my head. I can feel Jesse just behind me, lathering soap in his hand.

"I wanted to ask you . . ." Jesse says. "Why did you leave LA?"

"What do you mean?" I ask.

"I mean, I just assumed you'd still be out there. Why did you come back?"

"I like it here," I say.

"You liked it there, though," he says. "We both did. It was our home."

He's right. I loved my life in California, where it never snowed and the sun was always shining.

Now, my favorite day of the year is when daylight savings begins. It's usually when the air starts to thaw and the only precipitation you can be threatened with is a little rain. You're tired in the morning because you've lost an hour of sleep. But by seven o'clock at night, the sun is still out. And it's warmer than it was yesterday at that time. It feels like the world is opening up, like the worst is over, and flowers are coming.

They don't have that in Los Angeles. The flowers never leave.

"I just knew I needed to come home to my family."

"When did you move back?"

"Hm?"

"How long after . . . how long was it before you moved back to Acton?"

"I guess soon," I say, turning away from him and into the water. "Maybe two months."

"Two months?" Jesse says, stunned.

"Yeah."

"Wow," he says. "I just . . . all these years I always pictured you there. I never . . . I never really pictured you here."

"Oh," I say, finding myself unsure how to respond or what to say next. "Do you see the shampoo anywhere?" I say finally. But I'm not paying attention to the answer. My mind is already lost in the life that Jesse never pictured.

Me and Blair Books and my cats and Sam.

I close my eyes and breathe in.

It's a good life, the one he never imagined for me.

It's a great life.

I miss it.

Sam knows I can't eat cheese. And he knows that I never want to change my last name from Blair again. He knows how important the store is to me. He likes to read. He likes to talk about books and he has interesting thoughts about them. He never drives without a license. He never attracts police officers. He drives safely in bad weather. Sam knows me, the real me. And he has loved me exactly as I am, always, especially as the person I am today.

"Em?" Jesse says. "Did you want the shampoo?"

"Oh," I say, snapping out of it. "Yeah, thanks."

Jesse hands me the bottle and I squeeze it into my palm. I lather it through my hair.

And suddenly, it takes everything I have not to dissolve into a puddle of tears and go down the drain with the soapy water.

I miss Sam.

And I'm scared I've pushed him away forever.

Jesse notices. I try to hide it. I smile even though the smile doesn't live anywhere beyond my lips. Jesse stands behind me, putting his arms around me, his chest against my back. He nestles his chin into my shoulder and he says, "How are you?"

There is nothing like a well-timed "How are you?" to reduce you to weeping.

I have no words. I just close my eyes and give myself permission to cry. I let Jesse hold me. I lean into him, collapse onto him. Neither of us says anything. The air grows so hot and oppressive that eventually breathing takes more effort than it should. Jesse turns off the steam, turns down the temperature of the faucets, and lets the lukewarm water run over us.

"It's Sam, right? That's his name?"

I had split my world into two, but by simply uttering Sam's name, Jesse has just sewn the halves back together.

"Yeah," I say, nodding. "Sam Kemper." I want to pull away from Jesse right now. I want him to go stand on the other side of the shower. I want to use the water and the soap to clean my body and I want to go home.

But I don't do any of that. Instead, I freeze in place—in some way hoping that by standing still I can stop the world from spinning for just a moment, that I can put off what I know is eventually going to happen.

I watch as Jesse places the name.

"Sam Kemper?" he asks. "From high school?"

I nod.

"The guy that used to work at your parents' store?"

There's no reason for Jesse to dislike Sam other than the fact that I love Sam. But I watch as Jesse's face grows to show contempt. I should never have said Sam's full name. It was better when Sam was an abstract. I've done a stupid thing by giving him a face to match. I might as well have stabbed Jesse in the ribs. He bristles and then gets hold of himself. "You love him?" Jesse asks.

I nod but what I want to do is tell him about what Marie said, that she told me this isn't about who I love but rather who I am. I want to tell him that I've been asking myself that question over and over and it's starting to seem glaringly obvious that I am different from the person Jesse loves.

I am not her. Not anymore. No matter how easy it is for me to pretend that I am.

But instead of saying any of that, I just say, "Sam is a good man."

And Jesse leaves it there.

He turns off the water and I'm instantly cold. He hands me a towel and the moment I wrap it around myself, I realize how naked I feel.

We dry ourselves off, not speaking.

I'm suddenly so hungry that I feel ill. I throw some clothes on and head downstairs. I start brewing coffee and put bread in the toaster. Jesse comes down shortly after, in fresh clothes.

The mood has shifted. You can feel it in the air between us. Everything we've been pretending isn't true is about to come tumbling out of us, in shouts and tears.

"I started making coffee," I say. I try to make my voice sound light and carefree but it's not working. I know it's not working. I know that my inner turmoil isn't so inner, that trying to cover it up is like brushing a thin coat of white paint over a red wall. It's seeping out. It's clear as day what I'm trying to hide.

"I'm starting to think you don't want to be here," Jesse says.

I look up at him. "It's complicated," I say.

Jesse nods, not in agreement with me but as if he's heard this all before. "You know what? I gotta tell ya. I don't think it's that complicated."

"Of course it is," I say, sitting down on the sofa.

"Not really," Jesse says, following suit, sitting down opposite me. His voice is growing less patient by the second. "You and

I are married. We have been together, have loved each other, forever. We belong together."

"Jesse—"

"No!" he says. "Why do I feel like I have to convince you to be with me? This isn't . . . You should never have done what you did. How could you agree to marry this guy?"

"You don't—"

"You're *my* wife, Emma. We stood in front of a hundred people right down the road at that goddamn lighthouse and promised to love each other for the rest of our lives. I lost you once and I did everything I could to get back to you. Now I'm here, I'm back, and I'm in danger of losing you all over again? This is supposed to be the happy part. Now that we're here together. This is all supposed to be the easy stuff."

"It's not that simple."

"It should be! That's what I'm saying. It should be that fucking simple!"

I am both stunned at the anger directed at me and surprised it took this long for it to surface.

"Yeah, well, it's not, OK? Life doesn't always work out the way you think it will. I learned that when you left on a plane three years ago and disappeared."

"Because I survived a crash over the Pacific Ocean! I watched everyone else on that helicopter die. I lived on a tiny scrap of a goddamn rock, alone, trying to figure out a way to get back to you. Meanwhile, what did you do? Forget about me by August? Submit for a name change by Christmas?"

"Jesse, you know that's not true."

"You want to talk about the truth? The truth is you gave up on me."

"You were gone!" My voice goes from zero to sixty in three

seconds and I can feel that my emotions are bursting out of me like a horse kept too long behind a gate. "We thought you were dead!"

"I honestly thought," Jesse says, "that you and I loved each other in a way that we could never, ever forget about each other."

"I never forgot you! Never. I have always loved you. I still love you."

"You got engaged to someone else!"

"When I thought that you were dead! If I had known you were alive, I would have waited every day for you."

"Well, now you know I'm alive. And instead of coming back to me, you're sitting on the fence. You're here with *me*, crying about *him* in the shower."

"I love you, Jesse, and even when I thought you were gone, I loved you. But I couldn't spend my life loving a man who was no longer here. And I didn't think that's what you'd want for me, either."

"You don't know what I'd want," he says.

"No!" I say. "I don't. I barely know you anymore. And you barely know me. And I feel like you want to keep pretending that we do."

"I know you!" he says. "Don't tell me I don't know you. You are the only person in my entire life that I have truly, truly known. That I know loved me. That I have understood and accepted for exactly who they are. I know everything there is to know about you."

I shake my head. "No, Jesse, you know everything about the person I was up until the day you left. But you don't know me now. Nor do you seem to have any interest in seeing me for who I am today, or for sharing with me who you are today."

"What are you talking about?"

"I'm different, Jesse. I was in my twenties when you left. I'm thirty-one now. I don't care about Los Angeles and writing travel pieces anymore. I care about my family. I care about my bookstore. I'm not the same as I was when you left. The loss of you changed me. I changed."

"I mean, fine. You changed because I was gone, I get that. You got scared, you were grieving, so you came back to Acton because it felt safe and you took over your parents' store because it was easy. But you don't have to do any of that anymore. I'm back. We can go home to California. We can finally go to Puglia. I bet you can even sell some pieces to a few magazines next year. You don't have to have this life anymore."

But I'm already shaking my head and trying to tell him no before he's even finished. "You are not understanding me," I say. "Maybe at first I came home to retreat from the world, and sure, initially, I took the job at the store because it was available. But I love my life now, Jesse. I choose to live in Massachusetts. I choose to run my store. I want this for myself."

I look at Jesse's face as he searches mine. I try a different tactic, a different way of explaining to him.

"When I'm in a sad mood, do you know what I do to cheer myself up?"

"You eat french fries and have a Diet Coke," Jesse says, just as I say, "I practice the piano."

The difference in our answers startles him. His body deflates slightly, pulling away from me. I can see, as it quickly wipes across his face, that it's hard for him to reconcile my answer with who he believes that I am.

I imagine, for a moment, that the next words out of his mouth might be, "You play the piano?"

And I'd say yes and I'd explain how I got started and that I only know a few songs and that I'm not that good, but that it relaxes me when I'm feeling stressed. I'd tell him how Homer is normally asleep under it when I want to play, so I have to pick him up and put him on the bench beside me, but that it's so nice to sit there next to my cat and play "Für Elise." Especially when I pretend "Für Elise" is about his fur.

It would mean so much if Jesse wanted to fall in love with who I am today. If he opened up and let me fall in love with the truth about who he is now.

But none of that happens.

Jesse just says, "So you play piano. What does that prove?"

And when he says it, I know that the gap between us is even larger than I thought.

"That we are different people now. We grew apart. Jesse, I don't know anything about what your life has been like for the past three and a half years and you won't talk about it. But you are different. You can't go through what you went through and not be different."

"I don't need to talk about what happened to me to prove to you that I still love you, that I'm still the person you've always loved."

"That's not what I'm saying. I'm saying that I think you're trying to pretend that we can just pick up where we left off. I was, too. But that's not possible. Life doesn't work that way. What I've been through in my life affects the person that I am today. And that's true for you, too. Whatever you went through out there. You can't keep it bottled inside."

"I've told you I don't want to talk about it."

"Why not?" I say to him. "How are we supposed to be honest with each other about our future if you won't even tell me the most basic elements of your past? You say that you know that everything can be exactly how it was, but before you left we never had huge parts of our lives that we just *didn't talk about*. We didn't have any history that we didn't share. And now we do. I have Sam and, c'mon, Jesse, you have scars on your body. Your finger is—"

Jesse slams his fist into the pillow cushions underneath us. It would be a violent action if it hadn't landed in such a soft place, and I wonder if that was by design or by accident. "What do you want to know, Emma? For crying out loud. What do you want to know? That the doctors found two types of skin cancer? That when they found me, you could see the bone of my wrists and my ribs through my chest? That I had to have four root canals and it feels like half my mouth is fake now? Is that what you want to know? You want to know that I was stung by a Portuguese man-of-war as I swam looking for safety? You want to know I couldn't get it off of me? That it just kept fucking stinging me? That the pain was so bad I thought I was dying? That the doctors say I'll have this scar for years, maybe forever? Or maybe you just want me to admit how awful it was living out on that rock. You want me to tell you how many days I spent looking out at the sea, just waiting. Telling myself I just had to make it until tomorrow, because you'd come for me. You or my parents or my brothers. But none of you came. None of you found me. No one did."

"We didn't know. We didn't know how to find you."

"I know that," he says. "I'm not mad at anyone for that. What I'm mad about is that you forgot about me! That you moved on and replaced me! That I'm back and I still don't have you."

"I didn't replace you."

"You got rid of my name at the end of yours and you told

another man you'd marry him. What else could that possibly be? What other word would you use?"

"I didn't replace you," I say again, this time weakly. "I love you."

"If that's true, then this is simple. Be with me. Help me put us back together."

I can feel Jesse's eyes on me even as I look away. I turn to look out the window, to the blanket of snow covering the backyard. It is white and clean. It looks as soft as a cloud.

When I was a kid, I loved the snow. Then when I moved to California, I used to tell people I'd never leave the sun, that I never wanted to see snow again. But now, I can't imagine a green Christmas and I know that if I left, I would miss that feeling of coming in from the cold.

I have changed over time. That's what people do.

People aren't stagnant. We evolve in reaction to our pleasures and our pains.

Jesse is a different man than he was before.

I am a different woman.

And what has confused me ever since I found out he was alive is now crystal clear: We are two people who are madly in love with our old selves. And that is not the same as being in love.

You can't capture love in a bottle. You can't hold on to it with both hands and force it to stay with you.

What has happened to us is no one's fault—neither of us did anything wrong—but when Jesse left, life took us in opposite directions and turned us into different people. We grew apart because we *were* apart.

And maybe that means that even though we can finally be together . . .

We shouldn't be.

The thought cracks open my chest.

I am perfectly still but feel as if I'm caught in a riptide, barely able to see how I can get my head out and above the water.

I don't think I was ever afraid that loving both of them made me a bad person.

I was afraid that loving Sam made me a bad person.

I was afraid that I would pick Sam. That my heart would love Sam. That my soul would need Sam.

You're not supposed to forsake the man who journeyed home to you.

You're supposed to be Penelope. You're supposed to knit the shroud day in and day out and stay up every night unraveling it to keep the suitors at bay.

You're not supposed to have a life of your own, needs of your own. You're not supposed to love again.

But I did.

That's exactly what I did.

Jesse moves closer to me, gently puts his hands on my arms. "If you love me, Emma, then be with me."

It's a scary thought, isn't it? That every single person on this planet could lose their one true love and live to love again? It means the one you love could love again if they lost you.

But it also means I know Jesse will be OK, he will be happy one day, without me.

"I don't think I can be with you," I say. "I don't think . . . I don't think we're right for each other. Anymore."

Jesse's arms slump down around him. His posture sinks. His eyes collapse shut.

It's one of those moments in life when you can't believe that the truth is true, that the world shook out like this.

I don't end up with Jesse.

After all of this, all we've been through, we aren't going to grow old together.

"I'm sorry," I say.

"I have to go."

"Where are you going to go? We're snowed in."

He grabs his jacket and puts on his shoes. "I'll just go to the car. I don't care. I just need to be alone right now."

He opens the front door and slams it behind him. I go to the door and open it again to see his back as he walks toward the car, trudging through the snow. He knows I'm behind him but stops me before I can even say a word by lifting his arm up and giving me the universal sign for "Don't." So I don't.

I close the door. I lean against it. I slink down to the floor and I cry.

Jesse and I were once ripped apart. And now we've grown apart.

The same hearts, broken twice.

Over an hour has passed and Jesse has not yet come back. I stand up and peek through the front window to see if he's still in the car.

He's sitting in the driver's seat with his head down. I look around the front of the house. The warm sun has started to melt some of the snow. The roads in the distance look, if not cleared, at least a bit traveled. We could leave here right now if we wanted to. We'd just have a little shoveling to do. But my guess is Jesse is in no rush to be trapped in a car with me.

My eye drifts back to the car and I see him moving in the driver's seat. He's looking through my envelope. He's looking at pictures and reading notes, maybe even the *Beacon* article about his disappearance.

I shouldn't watch him. I should give him the privacy that he walked out there for. But I can't look away.

I see a white envelope in his hands.

And I know exactly what it is.

The letter I wrote him to say good-bye.

He fiddles with the envelope, flipping it back and forth, deciding whether he's going to open it. My heart beats like a drum in my chest.

I put my hand on the doorknob, ready to run out there and stop him, but . . . I don't. Instead, I look back out the window.

I watch as he puts a finger under the flap and tears it open.

I turn away from the window, as if he spotted me. I know that he didn't. I just know that I'm scared.

He's going to read that letter and everything is going to get worse. It will be all the proof he needs that I forgot him, that I gave up on us, that I gave up on him.

I turn back to the window and watch him read it. He stares at the page for a long time. And then he puts it down and looks out the side window. Then he picks it up again and starts reading it a second time.

After a while, he puts his hand on the car door and opens it. I run from the window and sit on the sofa, pretending I've been here the whole time.

I never should have written that goddamn letter.

The front door opens, and there he is. Staring at me. He has the letter in his hand. He's perfectly still, stunningly quiet.

I wrote the letter so that I could let go of him. There's no hiding that. So if that's the evidence he's looking for that I've been a terrible wife, an awful person, a disloyal soul, well, then . . . I guess he got what he was looking for.

But Jesse's reaction surprises me.

"What is this about going crazy on the roof?" he says calmly.

"What?" I ask.

He hands me the letter as if I've never read it. I stand up and take it from him. I open it even though I already know what it says.

The handwriting looks hurried. You can see, at the end, that there are splotches of ink where water must have hit it. Tears, obviously. I can't stop myself from rereading it, seeing it through new eyes.

Dear Jesse,

You've been gone for more than two years but there hasn't been a day that has gone by when I haven't thought of you.

Sometimes I remember the way you smelled salty after you'd gone for a swim in the ocean. Or I wonder whether you'd have liked the movie I just saw. Other times, I just think about your smile. I think about how your eyes would crinkle and I'd always fall a little bit more in love with you.

I think about how you would touch me. How I would touch you. I think about that a lot.

The memory of you hurt so much at first. The more I thought about your smile, your smell, the more it hurt. But I liked punishing myself. I liked the pain because the pain was you.

I don't know if there is a right and wrong way to grieve. I just know that losing you has gutted me in a way I honestly didn't think was possible. I've felt pain I didn't think was human.

At times, it has made me lose my mind. (Let's just say that I went a little crazy up on our roof.)

At times, it has nearly broken me.

And I'm happy to say that now is a time when your memory brings me so much joy that just thinking of you brings a smile to my face.

I'm also happy to say that I'm stronger than I ever knew.

I have found meaning in life that I never would have guessed.

And now I'm surprising myself once again by realizing that I am ready to move forward.

I once thought grief was chronic, that all you could do was appreciate the good days and take them along with the bad. And then I started to think that maybe the good days aren't just days; maybe the good days can be good weeks, good months, good years.

Now I wonder if grief isn't something like a shell.

You wear it for a long time and then one day you realize you've outgrown it.

So you put it down.

It doesn't mean that I want to let go of the memories of you or the love I have for you. But it does mean that I want to let go of the sadness.

I won't ever forget you, Jesse. I don't want to and I don't think I'm capable of it.

But I do think I can put the pain down. I think I can leave it on the ground and walk away, only coming back to visit every once in a while, no longer carrying it with me.

Not only do I think I can do that, but I think I need to.

I will carry you in my heart always, but I cannot carry your loss on my back anymore. If I do, I'll never find any new joy for myself. I will crumble under the weight of your memory.

I have to look forward, into a future where you cannot be. Instead of back, to a past filled with what we had.

I have to let you go and I have to ask you to let me go.

I truly believe that if I work hard, I can have the sort of life for myself that you always wanted for me. A happy life. A satisfied life. Where I am loved and I love in return.

I need your permission to find room to love someone else.

I'm so sorry that we never got the future we talked about. Our life together would have been grand.

But I'm going out into the world with an open heart now. And I'm going to go wherever life takes me.

I hope you know how beautiful and freeing it was to love you when you were here.

You were the love of my life.

Maybe it's selfish to want more, maybe it's greedy to want another love like that.

But I can't help it.

I do.

So I said yes to a date with Sam Kemper. I like to think you would like him for me, that you'd approve. But I also want you to know, in case it doesn't go without saying, that no one could ever replace you. It's just that I want more love in my life, Jesse.

And I'm asking for your blessing to go find it.

> *Love,*
> *Emma*

I know I'm adding new splotches, new tears, to the page. But I can't seem to stop them from coming. When I finally look at Jesse, his eyes are watery. He puts his arm around me and pulls me in tight. The pain between us feels sharp enough to cut, heavy enough to sink us.

"What did you do on the roof?" he says again, this time softer, kinder.

I catch my breath and then I tell him.

"Everyone said you were dead," I start. "And I was convinced they were all wrong and that you were trying to come home to me. I just knew it. So one day, when I couldn't take it anymore, I went up to the roof and saw this small sliver of ocean and I just . . . I became convinced that you were going to swim to shore. I got your binoculars and I . . . I stood there, watching the small little piece of shoreline, waiting for you to surface."

Jesse is looking right at me, listening to my every word.

"Marie found me and told me you weren't going to swim back to me. That you weren't going to just appear on the beach like that. That you were dead. She said that I had to face it and start dealing with it. And so I did. But it was the hardest thing I've ever done. I wasn't sure I'd make it through the day. Sometimes I was living hour by hour. I've never been more confused or felt less like myself."

Jesse pulls me in tighter, holding me. "Do you realize that we were both looking out at the same ocean looking for each other?" he says.

I close my eyes and think of him waiting for me. I remember what it felt like to wait for him.

"I had this idea in the car that I would look through that envelope and find all of the stuff in there, the memories and the pictures, and that I would show you how happy we were together. I thought I'd be able to make you see that you were wrong. That we are the same people we were when we loved each other. That we are meant to be together forever. But you know what I realized?"

"What?" I say.

"I hate your hair."

I pull back from him and he laughs. "I know that's not very nice to say but it's true. I was looking at those pictures of you back then with your gorgeous long hair, and I always loved how it wasn't really blond, but it wasn't really brown. I mean, I loved your hair. And now I'm back and you've chopped it off and it's blond and, you know, maybe I'm supposed to like it, but I was sitting in the car thinking, 'She'll grow her hair out again.' And then I thought, 'Well, wait, she likes her hair like that.'"

"Yes, I do!" I say, stung.

"That's exactly my point. This is you now. Short blond hair. My Emma had long, light brown hair. And that's not you anymore. I can't just look at you and ignore your hair. I have to look at you as who you are. Right now. Today."

"And you don't like my hair," I say.

Jesse looks at me. "I'm sure it's beautiful," he says. "But, right now, all I can see is that it's not like it used to be."

I find myself leaning back into him, putting my head back onto his chest. "The Emma I knew wanted to live in California, and she wanted to be as far away from her parents' bookstore as possible. And she wasn't going to sit still until she'd seen as much of the world as she could. She loved tiny hotel shampoo bottles and the smell of the airport. She didn't know how to play a single note on a piano. And she loved me and only me," he says. "But I guess that's not you anymore."

I shake my head without looking at him.

"And I have to stop pretending that it is. Especially because . . . I'm not the same, either. I know it seems like I don't know that, but I do. I know I've changed. I'm know I'm . . ." I'm surprised to see that Jesse has begun to cry. I hold him tighter, listening, wishing I could take the pain away, spare him any more hardship on top of what he's already faced. I want so badly to protect him from the world, to ensure nothing ever hurts him again. But I can't, of course. No one can do that for anybody.

"I'm messed up, Emma," he continues. "I'm not OK, I don't think. I keep acting as if I feel OK here, but . . . I don't. I don't feel like I belong anywhere. Not here, not there. I'm . . . struggling to keep it together almost every moment of the day. One minute I feel overwhelmed by how much food is around and then the next minute I can't bring myself to eat any of it. The night I landed I woke up around three and went down to the kitchen and ate so much I made myself sick. The doctors say that I still need to be mindful of what I eat and how much, but I just want to eat nothing or everything. There's no in-between. It's not just food, either. When we were in the shower earlier, I was thinking, 'We should get a bucket and save some of this water. Store it.'"

He's finally ready to say how he really feels and it's all spilling out of him like a turned-over gallon of milk.

"I can't even stand to look at my hand. I can't stand to see that my finger is still gone. I know it sounds so stupid, but I think I thought that if I could just get home, then things could go back to the way they were. I'd get you back, and I'd feel normal again, and my pinkie would, I don't know, magically reappear or something."

He looks at me and he breathes in and then breathes out, all with great effort.

"Do you want to sit?" I ask him, pulling him toward the sofa. I sit him down and I take a seat beside him. I put my hand on his back. "It's OK," I say. "You can talk about it. You can tell me anything."

"I just . . . I hate even thinking about it," he says. "It was . . . awful. All of it. Losing my finger was maybe one of the most painful things I've ever been through. I have been working so hard to block it out."

I am quiet in the hopes that he will keep talking, that he will continue to be honest with me and with himself, that he will share what he's been through, what plagues him.

"I sliced it almost clean through," he says finally. "Trying to open an oyster with a rock. I thought it might heal on its own but it wouldn't. I lived with it growing more and more infected until I finally just had to . . ."

I can see that he can't bring himself to speak the words.

But he doesn't have to.

I know what he can't say.

He had to cut off his own finger.

Somewhere in the years he's been gone, he was forced to save his hand the only way he could.

"I'm so sorry," I say to him.

I can't imagine what else happened, how many days he went without food, how near he came to grave dehydration, the searing pain of being stung over and over as he was trying to swim to rescue. But I am starting to think that he will tackle that pain when he is ready, talking and admitting more as he grows stronger. It will be a long process. It may even be years until he can unpack it all. And even then, he'll never be able to erase it completely.

The same way I'll never be able to erase the ache of grieving him.

These are the things that have made us who we are.

I step away from Jesse for a moment and head into the kitchen. I look through the cabinets and find an old box of Earl Grey.

"How about some tea?" I offer.

He looks up at me and nods. It is so gentle as to be almost imperceptible.

I put two mugs of water in the microwave. I grab the tea bags.

"Keep talking," I say. "I'm listening."

His voice picks up again and I realize that he must have, whether it was conscious or subconscious, been waiting for permission.

"I think I've been trying to *undo* the last however many years," he says. "I've been trying to put everything back the way it was before I left so it can be as if it never happened. But that doesn't work. I mean, obviously it doesn't. I know that."

I stop the microwave before it beeps, pulling the mugs out and putting the tea bags in. The smell of the tea reminds me of Marie. I sit back down next to Jesse, putting his steaming cup in front of him. He takes it into his hand but he doesn't drink it yet.

"I'm not the same person that I was back then," he says. "You know it and I know it, but I just keep thinking that with a little effort, I can change that. But I can't. I can't, can I?"

He puts the mug down and starts gesticulating with his hands. "I don't want to spend the rest of my life in Acton," he says. "I've spent too long trapped somewhere I didn't want to be. I want to go back to California. I respect that Blair Books means as much to you as it does, but I don't get it. We worked so hard to move away from New England, to get away from the life that our parents were pushing us toward. We sacrificed so much so that we could travel, not so that we could stay in one place. I don't understand why you came back here, why you chose to spend your life here, doing exactly what your parents always told you you should do.

"I'm really, really angry, deep down in my heart. And I wish that I didn't feel that way and I hate myself for feeling it. But I'm furious that you could fall in love with someone else. I know you say that it doesn't mean you forgot me, but, you know, at least right now, it sure sounds like it to me. And I'm not saying that we couldn't get past that, if everything else about us made sense, but . . . I don't know.

"I'm mad at you and I'm mad at Friendly's for turning into a Johnny whatever you called it. I'm mad at almost everything that changed without me. I know I need to work on

that. I know it's just one of the strings of issues that I'm facing. I know I said that now was supposed to be the easy part
but I don't know why I thought that. Coming home is hard.
This was always going to be hard. I'm sorry I didn't see that
until now.

"Of course I've changed. And of course you've changed.
There is no way we could be the same after losing each other;
we meant too much to each other for that to happen. So, I
guess what I'm saying is that I'm miserable and I'm angry, but I
guess I do get it. What you said in that letter makes some sense
to me. You had to let go of me if you were ever going to have
a chance at a normal life. I know you loved me then. I know it
wasn't easy. And, obviously, I know this is hard for you, too. I'd
be lying if I said that I didn't see what you see."

He puts his arms around me, pulling me close to him, and
then he says what has taken us days to understand.

"We loved each other and we lost each other. And now, even
though we still love each other, the pieces don't fit like they
used to."

I could make myself fit for him.

He could make himself fit for me.

But that's not true love.

"This is it for us," Jesse says. "We're over now."

I look in his eyes. "Yeah. I think we are."

After everything we've been through, I never predicted it
ending like this.

Jesse and I stay still, holding each other, not yet ready to
fully let go. His hands are still a little bit frozen. I take them in
my own. I hold them, sharing the heat of my body.

He pulls one hand away to brush a hair off of my face.

I think, maybe, *this* is what true love means.

Maybe true love is warming someone up from the cold, or tenderly brushing a hair away, because you care about them with every bone in your body even though you know what's between you won't last.

"I don't know where we go from here," I say.

Jesse puts his chin on my head, breathing in. And then he pulls away slightly to look at me. "You still don't have to be back until late tomorrow, right?"

"Yeah," I say.

"So we can stay," he says. "For another day. We can take our time."

"What do you mean?"

"I'm saying that I know what's ahead of us, but . . . I'm not ready yet. I'm just not ready. And I don't see why we can't spend a little bit more time with each other, a little bit more time being happy together. I've waited so long to be here with you; it seems silly to squander it just because it won't last."

I smile, charmed. I consider what he's saying and realize that it feels exactly right to me, like being handed a glass of water just as you realize you're thirsty. "That sounds good," I say. "Let's just have a nice time together, not worry about the future."

"Thank you."

"OK, so until tomorrow, you and I will leave the real world on the other side of that door, knowing that we will face it soon. But . . . for now, we can let things be the way they were, once."

"And then tomorrow we go home," Jesse says.

"Yeah," I say. "And we start to learn how to live without each other again."

"You'll marry Sam," Jesse says.

I nod. "And you'll probably move to California."

"But for now . . . for one more day . . ."

"We'll be Emma and Jesse."

"The way we were."

I laugh. "Yeah, the way we were."

Jesse builds a fire and then joins me on the sofa. He puts his arm around me and pulls me into the crook of his shoulder. I rest my head on him.

It feels good to be in his arms, to be satisfied with this moment, to not wonder what the future holds. I relish the way he feels next to me, cherish the joy of having him near. I know I won't always have it.

It starts snowing again, small flurries landing on the already white ground. I get up from Jesse's arms and walk over to the sliding glass doors to watch it fall.

Everything is quiet and soft. The snow is white and clean, not yet crushed under the weight of boots.

"Hear me out," I say, turning back to Jesse.

"Uh-oh," he says.

"Snow angels."

"Snow angels?"

"Snow angels."

As soon as we step out into the snow, I realize the flaw in my plan. We will sully the unsullied snow by walking in it. We will crush the uncrushed just by being here.

"Are you sure this is what you want to do?" Jesse asks me. "Imagine how good it will feel to watch a movie inside by the fire."

"No, c'mon, this is better."

"I'm not sure about that," Jesse says, and from the tone of his voice, I now understand why people sometimes describe the air as "bitter cold." The cold is not bitter. They are bitter about the cold.

I run ahead, hoping he'll catch up to me. I try to remember what it felt like to once be a teenager with him. I trip and let myself fall. I drop face-first into the snow. I turn around. I see Jesse running to catch up with me.

"Come on, slowpoke," I say as I stretch my arms out and widen my legs. I windshield-wiper them back and forth, until I hit the icy snow that has crystalized onto the grass beneath it.

Jesse catches up and plops himself down next to me. He extends his limbs and starts pushing the snow out of the way. I get up and watch him.

"Nice work," I say. "Excellent form."

Jesse stands and turns to look at his creation. Then he looks at mine.

"You can say it," I tell him. "Yours is better."

"Don't beat yourself up," he says. "Some people just have a natural raw talent for snow art. And I'm one of them."

I roll my eyes and then step lightly in the center of his angel where the footprints won't show. I lean forward and draw a halo where his head once was.

"There," I say. "*Now* it's art."

But I have made a rookie mistake, out here in the snow. I have turned my back to him. And when I stand up, he pelts me with a snowball.

I shake my head and then very slowly and deliberately make a snowball myself.

"You don't want to do that," he says, just a hint of fear in his voice.

"You started it."

"Still. What you're planning on doing would be a mistake," he says.

"Oh yeah? What are you gonna do?" I ask, slowly sauntering up to him, savoring the very trivial power I currently wield.

"I will . . ." he starts to say, but then he swiftly leans toward me and knocks the snowball out of my hand. It hits my leg on the way down.

"You just hit me with my own snowball!" I say.

I gather up another one and throw it at him. It hits him square in the neck. I have declared war.

Jesse gets in a snowball to my arm and one to the top of my head. I get one that hits him straight in the chest. I run away when I see a huge one forming in his hand.

I run and I run and then I trip on the snow and fall down. I brace myself, waiting for a snowball to hit me. But when I open my eyes, I see that Jesse is standing right above me.

"Truce?" he asks.

I nod and he throws the last snowball far out in the distance.

"How about that warm fire and those blankets?" he asks me.

This time I don't hesitate. "I'm in."

When we're thawed, Jesse heads to the stack of books and movies that have been sitting in this cabin for years. There are supermarket paperbacks so well-worn that they have white line creases on the spine. There are DVDs from the early 2000s and even a few VHS tapes.

We pick out an old movie and try to turn on the TV. It doesn't respond.

"Is it just me or does it appear that the television is dead?" Jesse says.

I look behind to see if it's plugged in. It is. But when I hit a few buttons, nothing happens.

"It's broken," he says. "I bet it's been broken for years and no one thought to turn it on."

"A book, then," I say, walking over to the stack of paperbacks. "I've come to realize it's a wonderful way to pass the time." I glance through the spines of the books on the shelf and spot a thin detective novel that I've never heard of among the John Grishams and James Pattersons. I pull it out. "Why don't we read this?"

"Together?"

"I'll read to you, you read to me," I say. Jesse isn't entirely sold.

The sun starts to set and even though we aren't in danger of being cold in here, Jesse adds logs to the fire. He finds an old bottle of red wine underneath the bar and I grab two jelly jars from the cabinets.

We drink the bottle as we sit by the fire.

We talk about the times we made each other blissfully happy, and we laugh about the times we made each other blisteringly mad. We talk about our love story like two people reflecting on a movie they just saw, which is to say, we talk about it with the fresh knowledge of how it all ends. All of the memories are ever so slightly different now, tinged with bittersweetness.

"You were always the voice of reason," Jesse says. "Always the one stopping us from going just one step further than we should."

"Yeah, but you always gave me the courage to do what I wanted to do," I say. "I'm not sure I would have had the guts to do half the things I did if I didn't have you believing in me, egging me on."

We talk about our wedding—the ceremony by the lighthouse, our brief dalliance here, our reception down the street. I tell Jesse that my memories of that day aren't darkened by what happened later. That it still brings me nothing but joy to think about. That I'm thankful for it, no matter where we have ended up.

Jesse says he's not sure he agrees with me. He says it feels sad to him, that it represents a painful naivete about the future, that he feels sorry for the Jesse of that day, the Jesse who doesn't know what is ahead of him. It feels like a reminder of what he could have had if he hadn't ever gotten on that helicopter. But then he says that he hopes, one day, to see it the way I do.

"If I ever come around to your way of thinking," Jesse says, "I promise I'll find you and tell you."

"I would like that," I say. "I'll always want to know how you are."

"Well, then it's a good thing you'll always be easy to find," he says.

"Yeah," I say. "I'm not going anywhere."

The fire slows and Jesse moves toward it, rearranging the logs, blowing on it. He turns back to me, the calm fire now starting to roar again.

"You think you would have ever gone to school in LA if it wasn't for me?" he says.

"Maybe," I say. "Maybe not. I know that I wouldn't have been as happy there without you. And I wouldn't have even applied to that travel-writing class without you. And I definitely wouldn't have spent a year in Sydney or all those months in Europe if you weren't with me. I think there were a lot of things I never would have done—good, bad, beautiful, tragic, however you want to describe them. I think there were a lot of things I wouldn't have had the nerve to do if it wasn't for you."

"Sometimes I wonder if I would have just let my parents push me toward pro training if I hadn't met you," he says. "You were the first person who didn't care how good of a swimmer I was. The first person who just liked me for me. That . . . that was life changing. Truly."

He turns and looks at me intently. "You're a lot of the reason why I am who I am," he says.

"Oh, Jesse," I say, so much tenderness and affection that my heart is soaked, "there is no me without you."

Jesse kisses me then.

A kiss is just a kiss, I guess. But I've never been kissed like this before. It is sad and loving and wistful and scared and peaceful.

When we finally pull away from each other, I realize I'm tipsy and Jesse might just be drunk. The bottle is gone and as I go to put down my glass, I accidentally tip it over. That unmistakable cling and thud of a wine bottle hitting the floor is not followed by the familiar crash that sometimes accompanies it. Grateful, I pick up the intact bottle and our glasses.

I think it's time to switch to the soft stuff.

I get us some glasses of water and remind him about the book.

"You really want to read a book together?" he says.

"It's that or Taboo."

Jesse acquiesces, grabbing blankets and pillows from the couch. We lie down on the floor, close to the fire. I open up the book I pulled aside earlier.

"The Reluctant Adventures of Cole Crane," I begin.

I read to children's groups on Sunday mornings sometimes. I've started getting more confident, making up voices for the characters and trying to make the narration come alive. But I don't do any of that now. I'm just me. Reading a book. To someone I love.

Unfortunately, it's a very bad book. Laughably bad. The women are called dames. The men drink whiskey and make bad puns. I barely get through five pages before handing it over to Jesse. "You have to read this. I can't do it," I say.

"No," he says, "c'mon. I waited years just to hear your voice."

And so I read some more. By the time my eyes feel dry from the fire, I'm reluctantly invested in what happens to the Crooked Yellow Caper and I find myself wanting Cole Crane to just kiss Daphne Monroe already.

Jesse agrees to read the second half while I lie in his lap with my eyes closed.

His voice is soothing and calm. I listen as it ebbs and flows, as his words fall up and down.

When he's been reading for over an hour, I sit up and take the book out of his hand. I put it on the floor.

I know what I'm about to do. I know that it is the last time that I will ever do it. I know that I want it to mean something. For years I never had a chance to say good-bye. Now that I have it, I know this is the way I want to do it.

So I kiss him the way you kiss people when it is the start of something. And it starts something.

I pull my shirt over my head. I unbutton the fly of Jesse's jeans. I lay my body flush against his. It is the last time I will feel his warmth, the last time I will look down to see him below me, with his hands on my waist. It is the last time I will tell him I love him by the way I sink my hips and touch his chest.

He never looks anywhere but at me. I watch as his gaze moves down my body, watching me, taking it all in, trying to pin it to memory.

I feel seen. Truly seen. Cherished and savored.

Don't ever let anyone tell you the most romantic part of love is the beginning. The most romantic part is when you know it has to end.

I don't know that I've ever been as present in a moment as I am this very second, as I make love to a man I once believed was my soul mate, who I now know is meant for some*one* else and some*thing* else, is meant to build his life some*where* else.

His eyes have never looked more captivating. His body underneath me has never felt safer. I trace my hands over the scars on his body; I intertwine my left hand with his right one. I want him to know he's beautiful to me.

When it's over, I am too tired and stunned to mourn. I crawl back into the crook of his arm and I hand him the book again.

"Read?" I say. "Just a little while longer."

All of this. Just a little while longer.

"Yeah," Jesse says. "Anything you want."

I fall asleep in his arms, listening to him read the end of the book, happy to learn that Cole grabs Daphne by the shoulders and says, finally, "My God, woman, don't you know it's you? That it's always been you?"

Falling out of love with someone you still *like* feels exactly like lying in a warm bed and hearing the alarm clock.

No matter how good you feel right now, you know it's time to go.

E*rrr Errr Errr Errr Errr.*

The sun is shining brightly in my face. And Jesse's watch is beeping.

The cover of *The Reluctant Adventures of Cole Crane* is bent back, underneath his leg.

The fire is out.

"Time to get up," I say.

Jesse, still trying to adjust to wakefulness, nods his head and rubs his face.

We both head into the kitchen and grab some food. I drink a full glass of water. Jesse drinks cold coffee from the pot. He looks out the kitchen window as he drinks and then he turns back to me.

"It's snowing again," he says.

"Hard?" I ask. I look around to the front window to see that there's a fresh blanket of snow on the driveway.

"We should get on the road soon," he says. "I think it looks pretty clear right now, but we don't want to wait too much longer."

"OK, good idea. I'm going to get in the shower."

Jesse nods but doesn't say anything else. He doesn't follow me up the stairs to join me. He doesn't make a joke about me being naked. Instead, he moves toward the fireplace and starts to clean up.

It is then, as I start walking up the stairs alone, that I feel the full weight of the new truth.

Jesse is home. Jesse is alive.

But Jesse is no longer mine.

Within forty-five minutes, Jesse and I have gathered our things and are ready to go. The dishes are done, the remaining groceries are packed up, the mess we made has been cleaned. Even *The Reluctant Adventures of Cole Crane* is back on the shelf, as if it had never been read. If I didn't know better, I'd swear we were never here.

Jesse grabs the keys and opens the front door for me. It is with a heavy heart that I pass through it.

I don't offer to drive because I know he won't let me. He's going to do things his way and I'm going to let him. So I get into the passenger seat and Jesse puts the car in reverse.

I take one last look as we pull away from the cabin.

There are two tracks of footprints leading from the front door.

They start out close together and veer off in different directions as our feet head for opposite sides of the car.

I know those footprints will be gone soon. I know they might not make it to tonight if it keeps snowing like this. But it feels good to be able to look at something and understand it.

The footprints start off together and they grow apart.

I get it.

It's fine.

It's the truth.

Two True Loves

Or, how to make peace with the truth about love

J esse and I are almost to New Hampshire by the time we start actually having a conversation. We've just been listening to the radio, stuck in our own heads for the past hour and a half.

I have thought mainly of Sam.

About the stubble that always grows on his face, about the fact that he's clearly going to go gray early, about how I am eager to go back to spending my evenings with him at the piano.

I hope that when I tell him he's the one I want, he believes me.

It's been rough going but I have finally figured out who I am and what I want. In fact, never has my identity felt so crystal clear.

I am Emma Blair.

Bookstore owner. Sister. Daughter. Aunt. Amateur pianist. Cat lover. New Englander. Woman who wants to marry Sam Kemper.

That doesn't mean that it's without pain and sadness. There is still loss.

I know, I know deep in my gut that the moment when I get out of this car, when Jesse drops me off and says good-bye, I will feel as if I am breaking.

I feel the same way I did when I was nine and my mom took me to get my ears pierced for my birthday.

My party was that night. I had a blue dress that I had picked out myself. My mom and I picked out fake sapphire stud earrings to match. I felt very grown-up.

The woman put the gun to my right ear and told me it might hurt. I told her I was ready.

The pierce shot through me like a shock. I wasn't sure which was worse: the pressure of the squeeze, the pain of the puncture, or the sting of the air on a fresh wound.

I shuddered and closed my eyes. I kept them closed. My mom and the lady with the piercing gun asked me if I was OK and I said, "Can you do the other one now? Please."

And that ache—that sense that I knew exactly what to expect and I knew that it would be awful—feels exactly like the ache inside me now.

I know exactly how much it hurts to lose Jesse. And I'm in this car, waiting to be pierced.

"When my parents have adjusted a bit," Jesse says as we approach the state border, "and I feel like they will be OK if I leave, I'm just going right back to Santa Monica."

"Oh, Santa Monica? Not interested in trying out San Diego or Orange County?"

Jesse shakes his head. "I think Santa Monica is my place. I mean, I thought you and I would spend the rest of our lives there. I wasn't sure what to make of the fact that you were back here. But you know what? I think it will be really good to go back on my own." He says it as if it's just occurring to him that by letting me go, he has freed himself of some things.

"If you do go, will you let us all know how you are?"

"I have no intention of ever leaving anyone wondering where I am again."

I smile and squeeze his hand for a brief moment. I look out the window and watch as we pass bare brown trees and green highway signs.

"And you," Jesse says after a while. "You're gonna marry Sam and live here forever, huh?"

"If he'll have me," I say.

"Why do you say that? Why wouldn't he have you?"

I fiddle with the heat controls on my side of the car, aiming the air right on me. "Because I've put him through hell," I say. "Because I haven't been the easiest woman to be engaged to lately."

"That's not your fault," Jesse says. "That's not . . . that's not the whole story."

"I know," I say. "But I also know that I've hurt him. And the last time I spoke to him he said not to call him. That he would call me when he was ready to talk."

"*Has* he called you?"

I check my phone again, just to be sure. But of course he hasn't called. "No."

"He'll take you back," Jesse says. He's so sure of it that it makes me realize just how unsure I really am.

I risked my relationship with Sam to see if there was something left with Jesse. I knew what I was doing when I did it. I'm not pretending I didn't.

But now I know what I want. I want Sam. And I'm afraid that I may have lost him because I didn't know it earlier.

"Well, if he doesn't take you back . . ." Jesse says, just as he realizes that he needs to be three lanes over. He doesn't finish his sentence right way. He's focused on the road. I wonder, for a moment, if he's going to say that if Sam doesn't marry me, he'll take me back.

I am surprised at how unnatural and inaccurate that would be.

Because I haven't been choosing between Sam or Jesse. It was never one or the other. Even though at times, I thought it was exactly that.

It was about whether Jesse and I still had something, or whether we didn't.

I know, like I know that stealing is wrong and my mom is lying when she says she likes my dad's mint juleps, that what has happened between Jesse and me is because of Jesse and me. And not because of anyone waiting in the wings.

We are over because we aren't right for each other anymore.

If Sam doesn't want me to come home after all of this, Jesse will call me to make sure I'm OK and send postcards from sunny places. And we'll both know that I could join him. And we'll both know that I'm not going to. And we'll be OK with that.

Because we had this.

We had three days in Maine.

Where we reunited and broke our own hearts.

And walked away in two pieces.

"Sorry," Jesse says now that he's been able to make it through the interchange and can focus on talking again. "What was I saying? Oh, right. If Sam doesn't take you back, I will personally kick his ass."

I laugh at the idea of Jesse kicking Sam's ass. It seems so absurd. Jesse could probably kick Sam's ass in about three seconds. It would be like one of those boxing matches where the one guy gets in a punch right off the bat and the poor sucker never knew what hit him.

Sam, my Sam, my adorable, sweetheart Sam, is a lover, not a fighter. I love that about him.

"I'm serious," Jesse says. "This is an insane situation. If he can't see that, I will personally see to it that he is in physical pain."

"Oh!" I say, joking with him. "No, don't do that! I love him."

I don't mean it as a profound announcement, despite how profoundly I feel it. But no matter *how* I say it, it's sort of an uncomfortable thing to say, given the circumstances.

I watch Jesse swallow hard and then speak. "I'm happy for you," Jesse says. "I am."

"Thank you," I say, relieved at his magnanimity. I don't think he's being honest, right now. But he's trying really hard. I have so much respect for him for that.

"And that's going to conclude our discussion of him," Jesse says. "Because otherwise, I'm going to be ill."

"Fair enough," I say, nodding my head. "Happy to change the subject."

"We'll be home not too long from now," he says. "We're almost in Tewksbury."

"Should we play I Spy or something?"

Jesse laughs. "Yeah, all right," he says. "I spy with my little eye . . . something . . . blue."

Maybe relationships are supposed to end with tears or screams. Maybe they are supposed to conclude with two people saying everything they never said or ripping into each other in a way that can't be undone.

I don't know.

I've only really ended one relationship in my life.

It is this one.

And this one ends with a good-natured game of I Spy.

We spot things and we guess them and we make each other laugh.

And when Jesse pulls the car into the front parking lot of Blair Books, I know I only have a moment before the piercing gun comes to my ear.

"I love you," I say. "I've always loved you. I'll always love you."

"I know," he says. "I feel the same way. Go grab the life you made for yourself."

I kiss him good-bye like you kiss your friends on New Year's. I don't have it in me to kiss him any other way.

I gather my things and I put my hand on the car door, not yet ready to pull the handle.

"You were a wonderful person to love," I say. "It felt so good to love you, to be loved by you."

"Well, it was the easiest thing I ever did," he says.

I smile at him and then breathe in, preparing myself for the piercing pain of leaving.

"Will you promise me that you will take care of yourself?" I say. "That you'll call me if you need anything. That you'll . . ." I don't know exactly how to phrase what I mean. He has been through so much and I want him to promise me, promise all of us who care about him, that he will work through it.

Jesse nods and waves me off. "I know what you mean. And I promise."

"OK," I say, smiling tenderly. I open the door. I put my feet onto the pavement. I get out of the car and close it behind me.

Jesse waves at me and then puts his car in reverse. I watch him as he does a three-point turn out of the lot. It hurts just as much as I thought it would. The pressure, the ache, the sting.

I wave as he makes a left onto the main road.

And then he's gone.

I close my eyes for a moment, processing what has just hap-

pened. *It's over. Jesse is alive and home and our marriage is over.*
But then when I open my eyes again, I realize where I am.

My bookstore.

I turn around and walk toward the door.

I'm walking toward books and my family and that one day
in spring when the sun feels like it will shine for you forever
and the flowers will bloom for months. I am walking toward
vegan cheddar grilled cheese and cat GIFs and "Piano Man."

I am walking toward Sam.

I am walking home.

And just like the day I got my ears pierced, once the pain
has come and gone, I've grown up.

M y mother and father are both in the store. Before I'm even close enough to say hi to them, I hear children crying in the far corner.

"Are the girls here?" I ask the moment I hug my parents hello.

"With Marie in the children's section," my mom says.

"How are you? How did everything go?" my dad asks.

I start to answer but there's so much to explain and I'm not up for getting into the details just yet. "I missed Sam," I say. Actually, that might just cover all of it. Succinct and painless.

They look at each other and smile, as if they are part of a two-man club that knew this is what I'd do all along.

I hate the idea of being predictable, especially predictable to my parents. But, more than anything, I'm relieved that I seem to have made the right set of decisions. Because, after all, they are my parents. And when you get to be old enough, it's finally OK to admit that they often do know best.

I can hear Marie trying to calm down Sophie and Ava. I come around the side of the register to get a better view. The two girls are crying, red faced. They are both holding opposite sides of their heads. I look back to my parents.

"Ava ran into Sophie and they hit each other in the head," my mom says.

My father puts his finger to his ear, as if the sound of their screaming is going to burst his eardrum. "It's been great for business."

As the girls' sobbing dies down, reduced to the far more quiet but equally theatrical gulping for breath and frowning, Marie spots me and comes walking over.

I turn to my parents. "By the way, we have to talk about Tina," I say.

Neither of my parents look me in the eye directly. "We can talk about it another time," my dad says. "When things aren't so . . . dramatic."

My mother averts her gaze, instantly focusing on straightening things underneath the register. My dad pretends as if he's deeply engaged in the store calendar sitting on the counter. I have been their daughter for too long to fall for this kind of crap. They are hiding something.

"What's going on?" I ask. "What are you two not saying?"

"Oh, honey, it's nothing," my mom says, and I almost believe her. But then I see the look on my dad's face, a mixture of "Is she buying this?" and "Oh, God, we should just tell her."

"We just have some, you know, ideas for the management of the store," my dad says finally. "But we should talk about it later."

When Marie makes her way to me and looks like she's afraid to tell me she borrowed my favorite sweater, I know she's in on it, too.

"C'mon, everybody, I'm dealing with too much stuff right now to have the patience for whatever this is."

"It's nothing," Marie says. I frown at her to let her know I don't believe it for a second. She folds like a cheap suit. "Fine. I want the job."

"What job?" I ask.

"The assistant manager position."

"Here?"

"Yeah, I want it. Mom and Dad think it's a great idea, but obviously it's up to you."

"You want to work here?" I say, still disbelieving. "With me?"

"Yes."

"At this store?" I say.

"See? I knew it wasn't the right time to talk about this."

"No," I say, shaking my head. "I'm just surprised."

"I know," she says. "But this could be my something. Like we talked about. Something outside of the house that has nothing to do with potty training or hearing and deafness. I think this idea is better than writing, actually. I'm excited about it and it's something with adults, you know? A reason to put on a nice pair of pants. Emma, I need a reason to put on pants."

"OK . . ." I say.

"I can't take on a full-time job but an assistant manager position could be really good. Especially because Mom and Dad could help fill in for me with the kids or here if need be. I guess what I'm saying is . . . Please hire me."

"But you used to be the manager. I'd be your boss," I say.

Marie puts both of her hands up, in mock surrender. "It's your show. I know that I gave up the position and you've done a great job at it. I'm not trying to usurp anything. If, later on down the line, I decide that I want to take on more or be a more vocal participant in the store, that's my problem and I'll deal with it. I can always take on a manager job at one of Mike's stores if it comes to that. But right now, what I really want is to spend my time here, with you."

Marie has said her piece and now it's up to me to respond.

I can feel my sister's, my father's, and my mother's eyes on me. Sophie and Ava, now calm, are pulling on Marie's leg.

"So?" Marie says.

I start laughing. It's all so absurd. All three of them start to worry, unsure what, exactly, I find so funny. So I get hold of myself in an effort to not keep them in suspense any longer.

It scares me, the idea of having Marie working under me. It makes me sort of uncomfortable and I'm slightly worried that it will undermine the good relationship we've started to build. But I also think that it could turn out to be great. I'd have someone to share this store with, someone who understands how important it is, who has a passion for not just books but this store's history. And working together, spending more time with each other, could bring us even closer.

So I think this is a risk I'm willing to take.

I'm ready to bet on Marie and me.

"OK," I say. "You're hired."

The smile that erupts across my father's face is so wide and sincere that the teenage version of me would have threatened to barf. But I'm not a teenager anymore and it won't kill me to give my father everything he's ever dreamed of. "All right, Dad," I say. "Your girls are running your store."

For the first time in my entire life, I wonder if perhaps Marie and I might actually prove to be greater together than the sum of our parts.

Emma and Marie.

Our moment of celebration is interrupted by a man who tells my dad he is looking for a book for his wife. I overhear as my dad asks what it's called. The man says, "I don't know and I'm not sure who wrote it. I don't remember what it's about, but I do remember that the cover was blue."

I watch my parents give each other a knowing glance and then both of them try to help him.

As they walk away, Marie looks at me. "So what happened in Maine? Are you going home to Sam?"

"I don't know, exactly."

"What do you mean?" she asks.

"I know that I want to be with Sam, but he told me not to call him even if I've made a decision. He said that he would let me know when he was ready to talk. Not the other way around."

Marie waves it off. "He just meant that if you were going to turn him down. He doesn't mean that if you have good news you shouldn't tell him."

"I don't know. I think he's really upset."

"Of course he's upset. But that's all the more reason to find him and talk to him."

"I want to respect his wishes," I say.

"Emma, listen to me. Go find him right now and tell him that you want to be with him."

"You mean like go to his office at school?" I say.

"Yes!" Marie says. "Absolutely do that. I mean, don't propose to him in front of band kids or whatever. But yes! Find him now."

"Yeah," I say, starting to build up the confidence. "Yeah, I think you're right."

My parents come over and ring up the man. He must not have found what he came in for. He is, instead, purchasing a copy of *Little Women*. No doubt my parents gave up trying to figure out what book he was talking about a few minutes into it and just decided to sell him on Louisa May Alcott.

They want to sell everyone a copy of *Little Women*. Because it's a great book, sure. But also because they are proud that it was written just a few miles away. They probably also tried to sell him any Henry David Thoreau or Ralph Waldo Emerson we have in stock.

I haven't been pushing the transcendentalists like they do. Copies stay on the shelf longer than they did when my parents were running things.

They have never given me a hard time about it. My father has never asked why there are copies of *Civil Disobedience* that have managed to earn dust on them.

My parents have given me an incredible gift: they gave me this store, and they set up a future for me, but they never told me theirs was the only way to do it.

We sell more journals and candles now. We sell tote bags with literary quotes on them. We sell more Young Adult than we have in years. And we sell less of the classics and less hard-covers. That all might be because of how the business is changing. But I also think it's because of me. Because I do things differently, for better and for worse.

Now, things might change again with Marie coming back. We might grow even stronger.

The man leaves and I prepare to head out to my car and try to win back the love of my life.

"OK," I say. "I'm out of here. Wish me luck."

I get to the door before I turn around. I decide that something I've left unsaid needs to be explicit.

"Thank you," I say to my parents. "For trusting me with this store and for waiting for me to fall in love with it on my own, in my own way. Thank you for guiding me toward a life that makes me happy."

For a minute, my mom looks like she might cry, but she doesn't.

"Of course, honey," she says as my dad gives me a wink. That's parents for you.

You say thank you for gifts they've given that have shaped your entire world and their answer is, "Of course."

As I'm out the door, I turn to Marie and say, "Welcome back."

As I get into my car in the back lot, I find my days-old sandwich sitting in the front seat. It has already given my car a sour, acrid odor. I grab it and throw it away in the Dumpster and then open up both of my car doors for a minute, trying to air it out.

That's when I see a car pulling in.

I don't need to look through the windshield to know who it is.

But of course I do anyway.

Sam.

My heart starts beating rapidly. I can feel rhythmic bass throbbing in my chest.

I run toward his car just as he steps out of it.

He's in slacks and a button-down with his tie untied and hanging loosely around his neck. His coat is unbuttoned.

It's the middle of the day and he should be at school.

Instead, he's standing in the lot of my store with his eyes bloodshot.

I look at him and I see a broken heart.

"I have to talk to you," he says, his breath visible in the cold.

"I have to talk to you, too," I say.

"No," Sam says, putting his hand up. "I'm going first."

I can feel my heart start to break in my chest. *Is it over?* I am devastated that my being unsure has led to the man I love being unsure about me. I feel the urgent need to stall, to draw out this moment, to spend as much time as possible with him before he leaves me for good—if that's what he's going to do.

"Can we get in the car?" I say. "Turn on the heat?"

Sam nods and opens up his car door. I run around to the passenger side, rubbing my hands together for warmth. Sam turns on the ignition and we wait for the heat to warm up. Soon, my hands start to thaw.

"Listen," Sam says. "I've spent the past four days thinking."

It feels like a lifetime has passed but it's only been four days.

"I can't do this," he says as he turns his whole body toward me. "I can't live like this. I can't . . . This isn't working for me."

"OK," I say. I can feel my chest start to ache as if my body can't stand to hear this.

"You have to come home," he says.

I look up at him. "What?"

"Fifteen years ago, I watched you go off with Jesse and I told myself that you had made your decision and there was nothing that I could do about it. And here we are, all this time later, and I'm doing the same thing. That's not . . . I can't do it again. I'm fighting for you.

"I left work after fifth period today because I was considering teaching the jazz band how to play 'Total Eclipse of the Heart.' I'm heartbroken without you. I have spent this time alone moping around like a bird with a broken wing just hoping that you'd come back to me. But it's not enough to hope. I'm an adult now. I'm not a teenager like I was back then, the first time. I'm a man now. And it's not enough for me to hope for you. I have to fight for you. So here I am. That's what I'm doing. I'm putting up a fight."

Sam takes my hand and implores me. "I am right for you, Emma. What we have is . . . it's true love. I love you. I want to spend the rest of my life with you. You're my soul mate. I can make you happy," he says. "I can give you the life you want. So marry me, Emma. Marry *me*."

"Oh, my God," I say, relief washing over me. "We are so ridiculous."

"What are you talking about?" Sam asks. "What do you mean?"

"You're fighting for me?" I say.

"Yeah."

"I was about to come find you at your job to fight for you."

Sam is disarmed and stunned. He is quiet. And then he starts to tear up and says, "Really?"

"I love you, sweetheart," I say to him. "I want to be with you for the rest of my life. I'm so sorry that I had unfinished business. But it is finished now. It's over. And I know that you are the man I want to spend every day of my life with. I want our life. I want to marry you. I'm sorry I was lost. But I'm so sure now. I want you."

"And Jesse?" Sam asks.

"I love Jesse. I'll always love him. But he was right for me then. You are right for me now. And always."

Sam breathes in, letting my words flow into his ears and settle in his brain.

"Do you mean all of this?" he asks me. "It's not just something you're saying to be dramatic and wonderful?"

I shake my head. "No, I'm not trying to be dramatic and wonderful."

"I mean, you've succeeded in it, for sure."

"But I mean it. All of it. Assuming that you can forgive me

for being uncertain, for needing to leave, for needing more time with him, to find out what I think I already knew."

"I can forgive that," Sam says. "Of course I can."

It's important to me that he knows what I've done, that I face it. "We went to Maine together, alone," I say.

I don't say anything more because I don't have to.

Sam shakes his head. "I don't want to hear about it. I don't want to know. It's over. It's in the past. All that matters is from here on out."

I nod my head, desperate to assure him. "I don't want anyone or anything except you from here on out, forever."

He takes it all in, closing his eyes.

"You'll be my wife?" he says, smiling wide. I don't know if I've ever felt more loved than in this moment, when the idea that I might marry a man brings that much joy to his face.

"Yes," I say. "God, yes."

Sam leans over to my side of the car and kisses me, beaming. The tears in my eyes are finally happy tears. My heart is no longer pounding but swelling.

No more conflicted feelings. No more uncertainty.

"I love you," I say. "I don't think I ever knew just how much until now." It's a good sign, I think, that our love has proven to grow, rather than wane, when faced with a challenge. I think it bodes well for our future, for all of the things ahead of us: marriage, children.

"Oh, God, I was so scared I'd lost you," Sam says. "I was capsizing over here. Worried I'd lose the greatest thing that has ever happened to me."

"You didn't lose me," I say. "I'm here. I'm right here."

I kiss him.

The two of us are sitting awkwardly half over the console

with cricked necks and the stick shift digging into my knee. I just want to be as close to him as possible. Sam kisses my temple and I can smell our laundry detergent on his shirt.

"Take me home?" I ask.

Sam smiles. It is the sort of smile that any minute might turn to tears. "Absolutely."

I move away from him, putting myself firmly in the passenger seat as he puts the car in reverse and backs out.

My phone and my wallet are in my car, as well as my weekend bag with all of my things. But I don't stop him. I don't ask him to wait just a minute while I grab them. Because I don't need them. Not right now. I don't need anything that I don't have right this minute.

Sam holds my left hand with his right. He does so the entire way home except for a twenty-second period when I lean forward and dig through his glove compartment for his favorite Charles Mingus CD that he keeps buried in the dash. I still can't stand jazz and he still loves it. In both important and unimportant ways, Sam and I are the same to each other that we were back then. When the music begins, Sam looks at me, impressed.

"You hate Mingus," he says.

"I love you, though, so . . ."

This seems like a good enough explanation for him and so he grabs my hand again. There is no tension, no pressure. We are at peace simply being next to each other. A deep calm comes over me as I watch the snowplowed streets of Acton turn to those of Concord, as the evergreens that hug the highway leading us through Lexington and Belmont turn to brick sidewalks and brownstones in Cambridge. The world feels like a mirror, in that what I see in front of me is finally in perfect synchronicity with what I am made of.

I feel like myself on these streets, with this man.

We park and head up to our apartment. I am tucked into the crook of his arm, using his body as a shield against the cold.

Sam turns the key and when the door shuts behind us, it feels like we've locked the whole world out. When he kisses me, his lips are still chilled and I feel them warm up with my touch.

"Hi," he says, smiling. It is the kind of "hi" that means everything except hello.

"Hi," I say back.

The smell of our apartment, a scent I'm not sure I've ever noticed before, is spicy and fresh, like cinnamon toothpaste. I spot both of the cats under the piano. They are OK. *Everything* is OK.

Sam pushes himself against me as I rest against the back of our front door. He puts his hand to my cheek, his fingers slip into my hair as his thumb grazes under my eye.

"I was afraid I'd lost these freckles of yours forever," he says as he looks right at me. His gaze feels comforting, safe. I find myself moving my head toward his hand, pressing against it.

"You didn't," I say. "I'm here. And I will do anything for you. Anything. For the rest of our lives."

"I don't need anything from you," Sam says. "Just you. I just want you."

My arms reach up around his shoulders and I pull him close to me. The weight of his body against mine is both stirring and soothing. I can smell the drugstore pomade in his hair. I can feel the short stubble of his cheeks. "You're it for me," I say. "Forever. Me and you."

I was wrong before, when I said there's nothing more romantic than the end of a relationship.

It is this.

There is nothing more romantic than this. Holding the very person that you thought you lost, and knowing you'll never lose them again.

I don't think that true love means your only love.

I think true love means loving truly.

Loving purely. Loving wholly.

Maybe, if you're the kind of person who's willing to give all of yourself, the kind of person who is willing to love with all of your heart even though you've experienced just how much it can hurt . . . maybe you get lots of true loves, then. Maybe that's the gift you get for being brave.

I am a woman who dares to love again.

I finally love that about myself.

It's messy to love after heartbreak. It's painful and it forces you to be honest with yourself about who you are. You have to work harder to find the words for your feelings, because they don't fit into any prefabricated boxes.

But it's worth it.

Because look what you get:

Great loves.

Meaningful loves.

True loves.

I wear a pale lavender dress at my second wedding. It is sleek and ornate. It feels like the wedding dress of a woman who has lived a full life before getting married. A dress that signals a strong, well-rounded person making a beautiful decision. Marie is my maid of honor. Ava is our flower girl; Sophie is our ring bearer. Olive gives a speech that leaves half the room in tears. Sam and I honeymoon in Montreal.

And then eight months and nine days after Sam and I say our vows in front of all of our friends and family, I am talking to Olive on the phone as I close up Blair Books on a balmy summer night.

Marie left early to pick up the girls from our parents'. We are all meeting up for dinner at Marie and Mike's house. Mike is grilling steaks and Sam promised Sophia and Ava he'd make them grilled cheese.

Olive is talking about the first birthday party that she is throwing for her baby, Piper, when I hear the familiar beep of call-waiting.

"You know what?" I say. "Someone's on the other line. I gotta go."

"OK," she says. "Oh, I wanted to ask you what you think about sea animals as a theme for—"

"Olive!" I say. "I gotta go."

"OK, but just . . . do you like sea animals as a theme or not?"

"I think it depends on what animals but I have to go."

"I mean, like, whales and dolphins, maybe some fish," Olive explains as I groan. "Fine!" she says. "We can FaceTime tomorrow."

I hang up and look at my phone to see who is calling me.

I don't recognize the number. But I recognize the area code. 310.

Santa Monica, California.

"Hello?"

"Emma?" The voice is instantly familiar. One I could never forget.

"Jesse?"

"Hi."

"Hi!"

"How are you?" he asks me casually, as if we talk all the time. I have gotten postcards from California a few times, even one from Lisbon. They are short and sweet, simple updates on how he is, where he's headed. I always know he's OK. But we don't text that often. And we never talk on the phone.

"I'm good," I say. "Really good. How about you?"

"I'm doing well, yeah," he says. "Miss you guys in Acton, obviously."

"Obviously," I say.

"But I'm good. I'm . . . I'm really happy here."

I don't know what else to say to him. I can't quite tell why he's calling. My silence stalls us. And so he just comes out with it.

"I met someone," he says.

Maybe it shouldn't surprise me—that he met someone, that he wants to tell me. But both things do.

"You did? That's wonderful."

"Yeah, she's . . . she's really incredible. Just very unique. She's a professional surfer. Isn't that crazy? I never thought I'd fall in love with a surfer girl."

I laugh. "I don't know," I say, locking up the shop, walking out to my car. It's still bright out even though the evening is fully under way. I will miss this come October. I make a point to appreciate it now. "It kind of makes perfect sense to me that you'd fall in love with a surfer girl. I mean, it doesn't get much more California than that."

"Yeah, maybe you're right." Jesse laughs.

"What's her name?"

"Britt," Jesse says.

"Jesse and Britt," I say. "That has a nice ring to it."

"I think so. I think we're good together."

"Oh, Jesse, that's so wonderful. I'm really so glad to hear it."

"I wanted to tell you . . ." he says, and then he drifts off.

"Yeah."

"I get it now. I get what you were saying. About how falling in love with Sam didn't mean that you forgot me. That it doesn't change how you once felt. It doesn't make the people you loved before any less important.

"I didn't get it back then. I thought . . . I thought choosing him meant you didn't love me. I thought because we didn't work out, it meant we were a failure or a mistake. But I understand it now. Because I love her. I love her so much I can't see straight. But it doesn't change how I felt about you or how thankful I am to have loved you once. It's just . . ."

"I'm the past. And she's the present."

"Yeah," he says, relieved that I've put it into words for him, that he doesn't have to try to find them himself. "That's exactly it."

I think you forsake the people you loved before, just a little bit, when you fall in love again. But it doesn't erase anything. It doesn't change what you had. You don't even leave it so far behind that you can't instantly remember, that you can't pick it up like a book you read a long time ago and remember how it felt then.

"I guess what I'm saying is I've come around to your way of thinking. I am immensely thankful I was married to you once. I am so grateful for our wedding day. Just because something isn't meant to last a lifetime doesn't mean it wasn't meant to be. We were meant to have been."

I am sitting in the front seat of my car with the phone to my ear, unable to do anything but listen to him.

"You and I aren't going to spend our lives together," Jesse says. "But I finally understand that that doesn't take away any of the beauty of the fact that we were right for each other once."

"True love doesn't always last," I say. "It doesn't always have to be for a lifetime."

"Right. And that doesn't mean it's not true love," Jesse says.

It was real.

And now it's over.

And that's OK.

"I am who I am because I loved you once," he says.

"I am who I am because I loved you once, too," I say.

And then we say good-bye.

ACKNOWLEDGMENTS

My grandmother Linda Morris lived her entire life in Acton. She passed away a few weeks before I sat down to start this book. It was my trip home that October for her memorial, with the beautiful leaves and crisp air, that made me realize just how deeply I love the place I am from. And just how much I wanted to write about it in tribute to my grandmother. The people in my life whom I have cherished the longest are people from Acton and its surrounding towns. So this is my way of saying not just *thank you* but also *I love you*.

This book—and every book I've written—would not be possible without three particular women: my editors, Greer Hendricks and Sarah Cantin, and my agent, Carly Watters.

Greer, thank you for seeing all the things I can't see and for having the faith to know I will find a way to fix them. Both of those qualities were in dire need this go-around and I could not be more grateful that you were on my team. Sarah, thank you for being such a great champion. I know that my work is in great hands at Atria and that is because of how good you are at what you do. Carly, thank you for always getting just as excited about my work as I do and for knowing what I'm going to ask before I ask it. Four books in, I still feel so lucky to have you as the face of this operation.

Crystal Patriarche and the BookSparks team, you are unbelievable publicity all-stars. Tory, thank you for handling every crazy question I have with patience and grace. Brad Mendelsohn, thank you for not only being an awesome manager who thinks ten steps ahead, but also finally putting together your daughters' trampoline.

Thank you to everyone at Atria, especially Judith Curr, for making Atria such an exceptional imprint to be a part of. I feel incredibly fortunate that my book travels from one talented hand to another on its way to publication.

To all the bloggers who have supported me time after time, this book exists because you've rallied readers. You make my job fun and your passion for great stories and characters is infectious. Thanks for always reminding me why I love what I do and for helping me reach a diverse and incredible readership. I owe you one (million).

To all the friends and family I've thanked before, I thank you again. To Andy Bauch and my in-laws, the Reids and the Hanes, I have dedicated this book to you because as much as I love Acton, I also love Los Angeles, and it is in no small part because of all of you. Thank you for always supporting me and for making this huge city feel like home.

To mi madre y mi hermano, Mindy and Jake, I love you guys. Mom, thanks for moving us to Acton so I had an exceptional education, an incredible support system, and, eventually, a place to write about. Jake, thanks for moving to LA so I have someone who I can talk to when I miss the Makaha and the Honey Stung Drummies from Roche Bros.

And last but not least, Alex Jenkins Reid. Thank you for reading all of my work as if it were your own—for being thoughtful enough to see what there is to love about it and honest enough to tell me when it sucks. And—on those occasions when it does, in fact, suck—thank you for going to get me an iced tea and a cupcake. Thank you for waiting until I'm ready to try again and then rolling up your sleeves with me and saying, "We'll figure this out." You're always right. We always do.

ONE TRUE LOVES

A Q&A with

TAYLOR JENKINS REID

When you set out to write *One True Loves*, did you know whether Emma would end up with Jesse or Sam? Did you find yourself rooting for one or the other as you wrote?

That is *the* question! I spent a lot of time, before I even sat down to write the first word of the book, trying to decide what I believed the truth of the situation would be. I asked myself (and a lot of my friends) what they thought they would do. I decided that there was one answer that simply felt more honest than the other answer. And I went with it. So when I started writing the first draft, I knew the ending.

As for whether I was rooting for either, I swear that I remained entirely neutral—and that I'm still neutral—about who I *wanted* to win out in the end. I only felt that one was more likely and I told the story I felt was the most real. But I love both Jesse and Sam madly and I worked hard in the hopes that readers would, too.

How have you developed as a writer over the course of crafting your four novels? Are there differences in how you approached writing *One True Loves* compared with your debut, *Forever, Interrupted*?

I'm embarrassed to say I don't have a concrete answer for this! I think my readers might be a better judge of that than I. I'm inclined to turn the question around and ask, of those who have read all of my work thus far, how do they see [my writing] changing?

One of the most obvious evolutions for me to recognize is that once I've talked about something in one book, I find myself working double time to avoid talking about it in another. So with *One True Loves*, I put in a great deal of effort to create challenges that my characters in other books haven't faced before. The more you write, the more you have to go out of your way not to emulate your past work—and that has led me to some really fun places I might not go [toward] as naturally.

What does "true love" mean to you? What about this concept did you want to explore in *One True Loves*?

My main goal was to put forth the idea that just because a relationship ends, it doesn't mean that it has failed. I don't think that true love means lasting love. If you remove that requirement and you start looking at the people you have loved in the past, you start to ask yourself: Did I love that person with all my heart? Did they change me for the better? Was I good to them? Am I glad it happened? And if that's the case, I think we should call that relationship a success.

What inspired you to set part of *One True Loves* in your hometown?

As I say in the acknowledgments, my grandmother passed away right before I was to start writing this story and it absolutely devastated me. My brother and I were raised by our mother with a lot of help from my grandmother, Linda. I dedicated my first book to her. She was so encouraging and believed in me with everything she had. I am a stronger and kinder person because of her influence on me. She lived her entire life in Acton, Massachusetts. I was lucky enough to spend what to me are my most formative years, from twelve to eighteen, living there. And I always took it somewhat for granted.

When my grandmother passed away in the fall of 2014, I went home to attend her memorial. I usually only go home during Christmas, or perhaps the summer. This was the first time I'd been home in the fall in probably a decade. When I got to town and saw how beautiful the changing leaves were, and how kind the people of Acton were in supporting my family during a very hard time, I realized I had not given enough credit to the wonderful town I am from.

Some of my very best friends—people that feel like my family—are people I met in Acton. And I have such fond memories of growing up there. So I decided to set the book in Acton as a way to honor both how much I appreciate the town and how much my grandmother loved it.

You based the bookstore Blair Books on Willow Books in Acton, MA. Do you have any memories of Willow Books you'd like to share?

My most fond—and very New England—story about Willow Books is from when I was about fourteen. My best friend, Erin, and I went to see *The Vagina Monologues* when it came to Boston. We were both completely riveted by it. We loved it. This was revolutionary stuff back then. So after we saw it, we decided we wanted to get the book, but it wasn't easy to find. We went into Willow Books and they kindly agreed to order copies for us.

A week later, I got a message on my family's home answering machine from this older woman who said, "I'm calling from Willow Books. The uh . . . the book that you . . . the monologues . . ." And then she just gave up and said, "The book you ordered is here." The poor woman couldn't bring herself to say the word "vagina." But she got me the book. And I read it cover to cover. That was probably my first unequivocally feminist moment, that book. No other store had it for me. But Willow did.

What is your favorite aspect of the writing process? What aspect is the most challenging for you? What are some things you do to overcome that challenge?

Oh, boy. When I'm writing a first draft, I'll tell you my favorite part is editing. When I'm editing, I'll say my favorite part is when it's done. When it's done, and I'm promoting it, I'll tell you that I want to get back to *writing*. I'm always convincing myself that the grass is greener on the other side of the street. I think, truthfully, the only part that is always as fun as I think it will be is coming up with ideas. The very beginning, when it's all potential, is very intoxicating.

And I find, somehow, even when I'm cursing whatever stage I'm in, the cumulative effect of all the stages still manages to be joy. Sort of [like] how they say, "The days are long but the years are short." Writing is frustrating, but being a writer is near bliss.

How were you able to imagine Jesse's mindset and experience after the helicopter crash? Did you do any research on crash survivors or near-death experiences?

I did some research about real people who have survived being lost at sea. There is a wide range of stories to pull from and no two stories are alike, which, at first, was very frustrating because there was nothing I could really pin down. But then I realized it was freeing because it gave me permission to be entirely unique.

The biggest research came from deciding where he could land, what he could live on, what challenges he would face. When I decided he would be in the Pacific, I had to narrow down what areas made the most sense, what vegetation was there, what the currents were like. And then comes the human element: What happens to the human body without protein? Without social interaction? What happens when you've cut yourself or been stung? What happens to your teeth when you can't brush them?

I wanted the reader to focus on Emma's tragedy, so I used only as much information about Jesse's as necessary to move the story forward. We've seen desert island stories. We've seen tales of men's adventures trying to get home. I wanted this to be about the woman left behind.

What do you think is the most important step in creating three-dimensional characters?

People don't make sense. They lie without even realizing they are lying. They are selfish while believing they are selfless, etc. I think the biggest thing I focus on is making sure that my characters are recognizable and knowable but not convenient or streamlined. Real people are messy. They are interesting because of the mess. I try to recreate that on the page.

In the book, Emma takes a circuitous route to becoming an avid reader and bookshop owner. What inspired you to have your protagonist have such a strong—and at times conflicted—relationship with a bookstore? Have you always wanted to be an author? What initially drew you to writing?

Yes, Emma definitely has an untraditional love story with books. And I did that because I think so often in the reading community, we focus on people who have loved reading their entire lives. But [in my case], I was not an avid reader until after college. And even then, I don't think I realized just how much I loved reading books until I realized I liked *writing* them. I feel vaguely embarrassed about that sometimes. Because I was the kid who didn't do her summer reading so that she could watch TV. I wanted to show a different story about how someone falls in love with reading.

It took me until I was about twenty-five to realize I wanted to be a writer and until [I was]about twenty-eight to admit it to people out loud. I floated around from job to job, attracted to various different elements of the work I was doing. And it wasn't until it occurred to me to try to write fiction that I realized being an author was exactly the thing I had been searching for. When I added up all of the elements of the other jobs I'd been doing, it hit me that writing fiction was my dream job.

It came as such a relief, honestly. To finally have that

direction. I knew it was a long shot but I also finally had a target to aim for.

You've also written for television and for film. How is this type of writing different from crafting a novel? How has your work as a novelist influenced your work as a screenwriter?

Writing for books, film, and TV are somehow all completely different and all essentially the same. In every medium, your goal is to connect with an audience, to bring them into a story, to thrill them, to make them feel. So the underlying skills are identical. How do I make this world seem real? How do I make this character someone people feel passionately about?

But of course there are different formulas for each one and different strengths to each. Part of what is the most fun about working in all three is coming up with an idea and then deciding how it will work best. Is this a book that could also be a TV show? Is it a book that would make a great film? Is it an idea that is really best only as a movie?

I've never painted or sculpted a day in my life but I'd imagine it's similar to having a vision of a woman in your head and trying to decide if she should be made out of paint, marble, or clay. Again, we're talking about the conception phase of a story—where you get to start making decisions about what it will be *someday*. And that is—and will forever be—the very thing that drives me.